THE DEVIL'S CHURCHYARD

A place named in hushed voices, a silent, shrouded place where lovers never wander...where great stone boulders bear mute witness to what evil men do in the name of dark powers....

THE DEVIL'S CHURCHYARD

Kate Evans and Jim Tranmire peeped through the mist from the cave where they had taken refuge from the rain. They could see the ancient circle, and watched with rising horror as a monstrous figure climbed and cavorted on the pale altar.

THE DEVIL'S CHURCHYARD
was originally published by
Doubleday & Co., Inc.

Other books by Godfrey Turton

Builders of England's Glory

The Emperor Arthur

My Lord of Canterbury

The Devil's Churchyard

GODFREY TURTON

PUBLISHED BY POCKET BOOKS NEW YORK

THE DEVIL'S CHURCHYARD

Doubleday edition published May, 1970

POCKET BOOK edition published September, 1971

This POCKET BOOK edition includes every word
contained in the original, higher-priced edition. It is printed
from brand-new plates made from completely reset, clear, easy-to-read
type. POCKET BOOK editions are published by POCKET BOOKS, a division
of Simon & Schuster, Inc., 630 Fifth Avenue, New York, N.Y. 10020.
Trademarks registered in the United States and other countries.

L

Standard Book Number: 671-77339-9.
Library of Congress Catalog Card Number: 79-103782.
Copyright, ©, 1970, by Godfrey Edmund Turton. All rights reserved.
This POCKET BOOK edition is published by arrangement with
Doubleday & Company, Inc.

Printed in the U.S.A.

Author's Note

As the custom of private patronage which survives in the Church in many parts of England may be unfamiliar to American readers an explanation is needed. The right to present a clergyman to a vacant living is known as an "advowson," and it is not uncommon—as in this story—for it to be vested in the lord of the manor, owner of the surrounding land, who bears the title of "patron" of the living and has the right when a vacancy occurs to choose whom he wishes to fill it. This is the limit of the patron's powers. Once the appointment has been made, and confirmed by the Bishop, he has no further say in Church affairs.

The Devil's Churchyard

Chapter 1

Years before the events to be related Kemsdale Wood held a
crop of sturdy oak; but it was sold for timber and felled, and
the ground left unplanted clothed itself as time passed with
stool-grown saplings and a dense scrub of birch, hazel and
thorn. Gutters silted up, watercourses brimmed over and
spread into bogs. Nature uncontrolled reverted to tangled
wilderness.

The wood dropped steeply into a gorge where the little
river Rune flowed through the hills. There was a field at the
bottom, long derelict, surrendered to bent-grass and rushes;
the cart track giving access through the wood was no longer
passable. Beyond the field and the river the opposite ridge
rose bare of trees, a cliff of heather and bracken, and there
was heather too above the wood, extending on up to the
skyline. The gorge was enclosed in moor on either side.

The upper fringe of the wood was marked off from the
moor by a road running straight as if drawn with a ruler. It
was only a secondary road connecting the market town of
Freeborough with the fishing port of Easby at the mouth of
the Rune; but on a fine Saturday afternoon in June it carried
a stream of motorists attracted by the cloudless sky and the
reputation of the scenery, which they found for once bathed
in sunshine equal to that of the tourist posters. There were
too many of them for the comfort of the girl on horseback,
who, edge as she might into the verge, earned eructations of
reproof from impatient horns. The narrow road bounded on
one side by a ditch, and from the moor on the other by a
steep bank rising to a wall, left her no choice beyond the
metalled carriageway, and her efforts not to obstruct it were
thwarted by her small white mare (she would not have liked
it to be called a pony), whose breeding was apparent not

only in flowing mane and tail and graceful limbs but also in a temperament which not even the firm seat and light hands of the rider could reconcile to the importunate noises. When a culvert in the ditch offered access to a track leading into the wood she turned aside without hesitation.

It was a wide path, and there were grooves like ruts as if it had once served as a cart track; but they were matted with rank grass, almost obliterated by clumps of tall weeds, it was evident that no traffic had passed for decades. Horse and rider both relaxed, the frantic urgency of the motor world dwindled muffled behind them. As they advanced at a foot's pace the wood encompassed, assimilated them, the mare's creamy white coat, the girl's green blouse and white jeans, her copper-red hair swaying with smooth tips on her neck. They became part of the light and shade, the dappled green and golden umber of their sanctuary.

The mood of relief did not last long. As the track bent downhill it entered a narrow cutting sunk between high banks. Falls of earth blocked the way in places, and a thicket of bushes and young trees sprang rooted in the bottom. There was barely passage for a man on foot, horse and rider were soon in difficulties; but she urged the reluctant beast on with her knees, bending forward pressed to its withers to elude the clutch of overhanging branches, undeterred by malicious switches of thorn that rebounded to whip and scratch her. No trace remained of any path; the ground became soft, the horse's hooves sank deeper, till it stopped abruptly, planted its feet and refused to move. Peering forward she swore to herself and accepted defeat, warned by the vivid green of the dell ahead fringed with grey patches of sphagnum moss. Pools of water glinted among the rushes.

As she turned back into the thicket the branches rustled; there was a patter of feet, and a shorn ewe black-faced and lean with two well-grown fleecy lambs emerged into the open. At sight of her they checked, stood and stared at her with suspicion, then as if they found her not too formidable, or their errand were too urgent to be postponed, they bolted on past her up the steep bank out of the hollow. She saw that they followed a track worn bare by sheep already, and when she urged her horse after them it responded with zest, thankful to escape the bog, took the climb at a canter and scrambled through bushes and over rocks to the crest. The ground dropped sharply again on the other side to an even thicker

2

belt of thorn, the overgrown ruin of a hedge; but between the gnarled trunks, through the mesh of leaves and twigs sunshine was streaming, this was where the wood ended. She lay prone, charged down at the weakest spot, leapt or crashed through a tangle of brushwood and briar and came out beyond scarred but triumphant in a field, an acre or so of rough pasture tucked away in the gorge between the wood and the river.

"What's this? The ride of the Valkyries?"

The voice was so unexpected that she scarcely took the words in. A young man stood in the shadow of the hedge. His khaki shirt and corduroy trousers bore evident signs of wear; he carried a crook, and a shaggy grey sheepdog waited at his heels.

She blushed: "I'm sorry. Am I trespassing?"

"Worse. You're committing sacrilege."

She glanced at him with curiosity. Neither his voice nor his words consorted with his shabby clothes. He was tanned, almost swarthy, but his features held an air of command, and his blue eyes were bold and teased her. They continued to rest on her when she looked away; they seemed to take pleasure in what they saw, ranging over her figure and her face, her full mouth, her own eyes grey and widely spaced.

"Do you know," he asked, "that this is the Devil's Churchyard?"

He was smiling, and she laughed: "No, I don't. What happens if he catches me?"

"I daren't tell you."

She blushed again: "Well, what are you doing here yourself? Or doesn't the Devil mind?"

"He won't have to. I'm gathering the sheep." He pointed up at the wood: "Once they get into that place they're rotten with maggots."

"I saw a ewe and two lambs there a few minutes ago," she told him.

"Did you?" His voice became earnest: "That's the old brute I'm looking for. Which way did she go?"

"She seemed to be aiming down here. We ought to see her."

They stared across the enclosure at an empty expanse of bent- and cotton-grass and scattered clumps of heather. There was no cover for the missing sheep except where a row of alder picked out the course of the river. The moor rose steeply beyond it with jutting crags.

"There's something moving in those trees," she muttered.

He nodded: "Yes, I'd better go and look." He made no attempt, however, stood silent beside her, absent-mindedly patting the mare's neck.

"We're beginning all wrong," he exclaimed at last. "We ought to introduce ourselves. I'm Jim Tranmire, and I live at Kemsdale Farm. I farm it myself."

"I'm Kate Evans, and I live at Saint Ursula's School at Easby. I teach there."

"I know it well. I wonder we've never met before, Kate." He added the Christian name deliberately as if to challenge the formality that had crept into her voice. As his eye caught hers she smiled shyly.

"I only started this term."

"Still you seem to find your way about. Does the school mount you?"

She shook her head and ran her fingers gently through the mare's mane: "No, Dinah's my own. I made friends with the man who does the grounds, and he keeps her for me on his holding. I'd suffocate if I couldn't sometimes escape from the school and be alone."

"What do you teach?"

"Anything from languages to arithmetic, whether I can or not. We're short of staff."

"Is English literature one of your subjects?"

"Yes. Why?"

"Thorough bush, thorough briar. You know Puck's song? You should sing it to your class, it suits you."

"A hobgoblin? You aren't very flattering. Instead of quoting Shakespeare oughtn't you to find your sheep?"

"It's all right. I'm watching. They can't stray far, the Rune will stop them. Let's go back to Shakespeare. I meant it as a compliment."

"Or the hideous truth? I expect I look awful." She squeezed her hand into the hip pocket of her jeans. They were tight, and she had to struggle to extract what she wanted, a gilt powder compact. When she tugged it out at last it slipped from her fingers and fell to the ground, hitting a stone. The clasp burst open, and the contents spilt out into the grass.

"Damn," she exclaimed. "It's bewitched, it did it on purpose."

4

He stooped to pick it up for her, saving as much of the powder as he could and replacing the pad. A small disc of paper was caught in the lid. He glanced at the design in surprise, a leering face wreathed with ivy.

She laughed: "Mr. Brink gave me that."

"It's copied from one of the carvings in the choir stalls, isn't it? The green man."

She nodded.

"Do you know Brink well?" he asked.

"Not really; but he comes to the church door to talk after the service. It's his duty, I suppose, as a parson."

"To talk to you?"

"Of course not." She blushed: "To all of us. Only I happened to ask about the carvings, and he said if I came some other time he'd show me them himself. So I took him at his word when I was free, and he showed me all over the church. He was very kind."

"I'm sure he was." His eyes were on her face as she dabbed it ineffectively, trying to obliterate the prickles and scratches of the hedge.

She paid no heed to his scrutiny: "At any rate I enjoyed it. He made it so interesting, and when we were in the vestry he brought out a lot of these little pictures from a drawer. The others were mostly saints and angels and things."

"What's it for? To stick in your prayer book? I'd have thought a saint or an angel would be more appropriate."

"He seemed pleased that I'd chosen the green man. He talked about the legend, he's very learned."

"Very." He spoke drily: "Did he talk of the Devil's Churchyard too? Is that why you came?"

She shook her head: "I'd never heard of it. Is that really its name? I thought you were joking."

"This is the Devil's Churchyard all right, at least that's what it's always called. There's an ancient circle of stones by the river. I'll show you if you like, but I'm afraid I haven't Brink's learning, or his charming way with it either."

"What do you mean?"

"I meant it as a warning."

She glanced at him thoughtfully, then nodded: "Yes, I wondered. Perhaps you're right."

"I don't want to be unjust to the man." He frowned: "Those who like him are all over him, women especially."

"Well, I wasn't."

5

"Not you of course. Only those who aren't in danger."

"You talk as if he were a satyr."

"And you a nymph? Perhaps you are."

"Not when I look in this mirror." She gave up her task with the pad, squeezed the reluctant compact back under her hip.

He watched her with amusement: "Let's go. I can round up the sheep at the same time."

He whistled to his dog nosing in an old rabbit hole, and they crossed the field in silence, he walking at the mare's side, the dog at his heels. Kate glanced at him once or twice with a puzzled frown, suddenly she exclaimed:

"I've got it. I know who you are, Mr. Tranmire."

"Jim," he corrected her.

"All right, Jim Tranmire. I know the name. I've heard it from Mrs. Buttle, our headmistress. You own most of Easby, you're her landlord."

He laughed: "I hope she isn't complaining still of the damp wall in the dormitory."

"She's full of your praises, says you're doing a lot for the estate." Her mouth curved into a smile: "You're a paragon in fact, except that you live on a farm and work it yourself."

"Do you think it odd of me?"

"Not if you're fond of the place."

"Well, I am. Kemsdale Farm was almost derelict when I took it over, I'm just beginning to pull it round. I wouldn't exchange it for anything, not if I was offered a yacht on the Riviera with a bevy of film stars thrown in."

"Film stars can look very charming."

"So too can dryads on horseback."

She leant forward to flick a dragonfly from the mare's ear. The posture hid her face, saved her from the need to reply.

As they approached the clump of alder the ground became softer.

"Shall I leave Dinah here?" she suggested. "It's getting boggy."

"I'm afraid you'll have to."

She turned over, slid to the ground and undid the halter coiled round the mare's neck, removed the bridle and fastened the halter to a low branch on a tree.

"Will she stand all right?" he asked.

"Yes, there's nothing to frighten her. You're used to this,

aren't you, Dinah?" She fondled the mare's head already lowered to graze.

The ewe and lambs were grazing too. Kate caught sight of them as soon as she entered the trees:

"Look, Jim." She pointed.

He whistled softly to the dog, which ran a short way towards the sheep, then crouched on its belly to watch them. The grass that held them was a promontory of turf enclosed in a loop of the river with only a narrow neck of land for access.

Jim laughed: "They couldn't have chosen a better place if they'd asked me. We can leave Fan to hold them there. Come on, let's call on the Devil."

Leaving the dog on guard he led her downstream along the bank. The alder encroached here to the water's edge, and they had to climb over prostrate trunks, duck under sagging branches to pass. There was a squeal behind him, a muffled curse, and he looked round anxiously:

"Have you hurt yourself?"

"Nowhere that matters." She scrambled to her feet, rubbing the seat of her pants, then bent suddenly to pick something out of the nettles.

"What is it?" he asked.

"A book, and it's bound in vellum. It can't have been here long, it's quite clean." She turned the pages, examining them with curiosity: "It's a sort of notebook, nothing printed, everything written in ink; but the handwriting looks very old, it's hard to read."

"Bring it along. We're almost out of the thicket."

She followed him across a morass, leaping from tuft to tuft of rushes, then crawled up through a last screen of leaves on to a knoll overlooking the river. The flat summit was bare of trees, the grass cropped close by sheep or rabbits. There was nothing to obscure the view of the ring of boulders that crowned it, some worn to mere stumps, others as tall as a man. Their plan remained undisturbed, a perfect circle.

Jim waited for Kate to catch up.

"The Devil's Churchyard," he told her.

They entered the precinct in silence. A huge slab embedded in the grass and protruding above it marked the centre, pale ganister scoured white by wind and rain, contrasting with the sombre sentinels surrounding it. At the farther end the ground rose again, and two adjacent monoliths set against the bank were joined by a crosspiece to form a cromlech giving entrance to a cave.

Kate pointed to it: "What's that?"

"The Devil's Parlour."

"Do people still believe all this?"

"I don't suppose so, but they keep the old names up. The ordnance survey helps, and the tourists like it."

"So do I." She stared round the enclosure, her eyes lingered on the cromlech, the gate to the underworld: "At least I'm not sure that I like it. Things can fascinate and frighten at the same time."

He nodded: "I expect that's what people felt in the past here, and if emotions can leave impressions this place ought to be full of them. It may be all nonsense about the Devil, but the men who put these stones up meant them for a place of worship." They were standing at the centre, and he touched the great slab with his crook: "That could be the altar."

"Yes, I wonder what rites it's known."

"If you want me to guess, human sacrifice."

She shuddered. A thundercloud reaching up over the hill clutched the sun, blotted it out for a moment, then crept on and released it.

"The Druids of course," she agreed. "This could have been one of their temples. They were priests in ancient Britain."

He smiled at her: "I don't only read books on agriculture." His tone had the effect that he wished, she blushed scarlet.

"I'm sorry. It's a dreadful habit, it comes from teaching in school."

"A charming habit." It was clear that he referred to her flushed cheeks rather than didactic manners. He added quickly: "Let's look at the book you found when you sat in the nettles. We'll read it together, Kate."

She held it out to him, glad of the diversion: "How did it ever get there? It's so well-bound, not the sort of book anyone would throw away."

He took it, examined it with interest. It was an octavo-sized volume whose binding of plain white vellum tooled with gold showed little trace of its recent misadventure. There was no title on the cover; the pages of thick handmade paper were covered with close handwriting, a florid and archaic script.

8

He whistled softly to himself: "More at home in a collector's library than in a bog in the wood."

He seated himself on the edge of the altar stone, drew Kate by the hand to sit beside him; but she shrank away, threw herself on her breasts in the grass.

"How can you? Think of the blood."

He laughed, got up and joined her: "Are you so superstitious?"

"We'd be sitting where the victims were killed. You said so yourself."

He did not reply, opened the book and turned the pages: "Can you read this scrawl? I can't."

"It's terribly difficult. Wait a moment, there's something here. Oh, it's Latin."

"I suppose you teach that too?"

"Only very elementary Latin. I'm sure you know as much as I do."

"I'm sure I don't. Go on, read it out."

She bent her head over the book: "*Alii animam ignem esse dixerunt, alii spiritum, alii sanguinem.*"

"You'll have to translate that for me, I need a dictionary."

"Some say the soul is fire, others breath, others blood." She frowned: "Blood again. It seems to haunt the place."

"Let's see what else it says." He flicked through the pages, but found nothing that either could decipher till near the end. Then almost at the last page he paused, dabbed the place with his finger: "Look, it's different handwriting, much easier."

She peered over his shoulder: "It's a list of names."

The list reached to a page and a half. From time to time a fresh hand took over as if this were a register kept up to date by a succession of clerks. All were personal names; they ceased halfway down the page, and the rest was blank.

Kate read the final entry, unaware that she was speaking aloud:

"Kate Evans."

Jim stared at her: "Is the book yours?"

She shook her head: "I've never seen it before."

Her face was drained of colour, her eyes remained fixed on her own name.

"It's in much fresher ink," she muttered. "It was added long after the rest."

9

She turned the pages back feverishly, poring over the unintelligible paragraphs that filled them. He watched her for a time in silence.

"Can you make any sense of it?" he asked at last.

"Very little. They seem to be notes jotted down at random. Here's something in Latin, and the next which looks like a recipe in a language I don't know at all. Ah, here's a text from the Bible, and in English." She read it out: "Labour not for the meat that perisheth but for that meat which endureth unto everlasting life."

"It sounds innocent enough."

"Yes, but what has it to do with me? Why should my name be written there?"

He was too puzzled himself to know what to say to comfort her.

Neither paid attention to the cloud advancing overhead, the ominous extinction of the sunshine. Their first effective warning of the storm was the splash of a raindrop on the book. More followed in rapid succession, the shower became a downpour.

Jim leapt to his feet. "Quick. You've only a thin blouse, you'll be soaked to the skin. We must run for it."

"But where?"

"The Devil's Parlour. There's nowhere else."

She grabbed the book, and they raced hand in hand across the grass to the dark entrance. It was low, and she had to crawl in on all-fours. He followed.

The floor of hard earth was quite dry, but there was not much room in the chamber. Jim and Kate crouched close together, his arm found accommodation round her waist. She accepted it without demur, thankful to have it to protect her from the shadows encroaching behind. In front, beyond the jambs of the cromlech, sheets of driven rain pelted down on the ring of standing stones and the pale altar in the middle.

She shuddered, and he laughed, squeezed her waist reassuringly: "We ought to be grateful to the Devil for so handy a shelter."

A peal of thunder reverberated, coinciding with a flash of lightning so dazzling that for a moment they were blinded. The storm was directly above them. As they recovered sight, peering out into the rain, Kate gasped, her voice sank to a whisper:

10

"What's that on the altar? There's something moving."

"Your eyes are still dazed by the flash."

"No, no. Look."

He could no longer deny it. The rain spread a veil that dimmed and distorted the view; nevertheless there could be no mistake, a figure was climbing up on to the altar stone. If it was an animal it was one of the larger sort, but it did not look like a sheep or a dog. In another moment it was standing erect on the top, a naked man. The limbs were human, but the head crowned with long horns was a goat's.

The two watching clung to each other in the darkness underground. The narrow orifice restricted their view, scudding rain obscured details and fostered illusion. The monstrous figure on the altar however persisted, refused to be explained away. A monotonous chant mingled with the storm, with the wail of the wind and the rustle of threshing branches. Time froze, the apparition seemed to last forever. Then the wind veered suddenly, a gust of rain drove in under the cromlech and they shrank back. When they looked out again the altar was empty.

They turned to each other, their eyes met.

"You saw it?" she asked.

He nodded.

"What can it be? It was as if the Devil stood there himself."

He laughed shortly: "Perhaps some madman with an urge to expose himself."

"However mad people are their heads don't grow horns like a goat."

He did not reply, and she sighed:

"Thank goodness at least that it's gone." Then she gripped his arm: "No, it hasn't. Listen, what's that?"

The noise came from a distance, out of the trees beyond the stone circle. It was like a yell of exultation, then again like the howl of an animal in pain. The two notes persisted, blending in infernal harmonics, till it was impossible to distinguish one from the other.

"Dinah," Kate cried. "What are they doing to her?"

She began to crawl out, but he caught her by the waistband: "No, stay here. I'll go and see." Then as she struggled against him he added: "That unholy row may be the Devil, but I'm damned if it's a horse."

11

She paid no attention, tugged herself free, ran across the grass into the trees. Unable to stop her he ran at her side.

The worst of the storm was over, the rain less heavy; but the wet leaves of the alder and the undergrowth into which they plunged drenched them as if they were bathing. The bloodcurdling clamour died down and was silent; still they pressed on in haste in the direction from which it had arisen, the direction in which Dinah was tied. As they approached the spot Kate raced on ahead.

Dinah was loose, had wrenched herself free; her halter trailed on the ground with a piece of the branch held fast in the knot, broken off by her struggles. She had not strayed far; but she still shivered, and fear and suspicion gleamed in the white of her eyes as she looked round. Kate walked quietly to her head, grasped and soothed her.

"She's been badly frightened," she called, "but she's all right."

The place where Dinah stood was a little hollow used by someone recently for the deposit of litter, painted cardboard, plywood and other less identifiable material crushed and scattered by the mare's hooves. Kate bent down to see what it was, but at that moment Jim called her:

"Here's where the trouble came from."

There was concern in his voice, and she made haste to tie Dinah to a securer tree, then ran to join him.

She found him on the bank of the river kneeling beside the dog, which crouched whimpering in the grass. The ewe watched defiantly, ready to repel attack. One lamb only was with her, panic-stricken, nuzzling her udder. There was a dark red stain in the ground, a pool of blood.

As Kate approached Jim raised his head:

"She's been beaten almost to death, with a heavy club from the look of her. It's a marvel she's alive."

Kate knelt, took the dog's head in her arms.

He nodded approvingly: "If you hold her I can make a proper examination. She won't bite."

"I'm sure she won't."

Fan confirmed the words by licking her hand.

He lifted each leg in turn and felt it carefully, then ran his fingers over spine and ribs. There was no protest except for a whine as he touched a tender spot.

"Poor old bitch," he muttered. "If I could catch the fiend who did this I'd break every bone in his body."

"Are hers broken?" Kate asked.

"I haven't found any yet, but I'm not sure. Let's see if she'll get up."

Kate released her, and Fan struggled to her feet, stretched herself.

"Come on, Fan," he urged. "Show us what you can do."

He took a few steps, and the dog followed limping.

"She's sore and bruised," he pronounced, "but with luck there's nothing worse."

"Poor, poor Fan." Kate rubbed her softly under the jowl. "Who could have been so cruel?"

He pointed to the pool of blood: "The swine who spilt that in the grass. It's pretty clear what happened. He took the lamb, Fan went for him, and he beat her off. What we heard was a mixture of his yells and her howls, all pandemonium let loose." He stared angrily round into the trees: "He seems to have got the best of it, killed the lamb and made off with the carcase."

Kate shuddered: "No wonder you call this place the Devil's Churchyard."

He frowned, spoke earnestly: "I wish I'd never told you the name. Look, Kate, you mustn't let it give you ideas. That figure we saw among the stones was no spook. How could a spook flog a dog and cut a lamb's throat?"

"What was it then?"

"A madman, a dangerous one to have about, but nothing uncanny."

She shook her head, the apparition remained vivid in her memory.

"I know what you're thinking," he persisted. "The horns and the goat's face. Perhaps we imagined them, we only caught a glimpse through the storm. Perhaps they were a disguise he was wearing."

"Perhaps," she replied unconvinced. "But nothing can explain away the feeling I had, the power, the evil."

He glanced at her with something of his former teasing expression: "All the same as I don't want to lose more lambs I'm going to report this to the police. They'll do more good, I think, than Brink with a service of exorcism."

She smiled despite herself: "Mr. Brink would love it, with all the words in Latin and tomes of learning to support each."

"Let him. There's nothing to stop him. Archangels for him, policemen for me, we'll try both. Meanwhile I'd better

13

drive this ewe to safer ground before she loses the other lamb."

"Fan won't be much help." She turned to look for the dog; but as if understanding what was said Fan advanced already towards the sheep, moving with discomfort, limping, but with firm purpose.

Jim laughed: "It takes more than the Devil to keep Fan from work."

Kate's face was grave: "She's very plucky, but she can't turn them if they bolt. Wouldn't you like me to come too?"

"There's nothing I'd like better." The warmth of his smile pleased and reassured her: "Get up on Dinah, and if the sheep go wrong you can gallop round them."

She ran back to the mare, untied the halter, put on the bridle and mounted. They all set off together, Jim, Kate, Dinah, Fan, the ewe and her lamb. The storm was past, the sun shone again.

As they followed the bank of the river in the direction away from the Devil's Churchyard the alder became sparser, the ground firmer. There was a clearly marked path to guide them, and the ewe as if subdued by recent experience trotted obediently in front with the lamb at her heels, demanding no effort beyond the strength of the crippled dog. Kate held Dinah back to walk at Jim's side.

"I'll put them in the long pasture beside the wood," he told her. "I've made the fence up, they won't get through. It's your easiest way back anyhow to Easby. The field runs right up to the road, and there's a gate in the wall at the top."

"I'm glad I haven't to go back the way I came." She laughed: "It was less a ride than an obstacle race."

"You came down through the wood?"

She nodded.

"You must be the first for more than a century. I don't know when that road was last used, not since the oaks were planted, and they were felled before I was born."

"What was the road made for?"

"This field here in the bottom was cultivated in the old days, and there was other traffic too. It's said that there used to be a festival, that crowds came to attend it at certain seasons of the year."

"What sort of festival?"

"Pagan in origin, I suppose. The rites weren't too decorous."

14

"Were they held in the Devil's Churchyard among the stones?" Her voice trembled.

"How should I know?" He spoke lightly: "I wasn't born, so I couldn't take part."

She rode on in silence, her face was clouded.

A hurdle made fast with wire barred the gap in the fence of the long pasture. He undid the fastenings, pulled it aside, and they put the sheep through. She followed, then waited while he restored the hurdle to its place. As he joined her he pointed up the hill:

"You can't miss the way. Make for that bush on the sky-line, the gate's not far beyond it."

"Thank you. I'll find it all right." She gathered her reins.

"Kate," he exclaimed suddenly. "You're not just going to gallop out of my life, are you?"

She hesitated, flushed, made no effort to urge the mare forward.

"I mean," he explained, "you've had a bad shock. Horrid things have happened this afternoon. I hope they haven't sickened you of my company."

"Why should they?" she asked. "They weren't your fault. They were just as horrid for you as for me, more so as it was your lamb that was killed."

"But your name in the book, though it's mere chance, I'm sure. You aren't the only Kate Evans in the world."

She stared at him in consternation: "Good gracious. The book. Where is it?"

"I thought you had it."

"I must have left it in the Devil's Parlour when we heard the noise and ran."

"I'll go back and get it."

"No, no. Not today."

"Why not? Because that madman may still be prowling there?"

She nodded.

"Look, Kate, you're not to worry. I know every inch of the ground. I'll come to no harm."

"Couldn't you wait till tomorrow?"

"All right, if it pleases you. The book's safe enough there. No one else is likely to find it. If I get it tomorrow, when shall I bring it so that we can look at it together?"

She hesitated: "The whole school goes to church in the

15

morning, and it's my Sunday on duty so I'll have to be there to help Mrs. Buttle."

"Like Fan to round up the flock?"

She nodded and laughed.

"What about later? I'd rather see you when you're free."

"I'll be pretty busy all day, except perhaps in the evening when I'm taking a few of the older girls to Mr. Brink's party."

"Yes, I'd heard of it. His midsummer orgy?"

"Not very orgiastic. We dance round a bonfire and jump over it, and end up by setting light to a straw wheel and rolling it down the rectory lawn."

"It all sounds very innocent and folksy."

"You won't be there yourself?"

"I've already posted a firm refusal, but I could change my mind."

"Oh, do come."

"You'll spare me a minute or two if I do? You won't be too absorbed in celebrating the solstice?"

She shook her head with a smile.

"Then I'll see you there. That's settled." He laid his hand on her thigh: "Why, you're soaked, and I've been keeping you all this time. I hope you don't catch cold."

"Or you either. You're just as wet as I am."

"All right, we'll both change our clothes. Goodbye till tomorrow."

The hill was steep, but the turf made the going easy. The mare broke into a canter, and Kate gave her her head. She looked round once to wave; Jim stood watching with Fan at his heels, he waved back. As she cantered on over the crest she had no room in her thoughts for the Devil, his churchyard, his parlour or even her name in his book. She was too busy thinking of Jim Tranmire.

She found the gate without difficulty and came out on the road. Cars strident and impatient, meeting or passing her, claimed her attention; but beyond the corner of the long meadow where the wood crept up to the roadside its tangled recesses reminded her of the secrets that it held. All looked peaceful in the dappled sunlight. A picnic party sat having tea against a backcloth of embroidered may-blossom.

A light blue car was parked at the other side of the road, a Ford Cortina. She supposed that it belonged to the picnickers, and she cursed them in her heart for making her ride into the path of oncoming traffic to circumvent it; but as she drew level she saw that it was occupied, and she recognised the man in clerical black who sat there. She smiled at him, but his eyes were fixed unseeing on the windscreen, and he paid no attention.

She was barely past him however before she heard his voice, and she turned. He was on foot hurrying after her, a man of rubicund complexion in late middle age whose tendency to corpulence was redeemed by his height, he was very tall.

"Miss Evans," he exclaimed. "My wits were wool-gathering when you passed, but I knew you at once from behind."

She smiled uncertainly: "Good afternoon, Mr. Brink."

"What a pretty picture, and to think that if I hadn't stopped to talk to these people I'd have missed it."

His eyes clung to her. She remembered that they had a habit of doing so when he showed her over the church, a scrutiny that provoked discomfort without sufficient cause to take offence. She felt herself blushing, tried angrily to control it, turning from him to stare at the picnickers:

"Are they friends of yours?"

"No, no, complete strangers; but I've lost one of my treasures, nothing really of value except to a collector like myself, and I fancy that it fell from my pocket the other day in the wood. As there are young people in the party it occurred to me they might have come across it in their rambles."

She glanced at him with interest and was about to ask what his lost treasure was, but he changed the subject abruptly, brought it back to herself:

"A transformation worthy of the classical poets, the new recruit at Saint Ursula's revealed as equestrian Muse. No, the Muses were draped, you tempt me to quote Ovid— *frenato delphine sedens, Theti nuda*."*

"Dinah isn't in the least like a porpoise." Her resentment arose even more from his description of herself as "naked Thetis."

His eyes twinkled placatingly: "Not a porpoise, my dear, a dolphin, but you're right, they're a similar species. You know too much Latin. I'll have to be careful."

She gathered her reins, resolved to be careful too: "Good-

---

*Naked Thetis, sitting on a bridled dolphin.

17

bye, Mr. Brink. I got wet through in the storm, I'm going home to change my clothes."

"Yes," he agreed, "I can see you're soaked to the skin."

She rode away, furious with him for the tone of his words, furious with her own too obtrusive contours, thankful only that he interrupted her before she could tell him about the book. Then she heard him start the car, and in another minute he passed her. She pretended not to see him when he saluted her with a hand raised in benediction.

She reached the brow of a long hill, and the town of Easby lay beneath her, the boats in the harbour, the ruined abbey on the cliff and the sea beyond. A bridle path offered escape here from the car-infested road, and she turned aside with relief into a field. The sky free again of clouds, the air fresh after the rain soothed her temper, discouraged lurid flights of imagination. What had the man's lost treasure to do with her? It was probably one of the knick-knacks that he showed her in the vestry. She recalled the nettle bed where the book was found, it was ridiculous to suppose that he would choose to walk there. Clergy in her experience did not go scrambling in bogs. It was sheer coincidence, nothing more, that the book held a list of names, that the last was Kate Evans.

Chapter 2

"I'm telling you for your good, Mother. You're only making yourself a laughingstock."

Pearl Corrington and her mother were helping to decorate Easby Church. They were an incongruous pair, the daughter tall, slim and stately, the mother amply cushioned and short, and while Pearl wore her clothes, a coat and skirt of navy-blue linen, with an elegance that disguised the art her mother's taste ran to loud patterns, garish colours. Both had fair hair, Mrs. Corrington's too fair to be credible, but Pearl's retained a natural gloss, skilfully waved. Her features were sharp but regular. She looked older than she was.

She turned away to adjust the sweet peas in a bowl on the font:

"If you don't care for your own sake you might at least for mine."

"You do make a fuss about nothing, Pearl." Her mother's voice was amiable, her double chin creased as she smiled: "I'm only trying to help the poor man. I'm sure he needs it without a wife or even a sister to look after him."

"Hasn't he got every old tabby in the town?" She glanced round the church at the women occupied there.

"That's naughty of you," her mother admonished her. "You shouldn't speak like that of pious ladies who give their lives to the church."

"To a bachelor clergyman, you mean, with a private income."

Mrs. Corrington stooped to her basket to sort out a bunch of roses. There was displeasure in her good-natured face:

"I don't know what Mr. Brink's income is, and I don't want to know. He's a dear man, and I'm glad to help him. People can say what they like."

"They do, and it's most embarrassing. I'm sure that's why Jim Tranmire was so curt the other day when I met him."

"Jim? What's he got to do with it?"

"Well, he's a friend of mine, or was. It isn't very nice to be dropped."

"Nonsense, Pearl. You imagine things." Mrs. Corrington found a bowl for the roses and filled it with water, her movements were flustered. "He's a very civil young man, always very pleasant. What did he say to offend you?"

"It wasn't what he said but what he didn't say. I might have been the dowdiest old frump, he was in such a hurry to be off."

"I expect he was busy, he has so much to do on his farm."

"Farm, farm till I'm sick of it. Baa-baa, black sheep. Why can't he leave his men to look after the wretched creatures? He ought to get about in the town more, mix with people of his own class."

"Yes, it does seem a pity," her mother agreed, glad that Jim Tranmire's failings should incur rebuke rather than her own. She added placidly: "I often think he'd do so well for you, Pearl."

19

"I wouldn't have him if he begged me on his knees, not till he rids himself of his barnyard habits." She turned away, devoted herself in glum silence to the flowers, venting her feelings in the violence with which she crammed them into place.

"I can't think why we're doing this," she exclaimed at last. "Who ever heard of decorating a church for mid-summer?"

Her mother glanced at her with an anxious frown: "You should ask Mr. Brink, he could tell you. I'm such a duffer, but of course this isn't only midsummer, it's Saint John's Day."

"Not much trace of Saint John. We've never had any-thing of the sort before, not till Mr. Brink came. He hasn't been here six months, and he's turning us all into pagans. I'm sure it isn't respectable."

"Pearl, you're very unkind. I refuse to listen."

"You'll have to listen when you hear it from others, from everyone in the town except his bevy of adorers." She glared at an old woman fitting a wreath of marsh-marigolds to a seventeenth-century dignitary recumbent on a tomb: "We aren't all so susceptible to his charm. Someone ought to complain to the Bishop."

"Nonsense. Everyone who matters is going to his party tomorrow to see the old customs revived."

"They'll go out of curiosity, but they aren't happy about it."

"Why not? These are sacred customs. He put it so nicely, they've the flavour of the age of faith; there's something very holy about them."

"Something very unholy, if you ask me, the flavour of the Devil."

A reverberating peal of thunder close overhead interrupted her. She paid no attention, but her mother looked up in alarm:

"What a sudden storm, almost uncanny, like an answer to blasphemy."

"Don't be so superstitious, Mother." She pursed her lips and went to the door, staring out at the rain pouring down in torrents: "In any case, I'm not the blasphemer. Serve him right if it's weather like this tomorrow."

The storm passed at last, the sun shone again. As the afternoon wore on the workers began to drift away for tea.

"Are you coming, Mother?" Pearl asked.

"Yes, I'm dying for a cup," she replied eagerly. Then her eyes fell on the pulpit: "Oh dear, they've given him no flowers when he's preaching."

"Why worry? He'll make up with flowers of speech. Forty minutes we got last week, and tomorrow's a special occasion."

"I can't leave it so bare for the poor man."

"I can, if he chooses to gallivant in his car round the country while we work."

"You're very unjust. He has a lot to do in the parish."

"So have I, and the first is to put on the kettle and make tea. You can follow when you like, Mother." She went out, slamming the door behind her.

The pulpit was a triple-decker, and by the time that Mrs. Corrington had adorned it to her satisfaction she was alone in the building. She was hot and tired, thought wistfully of Pearl with her cup of tea; but most of all she longed to take the weight off her legs, to ease her back which ached from bending, a posture unsuited to her stout figure. She sank with relief on her ample seat in a pew, an old-fashioned box pew with high sides like most of those in Easby Church. When a man came in from the porch she was out of sight, even the red and orange pattern of her blouse was lost in shadow.

She herself saw that it was Brink, but refrained for personal reasons from making her presence known at once. She had loosened the zip of her skirt, and it stuck fast now as she fumbled to adjust it. By the time that the difficulty was overcome he was at the steps of the chancel, and as she watched him his behaviour amazed her, held her silent. Awe restrained her from interrupting.

He seemed less to walk than to strut. His arms were stretched out before him in the hieratic pose of one performing a solemn ritual, and his hands supported a burden of which she could see little except a dull white. As he advanced along the choir stalls he stopped once or twice and knelt, laying down his burden and turning to the stall with a gesture as if he stroked the carving; then he rose in the attitude as before and went on again to the altar. He stood facing it, bowed several times and carefully deposited what he carried so that it rested in front of the cross. She could hear his voice chanting but could not distinguish the words. At last he removed the offering, bore it to a cupboard

21

in a recess used as an ambry and put it inside. He closed the door and locked it.

She was at a loss what to do. She felt that she was spying on him, witness of a secret act of communion between him and his God. He was coming back down the nave, and her heart sank as she saw him pause to examine the forms of service laid in the pews for the congregation tomorrow. Would he do the same when he came to hers? The deceit lay on her conscience, but her distress was too much for her. She put up her feet on the cushions and pretended to be asleep.

He reached her pew, leant over casually to rearrange the leaflets on the rack. Then he caught sight of her, exclaimed in surprise:

"Why, it's Molly Corrington."

She sat up, rubbed her eyes: "Oh dear, I must have dropped off. I was tired after doing all these flowers, so I took a little nap."

His face cleared, he collected himself: "No wonder you're tired out. You've made a magnificent job of the church." He glanced round at the decorations: "Have all the others gone home?"

"I think so."

"Leaving only my faithful Molly."

The use of her Christian name pleased and warmed her. They were not yet quite on those terms.

He surveyed her with a benevolence beneath which lay a trace of apprehension: "I disturbed you, I'm afraid. You were fast asleep?"

"Far away in dreamland." She could almost persuade herself that her words were true, that in fact she had dreamt it all.

He received her assurance with evident relief, held the door of the pew open for her as she rose to her feet to come out. She moved fussily, clutching her bag:

"I must be getting home for tea myself. Pearl will be wondering what's happened to me."

"No, I beg you. Let me give you tea here, I'm sure you're ready for it. I've an electric kettle in the vestry, we can enjoy a cup together."

It was an invitation that she could not resist.

The vestry to which a passage led from behind the pulpit was larger than its purpose needed. He used the farther end to accommodate a little museum, a collection of carved stones, scraps of documents and similar treasures, all that Kate Evans described to herself as his knick-knacks. There was a glass-topped case to hold some of these, a chest of drawers for others. An electric kettle stood on the latter, and he took it to the tap in the corner, filled it with water and inserted the plug.

As she sat in his armchair, soothed by the cup of tea that he brought her, Molly Corrington was able without difficulty to banish the memory of his odd behaviour from her mind. He went out of his way to charm her, plying her with chocolate biscuits of which she was fond, and leading the conversation by easy stages to Saint Ursula's School:

"You're among Mrs. Buttle's oldest friends, I believe?"

"Yes, I think I can say so." His interest flattered her: "Helen and I were ourselves at school together, and that's many, many years ago."

"Not so very many, if you ask my opinion."

Their eyes met and she dropped hers bashfully, hoping that he would say more. He was silent however, waiting, and she herself at last resumed:

"We drifted apart after I married. I'm afraid that Ernest wasn't her sort. He was a bookmaker, you know. Not at the races of course, but very high-class with offices in Mayfair, and he earned a lot of money and left Pearl and me very comfortably off." She sighed, took a handkerchief from her bag and dabbed her eyes.

"I bear Helen no grudge," she added. "She made up for it after his death, told me of this nice house at Easby, and Pearl and I came to live here. It was handy of course for Pearl to go to Saint Ursula's. That's where she got her fine manners, not from me."

He smiled: "You're too modest."

"I'm not, but I don't complain. We must take ourselves as we are. Anyhow, if I'd been Pearl's type I don't suppose Ernest would have married me."

He echoed her laugh politely: "Does Pearl keep in touch with her old school since she left?"

"Oh yes, she's a great favourite there. I tease Arthur about it, he spoils her."

"I wasn't thinking of Doctor Buttle, I meant the teachers. Aren't some of them about her age?"

"Only the new one, Kate Evans. The others are older."

"Kate Evans." He repeated the name slowly: "Yes, I've met her. So Pearl and she are friends?"

"Not really. Pearl's friends are all so classy. She gets quite cross with me, says I've low tastes; but I've taken rather a fancy to Kate myself. We can't all be ladies of leisure, not when so much goes in taxes."

He nodded: "If Pearl has these old-fashioned ideas I'm afraid she won't listen to my proposal."

"Proposal?"

He laughed genially at her tone of surprise: "No, no, not of marriage. It's just that I'm looking for a cast to act a sacred drama, and I haven't chosen my leading lady yet."

"She might be willing, but I doubt it. She doesn't much care for theatricals. Who else have you got?"

"My most enthusiastic support comes from the younger holiday-makers, especially from the caravan site by the harbour."

"Pearl wouldn't like that at all. She doesn't approve of them."

"Then I'll have to find someone else." He spoke without disappointment: "Who can you suggest? What about Kate Evans?"

"She's a very clever girl, she'd learn her part quickly. She was at college, you know, at Oxford, quite a bluestocking."

"She sounds just the thing. This is a rite of great antiquity, and I want to keep the traditional words, especially for the principal character. They're archaic, some even Latin."

"That won't trouble Kate. She teaches Latin, learnt it at college, took a degree with first-class honours, so Helen tells me."

He moved his chair towards her: "I want you to do me a favour, Molly. Talk to Kate and persuade her to accept the part, to make this event a success. Yes, and talk to Mrs. Buttle too, her permission will be needed for Kate to have time off to attend rehearsals. A word from you, Molly, can do so much."

The repetition of her Christian name had the effect intended. Molly Corrington beamed:

"Of course I'll do what I can—"

"Oswald," he pleaded.

"Oh, what a nice name. Of course I'll do what I can, Oswald, but if I'm going to talk to them I'd better know more exactly what you want. This is in connection with the church, I suppose?"

"Yes, with our celebration of the feast of Saint John. I hope to make an announcement tomorrow."

"But tomorrow it's midsummer already, Saint John's Day, I mean, and you haven't chosen your cast yet. You'll be too late with it."

He frowned: "An undertaking of this sort needs careful preparation, it can't be hurried. There are precedents for holding the final act over till the octave of the feast, which falls this year on the Sunday following."

"Of course you know best," she made haste to assure him; but the tone of his voice troubled her, and she recalled Pearl's warning, her unfavourable view of such rites. "I'm sure," she went on, "these old customs are very interesting and valuable, but I wonder if they aren't a little above our heads here in Easby. We haven't your learning, you see."

"If the priest understands the inner meaning it's enough."

"Yes, but other people may misunderstand and be difficult."

"You must help me to overcome difficulties. I rely on you, Molly." He patted her gently on the hand, then took her cup to refill it. As he reached for the teapot his sleeve rucked back, revealing an ugly wound on his forearm.

"Oh dear," she exclaimed. "You've hurt yourself. How did it happen?"

"It's nothing." He put down the pot, jerked his sleeve quickly into place: "I'd a little trouble with my car on the way home, a fault in the distributor. I'm a clumsy mechanic, I jabbed my arm with the spanner."

She accepted the explanation, but still regarded him with concern: "It looks horrid. Do let me bandage it for you."

"Really you're wasting your sympathy." He stood up, her cup was left unfilled. There was displeasure, ill-suppressed impatience in his manner, but he made an effort to control it: "Please don't think me discourteous, Molly. I'm expecting some young people very soon to discuss this project of mine, and I must look out a few books and things to show them." He moved across the room to the chest of drawers.

"Yes, of course. I know how busy you are." She clutched her bag, rose in some confusion to her feet: "I've taken up too much of your time already."

25

"You haven't, I assure you. I've much enjoyed our little talk. You won't forget to put in a word with Mrs. Buttle?" The smile with which he said it warmed her heart.

"Indeed I won't, Oswald." She hesitated: "I wish you'd do something for me in your turn, promise to show that nasty place on your arm to a doctor."

"I will if it doesn't heal." He turned abruptly, pulled open a drawer. It was very full, and some sheets of paper were shaken out; one of them fluttered to her feet.

She picked it up to hand back to him, glanced in surprise at the picture, a leering face wreathed in ivy.

He laughed: "The green man. Don't you recognise him?"

"No. Ought I?"

"Yes, indeed. He's among the worthies carved on the choir stalls. Keep him; he's rather good, don't you think?"

She peered at the little engraving: "I'm not at all sure that I like him, but I'll take him just as a keepsake. What's this pencilled on the back?"

He glanced at it over her shoulder: "Oh, a votive inscription, some verses I wrote in his honour."

"How interesting, with your name and the date."

"It's the date of my birth. It was the custom once, you may call it superstitious, to choose an influence to preside over one's life from birth to death, and I meant to invite the green man to play the part. He's always been a favourite of mine."

"What a quaint custom. What did you do?"

"Nothing in the end. I'd more important things to think about. Let me find you another copy, one that I haven't scribbled on. I've plenty more."

"I'd rather keep this, it's more personal, unless you still want to offer it to the green man."

"I can offer it to no one in whom I've more confidence than you."

"Thank you, Oswald." She beamed at him, put the engraving in her bag.

There were two doors to the vestry, the one giving access to the church, the other leading straight outside. Voices could be heard approaching the latter, the scrunch of feet on the gravel. She listened uneasily, remembering Pearl's admonition and shrinking from her disapproval. It would be awkward if the story went round the parish that she was found having tea with the rector alone in the vestry. She glanced at him appealingly:

"They're coming. I'd better be off."

He nodded, opened the door for her into the church, waited till it shut behind her before he went to the other to admit his visitors.

The church was filled with golden light where the sun streamed in through the immense haloes of the angels in the west window. Molly Corrington was a regular church-goer, she knew the building well; but she was accustomed to regard it as a setting for the performance of religious and social duties—the latter perhaps more than the former—and had little feeling for its beauty, its antiquity, being interested neither in ecclesiastical history nor in architecture. If she saw it now with changed eyes the enchantment arose less from the evening light on the mellow stone of walls and pillars, or the abundance of flowers and greenery adorning them, than from the association of all this with Oswald Brink. She felt his presence still with her as she stood beneath the pulpit, a presence dominating, disquieting but wholly fascinating her. The image returned to haunt her mind of a solemn procession, a hierophant offering sacrifice at the altar. It was like a dream troubling, bewildering, inspiring mystery and awe, but it gratified her to share such a secret even without his knowledge and against his will.

Sunbeams gleamed like points of fire from the polished oak of the choir stalls. She remembered how he paused there at intervals for mysterious rites, and her thoughts passed by association of ideas to the green man whose likeness she carried in her bag. It surprised him that she was not familiar with the carving; very well, she would look for it now, and when next she saw him she would tell him and earn his praise.

The figures were carved from bosses along the front of the stalls. She knelt to examine them, entertained by the vivid designs, expressions of racy humor more often than conventional piety. Here were imps, monsters, roguish monks, saucy nuns, fit company for the green man. She smiled as she recognised him, touched his face gently. It was wet, slimy. She stared in disgust at her fingertip, red with blood.

With difficulty she suppressed a scream. She rose to her feet, rushed in panic out of the church. In the open air she

27

looked at her finger again. The bloodstain was unmistakable. She wiped it off on the grass.

Easby Church, standing above the town near the abbey ruins, looked down on open sea in one direction and in another on the harbour at the mouth of the Rune, busy with fishing and pleasure craft. Molly Corrington hurried out of the churchyard on to the path at the edge of the cliff. A bench was placed there by the council for the benefit of those wishing to enjoy the view. She sank on it with relief, still trembling from her recent experience, lacking strength yet for the long flight of steps that led down between steeply clustered houses to the main street.

As she sat there she began to recover her equanimity, soothed by the great sheet of blue water glittering to the horizon and, when she turned, by the familiar faces of the buildings clothing and crowning the cliff opposite. Beneath her comfortable, rather commonplace appearance lay a fund of commonsense. What was she making all this fuss about? The man had a nasty cut on his arm, as she knew. What more natural than that, kneeling to make those gestures at the stalls, blessing them in all probability, he should inadvertently drip blood over them? She clutched at the explanation thankfully, reproved herself for her gruesome fancies. Her mind dwelt again with renewed tenderness on Oswald Brink, his learning, his odd ideas, but above all his charm. He was a great change from Ernest Corrington, and yet perhaps not so unlike. They were both men to make you feel warm inside.

She got up, rested and reassured, plodded cheerfully down the steps into the town.

More than an hour passed before the church disgorged the party conferring in the vestry. They came out chattering and laughing, young men dressed in the scanty shorts or dirty slacks that were the uniform of the camping site. Brink accompanied them as far as the wicket gate. As he stood there to see them off one of them hung back.

"Could I have a word with you, sir?" he asked.

"By all means." Brink glanced with curiosity at the puny, bespectacled figure remarkable only for the fervour glowing in the pale eyes.

The youth jerked his thumb contemptuously after his receding companions: "It's a lark to them, but not to me. I know what you're talking about. Those books you showed

28

us, I've read them, as many as I could find in the public library at home."

"You're a student of folklore?"

"Call it that if you like, but there's more to it than games on the lawn or whimsy-whamsy play-acting. They knew what they meant in the old days, and it wasn't too pretty."

"We're fellow workers, it seems, in the same field." His tone was not discouraging: "Let me see, do I know your name?"

"I don't suppose you do. It's Albert Dockin."

"What do you want to ask me, Albert? Is it something I didn't make clear in the vestry?"

"You made it clear enough as far as you took it. About the green man, I mean, that he reigns in the woods for a year from midsummer to midsummer, then the goddess tires of him and chooses another; but you didn't finish the story, that he comes to a sticky end."

"You're a purist, I see, you insist on the full text; but I'm a parson, remember, and this is a play to be acted in church. Parts of the ancient ritual aren't very suitable."

"They weren't content in the old days just to dance and sing."

"They weren't. Careful censorship is needed to produce an acceptable version."

Albert frowned: "What's the use of doing it at all if it's to be prettified out of all recognition?"

"The rites of midsummer are a pleasing tradition, and I try to reconcile them with Christianity." He broke off, laughed at Albert's expression of disdain: "Very well, I'll give you an honest answer. Religion has two faces, the one public, the other private. Among those attracted by the former a few are chosen to whom the latter can speak."

"That's better. Am I one of the few?"

"I can hardly know yet. Come and sit down. Tell me what you find in these ideas, and why you took them up." He led him to the bench formerly occupied by Molly Corrington. They sat for a time in silence, gazing out to sea at the shadows lengthening across the water as the sun crept down behind the coast.

Albert spoke first, his tone was defensive: "You'll laugh at me, I expect, but when I read about these people in the old days I feel they'd got hold of something true, something that matters. The tales may be bunkum, these legends about men and goddesses, but the meaning underneath makes sense, it's to do with power."

Brink nodded: "Go on."

"Power," he repeated. "That's what the green man stood for, that's why he had to die. There's no meat in the namby-pamby version these kids are going to act. Their goddess is a bit of a whore, always changing her man, but that's nothing."

"What else should there be?"

"You know yourself. She wasn't tired of him, she wanted his blood."

"Why?" Brink watched him intently.

"Because blood gives power, the blood is the soul. I've read that somewhere."

"So have I. We seem to read the same authors."

"Then you won't jeer perhaps if I tell you something. I've made experiments, first with animals, then with my own blood." He frowned: "They were rather messy and had no effect."

"I'm not jeering, but your experiments were hardly likely to succeed. The ancients prescribed severe training and elaborate forms for these rites."

"And that did the trick?"

"You're too impatient. Take care not to confuse the symbol with the thing in itself." His smile was as enigmatic as his words, and Albert stared at him glumly:

"I forgot you're a parson, I expect you disapprove."

"Disapprove? Why should I? Who despises power, unlimited power to transform the world?"

"And be top dog there."

"No, Albert, it would be blasphemous to seek the gift for so unworthy a purpose."

"What's it for then?"

"To enable men to live to the full, to unlock the gates of the New Jerusalem." His voice shook with exultation, he sat lost in his thoughts as if he were alone. Albert watched him in growing discontent:

"I hoped you'd tell me what they did in the old days, how they made the blood work."

"They used it to awaken the spirits." He spoke abstractedly, but he pulled himself together to add: "Or so they believed."

"Do you believe it?"

"When you've studied longer you'll see that isn't a question to answer, yes or no. Listen, you want to know what the ancients did. I'll tell you something that may be new to you. It wasn't always the green man they sacrificed at midsummer; a more potent rite was to drink the blood of the goddess herself."

"They sacrificed her?" Albert's eyes blinked excitedly behind his spectacles: "How did they go about it?"

"I ought to be able to tell you, but I can't. The fact is I found an old notebook belonging to a learned predecessor here, and among other scraps of interest he'd noted was an exact account of the rite. I read it through, even added a detail to bring it up to date, then I took it to an appropriate place for a little experiment and with incredible stupidity I lost it there. It must have fallen from my pocket."

"You mean to say you can't find it?"

"A small book isn't easy to find in Kemsdale Wood, as you'd know if you'd ever been."

"Kemsdale Wood? I know it well. It's the way to the Devil's Churchyard?"

"Quite right. So you know that too?"

"I do indeed. I've spent hours there. The others jeer at me, say there's nothing beyond a lot of old stones, but I know better. It's a haunted place, the circle and the altar and that underground chamber they call the Devil's Parlour. I've been there again and again, invoked every spirit I could name, but nothing seemed to happen, not till this afternoon."

"What happened this afternoon?"

"You can believe me or not as you like. I was on my way to the stones when that storm came on, and I sheltered in the bushes. I was too far off to see properly; but I could have sworn there was something moving in the circle, something like what they describe in the old books, partly a man and partly a goat, it might have been the Devil himself. I tried to get a better view, but there were too many leaves in the way, and then suddenly I heard a noise from the other direction. It was the Devil's own voice, the real thing." He paused morosely.

"Was it indeed? You made sure?"

"I never found out. The farmer and a girl came butting in from nowhere. I didn't want him to see me, he's got it in for me for leaving gates open. Anyhow the noise stopped, there weren't likely to be any secrets revealed with fools like that about. So I lay low and let them pass."

"The farmer was Mr. Tranmire?"

"Yes, that's his name."

"And who was the girl?"

"I'd never set eyes on her before. A strapping wench with carroty hair in a green blouse and white pants."

"Indeed? On horseback?"

He shook his head: "On all-fours crawling under a branch."

"You'd know her again if you saw her?"

"She was close enough, tempting to smack if I'd dared."

"Listen, Albert, this is important. Where did those two go after they passed you?"

"I didn't stay to look. I was too fed up with them. I made off."

Brink pondered frowning: "You didn't come across my book, I suppose, in your wanderings."

"Not likely in those bushes. Is that where you dropped it?"

"I don't know where I dropped it, but it must be found before it gets into the wrong hands."

"Would you make it worth anyone's while to find it?"

"Yes, indeed. A pound? No, thirty bob, if you like."

"I don't mean money. If I find the book I want to know everything that's in it."

"That's a tall order. It's a book of immense learning."

"I understand more than you think."

"Perhaps you do. Find the book, and we'll see."

"I'll find it, no matter if the Devil's hidden it himself." He glanced up at the sky: "There's daylight still. I'll get my bike and go at once."

Brink left alone stared across the harbour at the cliff encrusted with houses already twinkling with lights. He turned from it to the open sea darkening beneath him, but still lustrous in the distance with a sheen like silk. The sky was clear except for a cloud that reared itself above the horizon, so grotesquely shaped that its features assumed the likeness of a legendary monster. He smiled as he watched it, murmured aloud:

"And I stood upon the sand of the sea, and saw a beast rise up out of the sea having seven heads and ten horns."

He looked round quickly, no one was in sight. Fixing his eyes again out to sea, he rose to his feet and genuflected, then advanced to the edge of the cliff with his hands joined in prayer:

*"Pater noster qui eras in caelo."**

Chapter 3

Saint John's Day, the Christian heir of rites celebrating the summer solstice, is not among the principal festivals of the Church of England; but a large congregation assembled at Easby for the morning service. The rector's efforts to arouse interest in the old beliefs and customs were bearing fruit. He came to the door afterwards to exchange civilities with his departing flock. Molly Corrington responded to his greeting with an eager smile:

"I liked your sermon," she told him. "You put it so well. I never understood before why Saint John was beheaded."

"Yes, I mentioned it to show how the rites are present even in the New Testament. Salome played the part of the Midsummer Queen, the Baptist's head was the sacrifice."

Pearl watched them: "If that's the connection between midsummer and Christianity I don't think much of it. Salome may be your type, she isn't mine."

"You're irreverent, Pearl," her mother reproved her. "I'm sure that Oswald knows best."

Pearl raised her eyebrows, but his attention was claimed already by others, and he turned away. Mother and daughter walked on alone.

"Since when have you been on Christian name terms?" Pearl asked.

"Really, Pearl, haven't I known him long enough? He's an old friend."

"He was Mr. Brink yesterday."

---

* Our Father who wert in heaven.

33

Her mother's face set stubbornly, she kept her eyes averted:

"I can't think where you get your old-fashioned ideas from. Not from me, I try to keep up with the times."

"You can do that without keeping up with a lecherous old satyr. I'm surprised at you, Mother. Yes, you know very well whom I mean."

"I certainly don't."

"Well, you should. Haven't you noticed how he looks at a girl, strips her clothes off?"

"You're letting your fancy run away with you. I'm sure when he looks at you he only sees how neatly you're dressed."

Pearl glanced down with satisfaction at the chaste elegance of her churchgoing beige: "If he looked at me as he does at some others I'd smack his face."

"Which others?"

"Kate Evans for one, the new schoolteacher at Saint Ursula's. He never took his eyes off her as she came out of church."

"You're quite wrong. I happen to know. He has great respect for her mind."

"Minds have bodies, and she shows hers more than enough; but it's no business of mine, I couldn't care less what he does to her."

"Whatever he does it won't be anything he shouldn't. He wants her to act in a sacred play he's getting up."

"A play? Is that on the programme, as well as the childish games on the lawn?"

"No, it's not for this evening, not till next week. He needs time for rehearsals."

"Time for plenty of funny business with Kate Evans."

"Pearl, I can't have you talking like that, it isn't nice. If you want to know, he asked me if you'd take the part yourself; but I warned him it isn't really in your line, it seems that some of the young people from the caravan site are acting."

"That riffraff? He'd the cheek to ask me to join them?"

"He's so good with them, with all the poor in the parish. He's very popular."

"Not with his better-class parishioners. They're fed up with his cranky ideas, his midsummer madness. I've told you already, Mother, you do yourself harm in their eyes, and me too, by associating with him."

They were past the gate of the churchyard, out on the path skirting the cliff. Many people lingered there, strolling and talking, taking advantage of the occasion to enjoy the company of their friends. Molly Corrington glanced round at them, caught the eye of a handsome middle-aged woman whose grey dress with bold pattern of white moons enhanced her height and girth. She smiled at her and nodded, then turned to her daughter:

"He gets a good congregation, you can't deny it."

"They're regular churchgoers, that doesn't mean they approve of your Mr. Brink."

"Well, I do." The resolute words banished any lingering doubts of her own: "I don't care what anyone says."

"Or how they laugh at you behind your back?" She broke off suddenly, peered along the path towards the steps leading down into the town: "Why, it's Jim Tranmire. He hasn't been to church for ages."

"So long that he seems to have forgotten the time of the service. If he meant to come today he's much too late."

Pearl paid no attention: "He looks so distinguished in that smart brown suit. I wish he wore it more often."

"It wouldn't be smart long if he wore it on the farm."

"How stupid you are, Mother. Of course it wouldn't, but if he gave up farming, or at least the dirty work, he could dress respectably."

Jim Tranmire looked very spruce as he approached. He exchanged greeting with many whom he passed, but he did not pause; his step was purposeful, hurried.

"Oh, I must speak to him," Pearl exclaimed.

She darted forward, but either he did not see her or did not wish. The wicket gate of the churchyard intervened, and he strode through. The last of the congregation were still leaving, a multitude of schoolgirls in bright red, the uniform of Saint Ursula's. It was the rule for them to remain seated after the service till everyone else was gone so as to avoid congestion in the aisle and porch. They surged forward now towards the gate, but Jim slipped past in time into the churchyard. Pearl following on his heels found the passage impenetrably blocked by an endless flow of schoolchildren, who advanced laughing, chattering, unheeding. She retired in disgust.

Her mother stood talking to the tall woman in the grey dress, Helen Buttle, proprietress and headmistress of the
35

school. A bearded man, grizzled and benign, in formal black coat and pin-striped trousers accompanied them, Arthur Buttle. He practised as a doctor in the town, left the management of the school to his wife, except when medical attention was needed.

He smiled at Pearl: "You'll make no headway against Saint Ursula's in spate. Perhaps Helen can part the waves for you."

His wife looked round: "What is it, Pearl? Have you left something in church?"

"It doesn't matter." There was suppressed irritation in Pearl's voice.

"She wanted to speak to Jim Tranmire," her mother explained innocently. "He went through just now." An angry glance from Pearl checked her.

"Jim?" Helen Buttle took up the name with interest: "Has he started to come to church again?"

Molly Corrington shook her head: "He wasn't here till the service was over."

"What a pity. He ought to be more regular if only to set an example. I've the greatest admiration for the way he looks after the estate, but there's no need to turn himself into a hermit."

"He leads a quiet life," her husband agreed, "works hard, reads a lot, but he's no hermit when he gets among the farmers at a sheep sale or in the hunting field."

"A young man in his position ought to keep better company. Things have changed sadly since his father and mother died."

"If they were alive, Helen, Saint Ursula's would be homeless. Your house would still be Easby Hall, and they'd be living there. You should be thankful that Jim's content to pig it at Kemsdale Farm."

"All the same, Doctor Buttle," Pearl put in earnestly, "it's true what Mrs. Buttle says. He's wasted there, he needs to be brought out."

His eyes twinkled: "The tonic I prescribe for him is a smart and good-looking wife."

"You aren't a doctor, you're a wicked old matchmaker." There was no displeasure in her voice.

"An inspired soothsayer perhaps; but remember this, Pearl, Jim's wife mustn't turn out Saint Ursula's, leave us without

36

a roof. She must choose some other big house, mustn't she, Helen?"

"Don't talk nonsense, Arthur." His wife frowned: "We can think of that when the time comes. A more urgent question than Jim's marriage is the bad example he sets in the parish by his absence from church. After all he's patron of the living, he ought to support the rector, he appointed him himself."

"He probably wishes he hadn't."

"That's no excuse. I don't like these cranky ideas myself, I'd give anything to go back to the simple services we had before Mr. Brink came; but I bring the school every Sunday just the same, I don't let prejudice stand in the way of religion."

"Can you honestly call this religion?" Pearl asked. "All this pagan mummery?"

Her mother had been listening in silence, but she could contain herself no longer: "What's wrong with it? The church looks lovely decorated like this with flowers, and I'm sure it makes people more interested to give them something new."

Helen Buttle's eyes rested on her thoughtfully: "You won't hear a word against him, Molly. You're as stubborn as a mule."

"I have to be, you all misunderstand him. He's doing such good work in the town. Everyone's looking forward to the quaint ceremonies at the rectory this evening."

"The games and dances? Yes, those seem to be harmless enough; they may even be quite instructive, the man's a scholar. I'm letting some of the older girls go, Kate will take them."

"How sensible of you, Helen." She hesitated: "There's something else he has in mind, and he asked me to talk to you about it, a midsummer play. He can't get it ready till next Sunday, but that doesn't matter, it seems that in the old days the festival always lasted for a week."

"What has this to do with me?"

"He wants Kate Evans to take part in it, and to have time off for rehearsals."

Pearl looked down her nose, a prominent organ well shaped for disdain: "It's no business of mine, but she'll find herself in queer company."

"That's not true," her mother protested. "He needs young people for the cast, and some of them, I believe, are holiday-

37

makers; but I'm sure they're all perfectly nice, he wouldn't have them if they weren't."

Helen Buttle frowned: "What does Kate say herself?"

"I don't think he's asked her yet. Will you let her if she's willing?"

"Well, of course I could arrange her duties to leave the time free; but she's very young, I feel responsible. What do you think, Arthur?"

He shook his head doubtfully: "I hear a lot of gossip from patients, most of it probably quite untrue."

"Gossip can be so cruel," Molly Corrington insisted.

"Yes, it can; but you know the saying, there's no smoke without fire. I've no quarrel with Brink, he's pleasant enough to meet. The trouble is that parents in the town seem to find him too pleasant with their daughters."

"Oh, how can they say so? He's pleasant to everyone."

Pearl smiled acidly: "No matter how long in the tooth. You yourself find him extremely pleasant, don't you, Mother?"

"So he should be, Pearl." Helen Buttle's voice was severe: "Your mother and I were girls together, and that's a long time ago, but in all these years I've never had an unkind word from her." She turned quickly to her husband: "Will you see Mr. Brink and talk to him, Arthur, find out what's involved?"

"I doubt if I'll get much out of him. He always has plenty to say for himself, but he gives nothing away. I can hardly ask him out right if there's any funny business."

"No, but you can probe."

"If there's any probing to be done I'd rather tackle Jim Tranmire. I've an idea he could tell us quite a lot. After all he appointed the man."

"Well, if Pearl's right he's somewhere about. Why not take the opportunity?"

"If he hasn't already gone home."

She glanced at her watch: "Why, it's past twelve. We've dawdled here chattering, and the girls will be late for lunch." She turned to look for them: "Good gracious, what's happened? Where are they?"

No red-uniformed army waited marshalled at the gate. Some of the girls were still in the churchyard wandering round the graves, climbing on to tombs to spell out the epitaphs. Others were scattered along the path beside the

38

cliff or sat in the grass making daisy chains, little clusters of red frocks among the sober remnant of churchgoers.

Helen Buttle stared in dismay: "Where's Kate? I left her in charge."

She pounced on the nearest group of truants, scolded them, shouted to others farther off. "Where's Miss Evans?" she asked as she rounded them up.

They pointed to the church.

"All right, Helen," her husband called. "I'll find her while you gather your flock."

He strode through the gate into the churchyard. Pearl followed.

The blame for disrupting Saint Ursula's settled routine lay with Jim Tranmire. When he fled from Pearl into the church he found Kate emerging with the last of her charges. She greeted him with pleasure and surprise:

"I didn't know you were in church."

"I wasn't. I've only just got here." There was urgency in his voice and manner: "I must talk to you."

"Not now. I'm supposed to be keeping an eye on the children, to see them all out through the gate and deliver them to Mrs. Buttle." She glanced at the column of red uniforms; they still advanced in docile ranks, but inquisitive eyes peered round at her. Jim's arrival had not escaped remark.

"They're all right," he insisted. "Why worry?" He grasped her hand, drew her back into the porch where an alcove adorned with tall vases of lupins and hollyhock screened them from the children and the children from her.

She moved to free herself, but he shifted his grip to her bare arm, held her fast: "Listen, this is important, it can't wait. I went this morning to look for the book, and it wasn't there."

"Not in the Devil's Parlour?"

"I searched from end to end, every cranny. There isn't much room anyhow."

She stared at him in troubled concern: "Who could have taken it?"

"That's the point, that's why I came at once to warn you. I believe we've caught the man, the joker who danced on the altar and killed my lamb."

"You caught him yourself?"

"No, a policeman did. I've just heard."

39

There was a bench behind her beneath the notice board. She sat down abruptly, heedless of her duties, and he sat beside her:

"You remember I told you I was going to the police about this business? Well, one of the constables, Harry Bracken, lives in Kemsdale, and he's rather a friend of mine; so after leaving you yesterday I went to look for him at his cottage, thinking it would make less what-ho than a complaint to the serjeant at Easby. I was lucky, his wife was expecting him home off duty, and when he came I gave him the facts."

"Not about my name in the book?"

"No, only about the lamb and about Fan. She was with me, he could see the marks on her, and he agreed it was the work of a madman."

She smiled: "You couldn't ask him to arrest the Devil."

"Wait till you hear. Later in the evening he set out on a scouting expedition alone. If he'd told me of course I'd have gone with him. It's rather shaming that while I sat snug at home he was out there hunting a madman in the Devil's Churchyard."

"He probably didn't want anyone. You'd have been in the way."

He nodded: "Anyhow his hunch was right. The madman was back."

"Killing more sheep?"

"No, just slinking about. As a matter of fact he was doing nothing violent at all."

"Then what makes you think he was a madman?"

"When he saw Harry he bolted, but he was a puny specimen, he didn't get far. Harry caught and held him."

"There's nothing very mad in running away when you're chased."

He turned to her, laid his hand on her nylon-sheathed knee: "I'd think the same as you, Kate, that this was some ordinary trespasser, except that when Harry came to me this morning with his story I'd just come back from the place myself, and the book you left there has vanished."

"Had this man taken it?"

"I wish I knew; but of course Harry wasn't looking for it as I hadn't said anything about it. Still he isn't a policeman for nothing, he made the youth turn out his pockets in case he carried a weapon. There wasn't much in them, a few coins, a packet of fags and a torch. The last perhaps is suspicious."

"Anyone might carry a torch if he was likely to be out after dark."

"Or looking for lost things in dark places. Anyhow, there the facts are, the book vanishes and he was on the spot. If he didn't take it, who did?"

"If he did take it, where is it now? Did the policeman arrest him?"

"He couldn't, he'd no evidence. He took his name and address, gave him the rough side of his tongue and saw him home as far as the road where he'd left his bike. He's one of the campers, it seems, from the caravan site, the same youth, if I've got the name right, who left all my gates open last week and put the sheep into the barley."

"What name is it?"

"Albert Dockin. Do you know him?"

She shook her head: "I've never heard of him."

"Could he have seen you anywhere?"

"I suppose he could, but I've no idea when or where."

He frowned: "There's no sense in it, but if it's the youth I think, he's a stinker, he gave me the creeps. That's why I came at once to warn you."

"Aren't you jumping to conclusions? All you know is that this Albert creature was caught trespassing in your wood. He may have designs on your sheep. But why on me?"

"Don't be silly." The pressure of his hand enforced the words: "Why was your name written in the book? Why did he come searching for it? I'm sure he did, and I don't like it."

"Nor do I," she confessed.

The outer door creaked on its hinges. She shrank guiltily away from him, sprang to her feet. Arthur Buttle peered over the flowers into the alcove.

"Ah, there you are, Kate," he exclaimed. "My wife sent me to find you. Nothing wrong, I hope?"

"Nothing at all, Doctor Buttle." Her face was scarlet: "Oh dear, have I kept her waiting?"

Jim smiled unabashed: "It was my fault, I talk too much. If lunch is late at Saint Ursula's, blame me."

"The girls blame no one, they're having the spree of their lives."

Kate stared at him in dismay.

"When Kate's away the mice will play," he quoted.

41

"Yes indeed." Pearl followed him into the porch: "Every-one left to run wild, utter chaos." She turned to Jim: "Hullo, I heard you were here, I thought you might need me to rescue you."

"I'd say Mrs. Buttle needs you more." He scowled at her, and she bridled:

"It isn't my job to play nursemaid to a pack of school-children."

Kate was already darting across the churchyard, a green comet with hair and skirt streaming and long sleek legs.

Arthur Buttle sighed: "I'm afraid she'll catch it."

"So she should." Pearl nodded vigorously: "I've never known anything so disgraceful. She deserves to be spanked."

Brink coming out of the church overheard her words, caught a glimpse of Kate's retreating figure: "By all means." He rubbed his palms: "Will you let me perform the office on callipygous Atalanta?" He broke off, and his face fell: "Ah, Mr. Tranmire, we seldom see you here. You're quite a stranger."

Jim was silent, and he added uneasily: "My tongue ran away with me, a learned jest in compliment to Miss Evans, one that she'd appreciate."

"No doubt, but I'm not so brainy." Pearl smiled sourly: "Why can't you say what you mean in plain English?"

"Or in pig's grunts?" Jim strode past them and walked out.

"Dear me," Brink muttered. "I'm afraid I offended him."

"You did," Doctor Buttle agreed. "You're not my patient, Brink, and I don't want to be officious, but you're at an age when you ought to take care."

"Thank you, Doctor, I feel remarkably fit."

Pearl's eyes followed Jim's departure. She moved towards the door.

"Just a minute, Pearl," Brink called. "Is your mother outside?"

"She's gone home, I expect." Her tone was curt.

"That's a pity, I've a message for her. Will you wait, please, while I write her a short note?"

"Give it me by word of mouth. I'm in a hurry."

He shook his head, slipped back into the church.

She caught Doctor Buttle's eye and pouted impatiently:

"What's the great secret? I'll bet it's to mend the hassocks or wash his chasuble."

"Divine mysteries, Pearl." He smiled: "You and I are among the uninitiated."

Jim was by this time at the gate, beyond which the path was packed with red uniforms. Most of Saint Ursula's waited there, reassembled under the grim scrutiny of the head-mistress, while Kate, very red in the face, agitated and contrite, ran to fetch the last of the stragglers. He hesitated, it was not an auspicious moment to intervene. A mossy tomb protruded in the shelter of a spreading yew. He sat down on the plinth and lit a cigarette to soothe the rage provoked by Brink, and the growing uneasiness nagging him as he recalled the sequence of events in the Devil's Church-yard.

He could hear Helen Buttle's voice on the other side of the fence scolding, sternly exhorting. He waited for her to finish her lecture, then rose to his feet meaning to go out and appease her, bear his share of the blame. She was talk-ing in a lower tone now in conversation with Kate, and he was unable to distinguish what they said, till he caught the words:

"All right, Kate, you're forgiven, we'll say no more about it. I like a girl who's sorry and has the sense not to make excuses." She raised her voice: "Come on, children, make haste now, we'll get home to lunch. Those clouds look like rain."

He sat down again, content to leave good alone. The school moved off with a brisk patter of feet, shrill chatter of recovered spirits.

The sound dwindled in the distance, and he was about to depart himself when Pearl emerged from the church, and he drew back quickly, took cover in the thickest depths of the yew. She hurried towards the gate, walking as fast as her high heels allowed. Her eyes were fixed eagerly ahead, scanning what could be seen of the open ground beyond the fence. He guessed that she was looking for him, hoping to catch him up, but the tree screened him from view.

She reached the gate, stood peering towards the steps, turned to peer no less earnestly in the other direction, then swung round again towards the town with an angry mutter of disappointment. He could not see what happened next, but he heard her exclaim:

"Clumsy oaf. Can't you look where you're going?"

43

"Clumsy yourself, miss," a voice retorted. "It was your fault, not mine. You gave me a nasty jolt, I might have fallen over the cliff."

Pearl strode on without deigning to reply, and her victim came in through the gate, rubbing his shin. Jim's idea that he recognised the voice was confirmed when he saw that it was Albert Dockin. He remained hidden, busy with surmise, while Albert proceeded towards the church, avoiding the main entrance, slinking round the corner to the postern door into the vestry. As soon as he was out of sight Jim slipped out cautiously from his shelter and followed.

He was approaching the corner of the church when he heard his name called, and he looked back.

"Can you spare me a moment, Jim?"

Doctor Buttle stood outside the porch, beckoning. Jim hesitated, then with a frown he came back reluctantly to join him.

"This is luck," Doctor Buttle exclaimed. "I thought you'd gone back to the farm, that I'd lost my opportunity to talk to you."

Jim's face expressed no pleasure: "Is it something urgent?"

"Well, it is and it isn't. I want your advice, and if I don't ask it now I'm sure I never will. You're a difficult man to get hold of."

"As a matter of fact I was on my way to the vestry, and it's business that can't wait." He smiled disarmingly: "Please don't think me rude."

"Everyone's in such a hurry this morning. Pearl rushed off a minute ago as if she couldn't hold her water."

Jim grinned, and the other glanced at him shrewdly:

"Is there any connection, I wonder?"

"No, Doctor Buttle, there isn't. I'm sorry to make such a mystery of it. Could we meet later perhaps before I go home?"

"Why not? Will your errand take you long?"

"I don't know. I don't think so."

"Well, I'll wait for you, give Helen time to feed the children and calm down. You'll find me over there on the bench on the cliff." He glanced up at the sky: "Unless of course it rains."

He walked away, but Jim did not go back round the outside of the church to the postern door. Albert Dockin would surely be in the vestry now, closeted with Brink. Jim gambled on his hunch, strode in through the porch, met no one there, passed into the nave; the whole place seemed to be empty.

He knew its nooks and crannies well, having explored them often in his boyhood. On the threshold of the choir a door in the wall gave access to stairs leading to the top of the tower. He tried the latch, praying that as in the old days the door was kept unlocked; it opened creaking, and he slipped through as soon as it was wide enough, then climbed the steps to the belfry and on up the steeper, narrower flight which mounted to the leads. At a sharp bend another passage converged, an older shaft where steps so worn as barely to afford foothold wound down precariously into darkness. This was formerly an alternative way up the tower; but a short length only remained, cut off and sealed with a wall when the lower portion was demolished to make room for work of reconstruction in the chancel. Jim knew from his early explorations that a loose stone could be removed in the wall, affording a spyhole into the vestry.

He crept down encouraged by the sound of conversation below. The stone yielded as easily as ever when he grasped it; he put his face to the aperture, Brink and Albert were in conference on the other side.

Brink stood by the chest of drawers; one of them was open, and papers lay scattered on the floor while he rummaged among the others. On the glass-topped case beside him containing his antiquarian specimens a small book lay, bound in white vellum.

Albert sat in the armchair watching with a supercilious smile.

"I wish I weren't so untidy," Brink complained.

Albert nodded: "It isn't the way to success. I took prizes at school for my neatness."

"Well, I can't find what I want." His voice was irritable: "Perhaps you'll help me to pick some of these up and put them neatly away."

Albert rose unwillingly, stooped to collect the litter.

Brink was still peering into the drawer: "I've a full account somewhere of Parson Amos and his doings. Never mind, I can tell you most of it from memory." He broke off, glared: "What are you looking at?"

"This snap. Oh boy, she's a peach."

"Give me that photograph." He snatched it from him, tucked it away in the drawer under a heap of papers: "Mind your own business. I'll tell you what's for your eyes, and what isn't."

"No offence, Mr. Brink." He spoke sulkily: "Haven't I earned a bit of fun? Haven't I done everything I can for you, finding this lost book of yours in the wood? You gave me no help, never said you'd been in the cave."

"I never was. I can't imagine how it got there."

"Anyhow that's where I found it, and I kept it hidden from the cop, stuffed it down my shirt, and he never twigged it. I'd collywobbles, the way it bumped on my belly while he marched me back to my bike. Well, I've done my part, haven't I? You've got your book back, and I want to know what's in it. You promised to tell me."

"Didn't you take the opportunity to read it for yourself?"

"I could make no sense of it at all."

"So you're not as clever as you thought? All right, Albert, come here and sit down." He reached for the book from the showcase, took out his pipe and lit it:

"This book belonged, as I've just said, to my seventeenth-century predecessor, Amos Pounder, who used it to jot down excerpts from ancient authors and other memoranda appropriate to his studies. He was an odd character, Parson Amos, and such stories spread about him in the parish that a complaint was lodged with the Bishop. There's a copy of it in that report I was looking for. The charges range from black magic to lechery and murder."

Albert nodded: "The squares have it in for the adept. It's always the same, nothing but envy."

"Possibly, but it can't be denied that many of his parishioners, especially young girls, disappeared in circumstances hard to explain. The facts are reported, and I could give you them; but they don't really matter. What concerns us more is that Parson Amos ended his life in the Devil's Churchyard. He was found dead on the altar in the circle of stones."

"Is it known what killed him?"

"The Devil in person, according to contemporary opinion. My own is less crude, even if it amounts to much the same thing." He paused, added gravely: "He was attempting the great rite, and he failed."

"The great rite?"

"The rite of the goddess. It wasn't his first attempt either, to judge from the record he kept at the end of the book."

"What went wrong, do you think?"

46

"I can't say, but I can guess. He ought to have known, he'd got it all copied out there in fullest detail."

"Are you going to have a shot at it yourself, sir?" Albert's voice trembled with excitement.

"Of course. What else do you suppose these preparations are for?"

"The flowers in the church, you mean, and the games this evening in your garden?"

"Each has its place in the ritual." He glanced out of the window: "I can't command the weather, but if the games are washed out tonight no harm will be done. I'll postpone them like the play for a week, let everything mount together to the grand climax."

"So the play-acting makes sense after all."

"Wait and you'll see. It provides a purpose for enlisting a troupe of performers. That's where you can help me."

"To pick you a goddess?"

"No, she's chosen already; but there are other parts to fill, and you can find me suitable volunteers from the camp."

"I know one or two who might do."

"Tell them no more than you need. We've had enough meddling. Who set the policeman to prowl in the Devil's Churchyard? I've a suspicion it was Tranmire, and I don't like it. He was there himself, you say, yesterday afternoon?"

"Yes, and his girl with him."

"So you said, and I'd like to know what they're up to. I saw her later on horseback, and she looked more like swimming than riding."

"No wonder. The bushes were soaking wet, you should have seen her."

"A feast for the eyes, I'm sure." His tone was preoccupied: "It's his own land, and he runs his sheep there. He could have been shepherding, but it's the first I've heard that he employs Kate Evans as shepherdess."

"Is he sweet on her?"

"Apparently."

"Then I hope she's your choice for goddess. I haven't forgotten the way he cursed me just for a stroll in his fields. Filthy language he used."

Brink frowned: "Your personal feelings are of no interest, you must learn to control them."

"You wouldn't have liked it yourself, Mr. Brink; but he's civil enough to you of course, you're a gent."

47

"He wasn't so civil just now when I displeased him with a classical allusion, naughty perhaps but too apt to resist."

"Then we're both in disgrace with him, are we?"

"I don't care if we are or aren't, I'd like to be rid of him. He's a dangerous man, Albert, he knows too much and has too much influence."

Much of what was said was inaudible to Jim in his hiding place. He leant closer to the hole to catch the words, pressed inadvertently against the stone removed from the wall. It lay poised on the ledge beside him; his elbow pushed, and it fell to the ground with a crash.

Brink leapt to his feet: "Heavens above, what was that?"

Echoes rolling through the hollow of the church confused the sound; its source was lost in them. He darted to the inner door leading to the chancel. Albert followed white in the face, but there was exaltation in his voice as he muttered:

"That's how the power makes itself known, like a peal of thunder."

Brink did not reply. He entered the church, stared in all directions, no one was there. Still dissatisfied, he set about a rigorous search of every corner of the building. Jim crouching in the confined space at the foot of the disused steps could watch and hear no longer. He hoped fervently that Brink had had no occasion since coming to Easby to explore the tower, and did not know of this blind alley whose wall the vestry shared.

The door giving access from the church creaked loudly, the search was proceeding relentlessly to a higher level. There was a sound of feet on the stairs, then of voices in the belfry. They were too indistinct at first to distinguish the words, but Brink's rose as he called:

"No, not up there, it only leads to the top of the tower. That crash came from somewhere down inside the church."

Jim breathed a sigh of relief.

The others were silent till they stood again in the chancel. Albert spoke first:

"We could look forever, I tell you. It wasn't flesh and blood, it was power."

"You've much to learn, Albert. When you've studied as long as I have you'll know that the adept withholds judgement till every material explanation is eliminated."

"Is it my fault that I don't know enough? You swore to teach me what's in that book. When shall we begin?"

"In good time, not now."

"Why not?"

"For many reasons, not the least of which is that I'm going home for lunch."

He picked up the book as he passed through the vestry, and they walked together across the churchyard:

"Knowledge must be earned, Albert. You've done well, but I've another task to set you. I want to encourage the belief that the doings in the Devil's Churchyard are a threat to Tranmire himself."

"To stop him poking his nose in?"

"An even more important purpose is to persuade the girl to play the part assigned her."

"Kate Evans?"

He nodded: "The chosen victim, without whose consent the rite fails."

"It's a daft sort of persuasion to tell her there's danger in the affair."

"Not to herself, danger to Tranmire. Play on her fears, let her think she can save him by keeping an eye on the plot."

"Is she likely to believe me?"

"She will, if events prove the warning true."

"You want deeds as well as words, do you?"

"If he has an accident I shan't weep."

Albert's face was sullen: "I don't mind scaring the pants off the girl, but I'm not getting mixed up in a roughhouse with Tranmire, not on your life."

"There are other weapons than the fist. Your talents lie elsewhere, Albert. Obey the command of the Scriptures, be wise as the serpent, without need to be harmless as the dove."

"And my reward?"

"I've already promised to treat you as my pupil."

"Not pupil only but partner." A greedy leer shone in his eyes: "When you drink the victim's blood I want a sip too."

"Favete linguis." Brink's voice shook with anger: "In plain English, hold your tongue if you can't avoid inauspicious words."

They were at the gate, and he glanced towards the bench on the cliff where a man sat alone with his back to them. He turned again to Albert with a curt nod:

"Goodbye. I'll see you later." He strode quickly away.

49

Jim remained in the tower till the creak of the door announced that the stairs were clear, then he moved down cautiously to the chancel, found it empty, slipped on tiptoe through the nave to the porch. Watching from there, he saw Brink and Albert come round the corner of the building and cross the grass to the gate. They passed out of sight, and he made haste to escape. Although he heard nothing of the last part of their conversation he had enough on his mind to disturb him, and he was absorbed in thought when the sound of his own name aroused him with a start:

"At last, Jim. I was about to give you up."

He remembered with annoyance that Doctor Buttle was waiting for him, and reluctantly he turned to join him on the bench.

"I'm sorry," he greeted him. "I was kept longer than I expected."

"No matter. This is a favourite seat of mine. I'm fond of the view, and so far the rain's held off. Why, whatever have you been doing in your best suit? You're covered in dust and cobwebs."

Jim flicked the worst of the debris from his coat and trousers: "You want my advice about something?"

"Yes, about Brink." He hesitated: "You know more of him than I do."

"I don't hear many of his sermons."

"No, you don't, and I'm sure there's a reason. It isn't like you to refuse support to a man you chose yourself."

"The reason isn't much to my credit. I can't bear to be faced with my mistake."

Arthur Buttle glanced at him with concern: "You shouldn't take it too much to heart. He's a bit of a crank, but he does good work in the parish."

"I wish I could think so. It isn't as if I wasn't warned. When he applied for the living I wrote to people who knew him, and they told me about his odd interests, all this folklore business. I must admit that I put it in his favour. He sounded rather fun."

"Did they say anything about his morals?"

"Yes, that he was too forthcoming with the girls, but it was all so vague, mere tittle-tattle. I didn't want to be unjust; you know the proverb, give a dog a bad name and hang him. I was sorry for the man, anxious to give him a chance."

50

"And now you wish you hadn't?"

"Yes, when it's too late."

Arthur Buttle stroked his beard thoughtfully: "Whether it's his fault or his misfortune he seems to provoke gossip wherever he goes. There's plenty already in Easby, yet as far as I know he's done no wrong." He paused awaiting Jim's comment, but as none came he went on: "He's too free with his tongue of course, as you heard just now. There's probably glandular trouble, erotic hypertrophy. The symptoms are not uncommon among men of his age."

Jim's face darkened: "What do you want my advice about?"

"I'll tell you. He's getting up some midsummer play or other, and we've heard that he's going to ask Kate to take a part. Helen isn't happy about it, she feels responsible. Of course it may all be perfectly aboveboard, there shouldn't be anything wrong in a play in church, and with any other parson we shouldn't have hesitated; but as things are I thought I'd better investigate. I picked on you because you know more than most of us about the man's past."

"Has Kate agreed to act?"

"I don't suppose she's been told yet. I doubt if Helen was in a mood on the way home."

"Well, she'll hear of it from me, and she can tell Brink to go to hell."

"Wise advice, I'm sure, but perhaps it won't carry as much weight with her as it does with me." He glanced at him quizzically: "I didn't know till I saw you with her that you were even acquainted."

"Yes, we met." He offered no explanation, but returned to the theme that was on his mind: "I've a good mind to go to Brink and give him the answer myself."

"Is he still in church?"

"No, he went back to the rectory a few minutes ago."

"Ah, I was right, it was his voice I heard just before you came. I didn't look round, but there were two men talking at the gate, something about the communion service."

"The communion service?"

"Yes, transubstantiation. I thought I caught the words, drink the blood. It isn't a doctrine that appeals to me."

Jim shuddered. He saw again the pool of blood from the lamb in the Devil's Churchyard, and when he spoke it was as if he uttered his thoughts aloud, more to himself than his companion:

51

"No, I'd do more harm than good. I don't want him to know I'm on the scent till I've something better to go on."

Drops of rain began to fall. The storm threatened so long was breaking. Doctor Buttle rose to his feet:

"We'll be wet through if we don't move. Shall we shelter in the church?"

Jim looked up at the sky heavily overcast: "We might have to stay there all day. I've left my car at the bottom of the steps. If we hurry we can make it before the downpour."

He ran on ahead. Doctor Buttle, less agile, followed as fast as he could.

The church steps led down the cliff to a street that skirted the harbour. It was very narrow for most of the way, winding between encroaching houses, but where the steps debouched it widened and cars could be parked. Jim's, an open convertible, remained alone there; everyone else had already driven off. As he approached he saw an envelope on the driver's seat, and he picked it up, tore it open without looking at the superscription. It contained a short note, a hurried scribble without formal greeting:

Don't say anything to Doctor Buttle about the wound on my arm, Oswald Brink.

He stared at it in surprise, examined the envelope, saw that it was addressed to Mrs. Corrington. Doctor Buttle arrived panting, and he hesitated, then crammed the note into his pocket and made haste to put up the hood. Rain was falling steadily.

"Get in." He held the door open for his passenger: "I'll put you down at Saint Ursula's."

"You're a Good Samaritan, Jim. I've neither coat nor umbrella."

They drove in silence, and when they reached the school Jim refused the offer of hospitality, and Doctor Buttle entered alone. He found a cold meal, bread, cheese and salad, laid out for him, and as he sat down to eat it his wife looked into the room:

"Did you get very wet?"

"No, Jim brought me back in his car."

"Jim? Oh, you found him, did you?"

"Yes. In the porch, talking to Kate."

"So that's why Kate neglected her duties."

"I hope you weren't too hard on her, Helen."

She smiled indulgently: "If you had your way, Arthur, no attractive girl would ever incur rebuke. Well, if you want to know, I wasn't too hard on Kate, we've made it up and are friends again. She's a good girl, and when she does wrong she admits it and wastes no time on excuses."

"She could well have excused herself by laying the blame on Jim. I came on them suddenly and saw more than they intended."

She raised her eyebrows: "When did they get to know each other?"

"I've no idea, but I'm not as sure as I was about Pearl's wedding bells. Unless she takes care she'll find me a false prophet."

"I hope you are. I know which I'd choose if I were Jim."

Chapter 4

Rain fell in torrents. It gathered in pools in the grass on the rectory lawn, dripped from the leaking gutters of the roof; gusts of wind scattered spray in showers from laden branches of trees and bushes. The great heap of straw prepared for the fire-leaping rites of midsummer floated sodden in a waste of mud.

Oswald Brink stared at it from his study window: "The altar on Carmel was more inflammable, and I haven't Elijah's skill in miracles."

"It's a shame," Molly Corrington declared. "I could cry my eyes out."

She alone of the promised helpers had arrived, undeterred by the weather. The rectory, an ancient house of grey stone, stood on the top of the hill behind the abbey ruins, too far from the town to tempt the faint-hearted out on such an afternoon. They assured themselves that their services were not needed.

Brink himself was inclined to agree: "Never mind, Molly. We'll hold the rites on the octave instead."

"At the same time as the play?"

He nodded: "Did you have a word about that with Kate?"

"No, I haven't seen her yet to talk to, but I spoke to Helen."

"What did Mrs. Buttle say?"

She hesitated: "I'm afraid she was rather doubtful. She told Arthur to see you and discuss it."

"He said nothing about it when he saw me after church."

"Didn't he? Oh, I remember, he wanted to consult Jim Tranmire."

"Tranmire? What the—" He checked himself: "Forgive me for saying so, but Doctor Buttle seems to be rather a busybody."

"He's so kind, Oswald, and such a clever doctor too."

"He doesn't let anyone forget it. You got my message?"

"Message?"

"Yes, a written note. I asked Pearl to give it to you."

"She gave me nothing, she was too full of her own plans when she came in, inviting Jim to dinner and making up a party to meet him. Oh dear, what a tiresome girl she is. Was the message urgent?"

"It was to ask you to say nothing to Doctor Buttle about the sore on my arm."

"Well, I haven't, so there's no harm done; but I might of course if I'd thought of it. Your poor arm. Why don't you want Arthur to look at it?"

"Because he'd have a shrewd idea what caused the wound."

"Something to do with your car, you said, didn't you?"

"Yes, and I deceived you, Molly. You took me by surprise; but now I've had time to think it over, and I know I can trust you. The truth is, I was bitten by a dog."

"A mad dog? Oh, Oswald, you could die if the place isn't treated."

"The dog wasn't mad, and I haven't died; but I've reasons of my own for wanting to keep the incident secret. I'll tell you this much, the dog was Tranmire's."

"You don't mean to say he set it on you?"

"No, he wasn't there, but I was on his farm near the circle of stones they call the Devil's Churchyard. Ancient monuments of that sort have a fascination for me, and I was pot-

54

tering round there when I came on something very sinister. You've heard of the Black Mass?"

"Yes, it was in the papers about a year ago. A shocking case, I hardly liked to read it. A girl tied across the altar in a church with no clothes on and a foreign word scrawled on her in paint where she sits down."

"The Tetragrammaton." He nodded: "The rite was uncompleted, she was lucky. You wouldn't want anything similar to happen at Easby?"

"Oh, but it couldn't. Ours is such a respectable town."

"You can't judge people by what appears on the surface."

"What do you mean?" She stared at him wide-eyed: "What did you find in the Devil's Churchyard?"

"Evidence that leaves no room for doubt, but for the present I can tell you no more."

"I'd never repeat it."

"I'm sure you wouldn't, but my lips are sealed. I can't explain why, I can only ask you to take my word for it."

"You know best of course." Her disappointment was plain: "There's just one little question, you'd relieve my feelings so much if you'd answer it. Is Jim Tranmire mixed up in this?"

"I don't know. It might have been chance that his dog attacked me."

"He's such a nice young man, and Pearl's becoming so fond of him."

"Then I hope for Pearl's sake he isn't implicated either as practitioner or victim."

"You mean, he may be in danger? Oughtn't we to warn him?"

"It isn't as simple as that. I don't want to bore you with a long story."

"But it won't bore me. If you're in trouble I want to help you."

"Yes, I'm in trouble indeed, and of a sort that seems to dog me."

He drew her to the sofa, and they sat there side by side. She listened to him with rapt attention.

"You spoke of this Black Mass which you read about in the papers. You probably don't know that the church was in my own parish, the last that I held before I came here."

"How dreadful for you. So you knew the girl?"

"Her father was my churchwarden."

"Fancy a churchwarden's daughter wearing no clothes in church."

"An unusual fashion," he agreed, "commoner in a pagan than a Christian shrine; but you remember what our Lord said, judge not that ye be judged. We can only cast out evil by patience and understanding."

"How can we be patient with blasphemy, or begin to understand it?"

"To understand is not to condone. These people are deluded, they believe that their rites are the means of acquiring supernatural power. Many who seek it care only for themselves, to feed their own self-conceit; but there are some whose motives are truly spiritual, who seek power to be able to help others and make the world a happier place to live in."

"You mean that they do these shocking things for a good purpose?"

"They believe that the end justifies the means."

She frowned as she thought this over: "I'm not very bright. Have I got it wrong, or is there a sort of magic in this power? Does it really turn them into supermen?"

"Even if I were much brighter than I am I'd find it hard to answer that question. Where does faith end and superstition begin? Is it magic or our own will that gives us strength to do what we believe we can?"

"Oh dear, my poor brain's in a whirl. This is what's troubling you, is it? You're afraid that the same sort of thing may happen at Easby?"

"More than afraid, I'm convinced that it will, and as you see I know what I'm talking about."

"I still don't see why you have to keep it so secret. Even if you don't want advice from Arthur Buttle you could surely warn Jim Tranmire."

"There are many reasons why I can't. For one thing he'd probably laugh at me, tell me not to waste his time with fairy tales."

"But I thought you said that he might be mixed up in it himself, that his dog attacked you."

"That makes it all the more inadvisable to reveal my suspicion. The fact is, he knows too much about the doings in my old parish, and if I go to him now with stories of the same sort of thing here he'll think, or at any rate make
56

people think, that my own hands are stained with the mud."

"He'd never make me believe anything wrong of you."

"I wish all were like you." He patted her hand gently:
"Calumny was the weapon my enemies used against me last
time, and I'm afraid they'll try it again when they find out
I'm on their track."

"You mustn't do anything rash, Oswald."

"I mean to turn the tables on them, to make the ancient
wisdom on which they rely serve God rather than the Devil.
That's why I've been so anxious to revive the midsummer
rites and associate them with the church. You see it now,
don't you?"

"Not altogether, but I'm trying my best."

"Never mind, you will if my plan works out as I hope.
All depends on the final event, this mystery play for which
I need Kate Evans."

"Couldn't someone else play the part if she can't?"

"No one else." He shook his head gravely and turned
away to stare in silence at the window.

"Talk of the Devil—" he exclaimed suddenly. "Here she
comes."

"Who?"

"Kate Evans herself."

Molly Corrington rose quickly from the sofa, unwilling to
be found in such proximity to him. She walked across to the
window and peered out.

The girl in a green raincoat who approached round the
corner of the drive held an umbrella which hid her face.

"It's Kate all right." Molly laughed: "I'd know her anywhere by her stride."

Brink left the room, hurried to the door to admit his
visitor. The rain was less heavy, little more than a drizzle.
She lowered her umbrella and closed it, revealing a stream
of copper-red hair.

"Have you come to cheer me up?" he greeted her.

She hesitated as he beckoned her in, but the draught ruffled a heap of papers and blew them to the floor, and she
walked past him into the hall so that he could shut the door
behind her. She looked round her in surprise and some
dismay.

"What's happened to everyone? I thought you'd have
crowds here to help you."

57

"Their enthusiasm for the party is as damp as the garden. Many were chosen, one only obeyed the call, faithful Molly Corrington."

"Mrs. Corrington?" There was relief in her voice: "She's here, is she?"

"Yes, I'm here, Kate." She came from the study to join them: "Isn't this heartbreaking? Poor Mr. Brink."

Kate nodded sympathetically: "The rain seems to be stopping, but everything's soaking wet."

"Soaking wet," he repeated, "fit only for the gambols of Thetis."

She glared at him, but she kept her voice under control: "Mrs. Buttle sent me to tell you that no girls from the school will be coming after all, she's afraid they'd catch cold. She thought I'd better let you know at once."

"I'm grateful to her for the message and even more for the messenger, no longer Thetis on her dolphin but another favourite of mine, long-legged Atalanta."

"I don't understand a word you're saying," Molly Corrington exclaimed, "but you're teasing her and she doesn't like it. Pay no attention, Kate, to his learned nonsense."

"Yes, forgive me." He smiled: "I spoke in riddles to spare you the news that you've had your errand for nothing, the girls of Saint Ursula's won't be alone in missing the party. To put it plainly, the midsummer rites are postponed till next Sunday. Don't you think I'm right, Molly?"

"Absolutely right, and everyone, I'm sure, will agree. They can't dance in the mud, and wet straw won't burn."

"Then I'll tell Mrs. Buttle." Kate edged towards the door: "Perhaps the children can come next week if it's fine."

"Just a minute." He laid his hand on her arm: "I want to talk to you about next week. Take off your wet coat, and we'll go into the study."

"No, I'm sorry, I haven't time. I must get back quickly."

"Will this morning's riot be repeated if you aren't there to quell it?"

"It wasn't a riot, and it won't." Her eyes met his hotly.

Molly Corrington made haste to intervene: "I promise we shan't keep you long, Kate. I'm sure that Helen can spare you just while Oswald explains what he wants."

"I don't know, she might need me." She hesitated, however, and fumbled with the belt of her coat. Brink helped her off with it and hung it up.

58

She tugged down her short skirt as she preceded him into the room.

Molly Corrington spoke first when they were seated: "Helen may have mentioned this already. We're planning something more ambitious for next week, a mystery play. Isn't that right, Oswald?"

He nodded: "A symbolic drama enacting the spirit of the season."

"Yes, Mrs. Buttle said so." Kate's tone was aloof.

"Did she tell you we want you to play the principal part?"

"I'm sorry, I can't."

"Why not?" he asked sharply.

"I haven't the time for rehearsals, and I'm no good anyhow at acting."

"I'm sure you've talent if you tried." Molly smiled encouragement.

"As for rehearsals," Brink declared, "we'll make them suit your convenience. You'll pick up your part so quickly you won't need as many as the others. I could even rehearse you alone."

"Thank you. I'd rather not."

Molly turned to her reproachfully: "Do be reasonable, Kate. I'll speak to Helen, persuade her not to stand in your way."

"I'm sorry, Mrs. Corrington." She shook her head: "It's nothing to do with Mrs. Buttle. I don't want to."

"Listen, my dear." Brink leant forward towards her: "Let me tell you the story, and perhaps you'll change your mind. The Midsummer Queen is the darling of gods and men; she swims as Thetis in the sea, runs as Atalanta through the woods, rides as Kate Evans on a milk-white mare."

She looked up at her own name but did not interrupt.

"Like Thetis and Atalanta," he went on, "and perhaps not unlike Kate Evans either, she falls in love with a mortal, the green man. She marries him at the summer solstice, but at once his strength begins to wane. Month by month he grows weaker, all her joy is turned to sorrow, till midwinter comes, the longest night in the year, and he lies dying. She saves his life by giving him to drink of her own blood."

He paused for a moment with eyes fixed on her intently: "Her blood restores his strength. It's spring, the whole living earth rejoices, but with summer again the fatal solstice draws near. What should she do, allow the process to repeat

59

itself? May she not escape the curse by changing her lover? Year by year at midsummer she chooses her green man afresh, hoping against hope that the next will enjoy her own everlasting youth."

"What a quaint legend," Molly Corrington exclaimed, "and how well you told it. You made it seem so real."

"It's a horrible story." Kate spoke gravely: "What happens to the man she casts off?"

"You can probably guess. Which should it be, his blood or hers?"

She did not reply.

He addressed her with earnest solemnity: "This is more than a myth, it's a rite that people once practised, believing it had virtue to replenish the fruits of the earth. They were pagans, their knowledge of the spirit fell far short of ours; but instead of despising we should respect them for a glimpse of truth, while we enlarge and purify it in the light of the Christian revelation." He glanced at Molly Corrington for support, and she beamed at him:

"Yes, indeed. That's what you were saying before Kate came."

"And Kate? Do you see yourself what I mean?"

She shook her head.

"You're being perverse," he reproached her. "A brilliant girl like you who took a degree with first-class honours. Have you never read the *Golden Bough*, never heard of the White Goddess?"

"Yes, I have, enough to know what you're talking about."

"But not enough, if you'll forgive my saying so, to understand the inner meaning. Won't you let me explain it to you?"

"You'll only waste your time."

"Why so, with so intelligent a pupil?"

"No, no, please not. I can't help it, you'll never make me see truth in a cruel superstition."

He rose to his feet with an exasperated sigh, paced to and fro, but as he was about to speak a sound of voices outside distracted him. A party in waterproof capes flocked past in the drive.

"The midsummer mummers." He laughed: "Hope springs eternal, but I fear it must be hope deferred." He opened the window and leant out: "The rites are sunk in the Flood, but there's room for all in the Ark. Come round to the door and I'll let you in."

Molly stared after them with curiosity: "The young people from the camping site?"

"True enthusiasts." He nodded, with a malevolent glance at Kate: "No overeducated sceptics, none of this squeamishness there; but I suppose they're too common for a graduate of Oxford University to consort with." He darted out into the hall, forestalling any reply.

"He's quite wrong, Mrs. Corrington," Kate protested when they were alone. "I don't despise his friends at all."

"I'm sure you don't, dear. They mean well, I've seen them in church." She hesitated and added: "All the same, perhaps there's something in what he says, they're not your sort."

"That hasn't anything to do with it. Really it hasn't."

"Then what's the matter? Tell me, Kate, and we'll think of some way between us to get over the difficulty. He'd be so delighted if you took the part."

"Why can't he find someone else? There are lots of girls in the town who'd love to play the part of a goddess."

"He's set his heart on your playing it. You ought to be flattered."

"I suppose I ought, but I'm not."

"Why aren't you? Has Helen said anything to put you off?"

"Only that it would be difficult to fit the rehearsals in, but if that were all I could probably manage by learning my part alone, as Mr. Brink himself suggests. Mrs. Buttle isn't to blame, no one is except myself. You probably think me very obstinate, but I can't help it."

"I do think you're being rather unreasonable to disappoint poor Mr. Brink when he's taking such trouble to arrange this entertainment, something for everyone in the parish to look forward to. He's so anxious to draw people together, to arouse interest in the church. It's our duty, don't you think, to help him?"

"No one could do more than you, Mrs. Corrington."

"Thank you, dear, but we're talking of your duty, not mine."

"Oh, I wish I could explain, but I can't, I don't want to upset you." Her eyes filled with tears: "You're too sweet, Mrs. Corrington, to think evil of anyone."

"Of whom should I, Kate? Not of you?"

"No." She shook her head and laughed, leaving the rest of the question unanswered. She stood up: "Anyhow I ought to go back. I've taken too long as it is over this errand."

"Tell Helen that I kept you."

The door opened. Brink returned, followed by an eager retinue disencumbered of waterproofs and gum boots.

"What's this?" he exclaimed sternly to Kate. "An attempt to escape the proletarian invasion?"

"An attempt," she replied tartly, "to escape the sack. I'm neglecting my work at the school." She glanced longingly at the window which he had left open.

He turned to his flock: "Let me introduce the reluctant goddess. Here we are all ready to rehearse, and the star succumbs to temperament, a crisis of nerves."

Albert Dockin stepped forward, held out his hand: "Pleased to meet you, Miss Evans. I've heard no end about you from Mr. Brink."

She shook hands politely, without interest.

"Name of Albert Dockin," he added.

She stared in alarm, disengaged her hand as abruptly as if it touched a snake. "I'm sorry, Mr. Brink," she insisted, "but I can't stay. I only came to give you Mrs. Buttle's message."

The door was blocked by his followers, he smiled at them: "What shall we do to her? What does she deserve?"

"Give her what that sweetie got." Albert's eyes gleamed, he ignored Brink's frown: "The stunner in your drawer in the vestry."

Kate advanced on them with flaming cheeks: "I warn you, I'm strong, and I scratch and bite and kick."

"Don't be silly, Kate." Molly Corrington laughed nervously: "He's only teasing you, only joking."

"Very true, Molly." Brink nodded: "Yours as always is the voice of sanity. This is a rectory of the established Church of England, not Bluebeard's castle." He raised his arm with a mocking air of authority: "Hosanna, hosanna, make way for the Midsummer Goddess."

She strode out between them, embarrassed but thankful.

Brink followed her into the hall. She made haste to grab her raincoat and tug it on, shrinking back out of his reach when he tried to help her. He smiled unperturbed, opened the outer door for her, handed her her umbrella.

"Thank you." She controlled her voice with an effort: "I needn't put it up, the rain's stopped."

"Why should you ever? You look so charming when you're wet."

As she walked down the drive she let indignation take possession of her. All the fear aroused by the uncanny events in the Devil's Churchyard and the discovery of her own name in the mysterious book was transmuted into passionate hatred of the Reverend Oswald Brink and Albert Dockin. She was convinced that they were fellow conspirators. Albert who came by night to look for the book, Brink who sent him. It did not matter whether she had evidence, it was enough for her that both inspired the same repulsion. She remembered how Jim had said that Albert gave him the creeps, the description fitted her own feelings exactly.

The memory of Jim helped to restore her equanimity, re-quickening the glow of excitement which, proof against shock and agitation, persisted in her heart since she met him. His image engrossed and exhilarated her thoughts as she came out of the rectory gate into the lane that ran inland along the crest of the ridge overlooking the clustered houses of the town and the gorge of the Rune. This was the shortest way on foot from the church to the school, but motorists avoided it; the lane was narrow and winding, the surface pitted, merciless to tyres. She had it to herself on this grey afternoon under clouds that threatened any moment to resume their downpour.

She passed a solitary cottage with a few outbuildings, paused to lean over the gate of the field beyond it.

"Dinah," she called.

The mare was grazing, but she raised her head at the sound of the voice and came trotting up with a whinny of recognition. Kate stroked her nose, groped in the pocket of her coat, extracted the crumbled remains of a bar of chocolate. Dinah devoured the offering greedily, craned her head over the gate to snatch at the pocket in hope of a second helping.

"No, there's no more." She laid her hand on the importunate mouth; but her thoughts were of the last occasion when she rode Dinah, of the final scramble through the thorns, of the man who awaited her there. Lost in her dream she was taken by surprise, almost knocked over by the blow when Dinah suddenly jerked her head up, started back in alarm into the field.

"What's the matter, Dinah? Have you seen a ghost?"

She looked round, stared in dismay with rising temper. Albert Dockin approached behind her, wheeling his bicycle.

63

"Pardon me, miss. Can I have a word with you?"

"No, you can't. I haven't the time."

His pale eyes glinted, but he averted them: "You've time enough, it seems, for the nag."

"That time isn't wasted."

"Now look here, Miss Evans," he complained, and his voice reproached her. "You're not being fair to me. I've sweated my guts out to catch you up on this filthy road, all to do a good turn to you and Mr. Tranmire."

She glanced at him sharply, and he nodded:

"Return good for evil, as the Bible says. That's my motto."

"What's Mr. Tranmire got to do with it?" she asked.

"Ah, you'll listen to me now perhaps. He's in danger, there are queer goings-on on his farm. He's been losing lambs, hasn't he?"

"He can tell you better than I can."

"Never mind, I know he has, and unless he takes care it won't be only the lambs that get their throats cut."

"You mean that someone wants to hurt him?" her voice trembled.

"Put it that way if you like. He won't let me come on his land, sets the police on me; but if he only knew he'd do better to keep his eye on others."

"If you know of any plot it's your duty to report it to the police."

"Do you suppose they'd believe me? They'd haul me in as likely as not for making mischief."

"Not if you can prove what you say."

"I can't miss, I haven't the facts. That's the trouble, that's why I've come to you now. If you could see your way to play ball with the rector, join in his midsummer romps, you'd be better placed than anyone to find out the truth."

"The rector? You suspect Mr. Brink?" Her eyes rested on him, doubtful and suspicious: "Aren't you a friend of his?"

"What if I am? I haven't said anything against him, have I?"

"You said that if I played ball with him, your own words, I'd find out what's being plotted against Mr. Tranmire."

"I never said the rector was behind it."

"I thought that was what you meant."

"Well, I can't help it if you let your thoughts run away with you."

"Perhaps you'll tell me just what you do mean."

64

"No, I've said more than I should, you're too quick for me. You'll twist whatever I say, turn my meaning upside down."

"I'm only trying to get things clear."

"Haven't I warned you clearly enough? If something nasty happens to Mr. Tranmire you'll be sorry you threw away your chance to stop it."

"Why can't you talk plainly, tell me what I'm to do?"

"I've told you, take your part in this play and keep your eyes open."

"Yes, but open for what, open for whom?"

"Ask me no questions and I'll tell you no lies." He turned with a snigger, pushed his bicycle back on to the road, leapt into the saddle and pedalled off vigorously towards the rectory, crouched over the handlebars. She watched his retreating figure with distaste and distress.

The field where Dinah grazed was on the edge of the school grounds. In former days when the house was Easby Hall and Jim's parents lived there this land gave pasture to a stud of hunters, and the cottage was occupied by the groom, Charlie Bracken—father of Jim's friend, the policeman. When Easby Hall became Saint Ursula's the old man was left in residence with a few small fields for cow-keeping in return for his services as gardener and groundsman.

He came to the door as Albert rode away, and seeing Kate he walked across to her. She recovered her composure and smiled at him:

"Good afternoon, Mr. Bracken. Is it going to clear up, do you think?"

"Good afternoon, miss." He touched his cap and stared up at the sky: "I doubt there's more coming. It's hard on those with their hay out."

"You got yours all right, didn't you?"

"Yesterday." He nodded: "I never thought we'd do it when that storm blew up, but we did just in time, except for a little jag hardly worth the gathering."

"You've a lovely stack. I saw it when I came back with Dinah."

"Were you in trouble, miss? The mare's legs were caked with mud. I gave them a good wash."

"Oh, how kind of you. No, we weren't bogged, but there's a lot of soft ground in Kemsdale Wood."

"It's an awkward place," he agreed.

"You didn't find anything wrong when you washed Dinah?"

"No, she'd taken no harm, but she'd picked up a bit of decoration." He grinned: "I thought you'd been fitting her with a bracelet."

"A bracelet?"

"I'll fetch it and show you."

He went back into the house and returned with a strip of metal. Kate examined it with puzzled interest:

"This was sticking to her leg, you say?"

"Wound fast about it, just above the fetlock. I'd a job to free her."

The metal was pliable like a stout tinfoil, and where he had washed off the mud the surface shone bright and new. There were words engraved on it, she licked her finger and rubbed them to make them more legible:

Frolic and Fancy Ltd, Theatrical Costumiers, Wimbledon. On the other side there was a further inscription: *Satan size 3.*

She raised her eyes and spoke calmly: "There was some litter in the wood, an old box or something, and Dinah trod in it and got rather entangled. This must be part of it." She slipped it into the pocket of her coat.

"Those campers," he growled. "They leave their nasty litter everywhere. They might have lamed her."

"They aren't all so thoughtless. They're a mixture like the rest of us, some very nice."

"Maybe, but more of them like that chap who passed on the road just now."

"Albert Dockin?"

"You know him, miss?" His tone was surprised.

"Mr. Brink does. I met him at the rectory."

"The rector can look after himself, but if you take my advice you'll have nothing to do with that Albert Dockin. He's a bad lot, our Harry could tell you a thing or two about him."

"He suspects him, doesn't he, of stealing Mr. Tranmire's lambs?"

"He was up to no good at that time of night in the Devil's Churchyard."

"You call it that too?"

"We all do. It's a daft name, but I've never heard any other."

She nodded: "Has it always been called that?"

"As long as I can remember, and that's more than three-score years. If you ask me I'd say it's as old as the hills."

"I wonder what the reason for it was. Does no one know?"

"There were tales when I was a bairn, but they're mostly forgotten now. Things have changed with all this schooling and TV."

"What tales? Do tell me."

He shook his head: "None fit for a young lady's ears. There were queer doings in the old days. Folks were afraid, they kept clear of the Devil's Churchyard if they could."

"Aren't they afraid any longer? Wasn't Harry at all worried last night?"

"If he was he wouldn't let it interfere with his duties."

"He must have strong nerves. It's an uncanny place, I'd hate to be alone there after dark."

"No, that wouldn't do at all. You might meet worse than bogies."

Her fingers thrust in her pocket closed on the strip of metal: "Perhaps it was the same in the old days too. Bogies of flesh and blood."

"I shouldn't wonder, miss."

His wife came to the door, called to him that his tea was ready, and he went back in.

Kate walked on towards the school. The house stood on high ground looking down the valley of the Rune over the town of Easby and beyond the twin moles guarding the harbour to the sea, silver-grey this afternoon and flecked with white horses. The heavy canopy of clouds was frayed in places by rifts of blue sky, but thundery peaks looming up from the horizon discouraged any hope of a long respite from rain. Kate, pausing to look back as she turned in at the gate, stared in fascination at their fantastical shape. Like Brink the evening before, she was reminded of the vision in the Apocalypse, of the beast having seven heads and ten horns. She turned her back on it with a shudder.

"What a hell of a time you've been. I thought perhaps something had happened to you."

She smiled at the sound of the voice and quickened her pace. Jim was coming down the drive to meet her.

"I called," he explained, "to find out if the contingent from Saint Ursula's would be going in spite of the rain to the frolic at the rectory. I gather from Mrs. Buttle that you aren't, she said she'd sent you to tell Brink. I shan't bother to go myself if you won't be there."

"You'd find nothing happening if you did. It's too wet, he's putting it all off till next Sunday."

"He isn't as mad as I thought."

"Did Mrs. Buttle think I'd taken too long?" she asked uneasily. "I walked as fast as I could, but I got rather caught at the rectory."

"By Brink?" He frowned.

"Mrs. Corrington was there too."

"Molly Corrington?" He whistled softly to himself: "Well, I suppose she's better than no one."

"You haven't answered my question, Jim. Was Mrs. Buttle annoyed?"

"Not in the least. She was doing very nicely without you. Most of the children seemed to be watching TV, and a colleague of yours, the horn-rimmed blonde festooned in beads, was reading to the little ones."

"Doris Wayworth? She's sweet really, you can't judge her by her taste in necklaces."

"I wasn't, I was only describing her. Anyhow, all's quiet at Saint Ursula's. No one was missing you except me. I sat down to wait, hoping you'd soon be back, then as you weren't I thought I'd walk to meet you."

"I'm afraid I'll have to go straight back in. I'm on duty."

"No, you aren't. I took the chance while I was with Mrs. Buttle to beg the rest of the afternoon off for you, and you're coming into the town to have tea with me. We'll be rather late, but they'll serve us at the Angel, they know me."

"Are you sure it's all right with Mrs. Buttle?"

"She'd have said if it wasn't. She's a woman who knows her own mind."

"That's true." She laughed: "She's very outspoken."

"She was just now about you. Don't be alarmed, she was full of your praises. She has sound judgement, she likes you, Kate."

The startled expression on her face yielded to a blush, his eyes were fixed on her.

"So it's all arranged," he added. "She's free, she says, and can take over for an hour or two herself, but you're to be back before the girls have their supper."

"How very kind of her."

"She's got Miss Wayworth and her beads to help. Let's hurry before all the crumpets are eaten."

"I can't go to the Angel like this." She opened her coat to show him her blouse and skirt.

"Why not? What's wrong?"

"I must change into a dress, put on beads, if you like, from Doris."

"Don't be long. Beads alone, if it's quicker."

"Thank you." Her eyes mocked him: "They'd either leave too much bare or be uncomfortable to sit on."

She ran on ahead of him, disappeared into the house.

When she joined him at the car drawn up outside the front door no coat covered her short dress of yellow silk tight-waisted, splayed at the hips; her hair shone smooth and lustrous, her only beads were a short string of amber round her neck.

"Seven minutes exactly," she told him.

"Magic." He surveyed her with approval: "I might have known you're a witch."

Her face fell: "Witches and warlocks. Don't let's talk of them."

"I'm sorry, Kate."

She smiled at him, turned to get into the car: "It isn't raining. Shall we have the hood down?"

"Yes, of course. I was afraid you'd be cold."

"I love the feel of the wind."

"So do I." He pushed the hood back and fastened it.

She sat silent at his side as he drove out of the grounds into the lane, turning downhill to join the main road into Easby. Her hair streamed in the wind; the rush of damp air exhilarated, reassured her.

"It's silly to put it off," she murmured at last.

"Put what off?"

"The forbidden subject."

"Let it wait if you'd rather."

She shook her head: "The sooner you know the better." She described what Charlie Bracken had found round Dinah's leg, the strip of metal and its inscription: "I haven't it here," she concluded, "it's in my coat pocket in my room; but I'm quite sure what it is, it's the band belonging to a mask, a goat's mask for Satan. That's what the manufacturers had written on it."

He nodded: "I never thought that Devil was supernatural."

"I did, and I wish I'd been right."

"What, a diabolic apparition? You didn't seem to like the idea when we watched it yesterday."

"I like even less to know there's a madman in your wood killing lambs and busy plotting crimes more horrible still."

"What crimes?"

"I don't know. I wish I did." She hesitated, frowning: "Don't go near the Devil's Churchyard, Jim. There's no real need, is there?"

"There's every need when I'm looking for sheep."

"Can't you take the policeman, Harry Bracken, with you?"

He laughed: "I can hear the rude remarks at the police station if I asked them for an escort when I go shepherding. Who's been putting these ideas into your head? Has old Charlie Bracken been telling you gory legends?"

"You yourself told me Harry found a trespasser in the wood last night."

"Yes, he found Albert Dockin, but it couldn't have been Albert with that goat's mask on his head. Our Devil was tall and heavily built, Albert's puny and weedy."

"It could have been a friend of his."

"It could, but we've no proof. He spared us nothing of his anatomy except for the only part that interests me, his face."

They were in the streets of the town, crossed the bridge over the Rune, climbed the steep hill up the cliff facing the abbey. Terraces of early Victorian lodginghouses occupied the crest, and beyond them the Angel stood in its own grounds overlooking the sea, a handsome building whitewashed and dignified with a pillared façade that imitated the Palladian style. It was the best hotel in Easby, a haunt of local society no less than of summer visitors.

Jim turned into the car park and drew up. He laid his hand on her knee:

"You're not to start fussing about me, you've got to look out for yourself. I've an idea who our Devil is. Come in and have tea, and I'll tell you."

They were late but not too late. The lounge was still crowded, but most who sat there lingered talking over empty cups and plates. The headwaiter who knew Jim found him a secluded table in a corner and took his order for tea, crumpets and cakes.

70

Kate, who had never been here before, stared round the room with interest: "Most of them look as if they'd stepped out of an advertisement in *Vogue*."

"So do you."

"Not unless it's advertising Marks and Spencers."

"All right, I can't argue. I don't take *Vogue* in. I like pictures better of nymphs on horseback appearing hey-presto out of a briary bush."

Not knowing what to say, she was silent.

The waiter brought tea, and she ate and drank with appetite. He too at first; but after a time his face clouded, and she was still eating when he lit a cigarette.

"It's a damned shame," he exclaimed. "Why can't we sit here and be happy? Why must I spoil everything by talking of that Devil?"

"I felt the same," she reminded him, "when I got into the car."

He nodded: "I can't put it off. If anything happened to you because I hadn't warned you I'd never forgive myself."

"Warn me?"

"Yes, it's you, not me he has designs on."

"You haven't told me yet who you suspect."

"The Reverend Oswald Brink. Listen, Kate, I know quite a lot about this man. After all, I appointed him to the living. I expect you wonder why."

"I do rather."

"I was sorry for him. He'd made enemies in his last parish, and they spread stories against him, such nonsense, it seemed, that I put it all down to malice, sensational gossip, and was anxious to give him a fair chance. I was a fool of course."

"I'm sure I'd have done the same. What were the stories about?"

"Black magic, I thought it fantastic; but in fact there'd been a scandal in the church, a girl found tied to the altar with some abracadabra written on her bare bottom. She wouldn't say who'd done it, probably a gay youth on the spree. There was nothing to implicate the rector."

"I should hope not. Why should there be?"

"People talked, they said he was too free and easy with the girls, and things got so hot he resigned. I can't remember the details; but I went into them carefully at the time and came to the conclusion he was a crank, but otherwise harm-

71

less. So I offered him Easby, he sounded an amusing character."

"He is, I suppose."

"He doesn't amuse me any longer. I've been hearing things for months that made me doubtful, and now this business in the Devil's Churchyard puts the lid on it."

"You're only guessing, you don't know it was him we saw wearing the mask, who killed your lamb and beat Fan so cruelly. Poor Fan, how is she? I forgot to ask."

"A bit stiff, but otherwise quite herself again, gulping down Winalot by the bushel. She's all right, it's you I want to talk about."

"I don't see what I've got to do with it."

"You will in a moment. This morning after church Albert Dockin was with Brink in the vestry, he gave him the book from the Devil's Churchyard."

"So he had it all the time when the policeman caught him?"

"Evidently, but Harry of course wasn't looking for it."

"How do you know all this?"

"There's a spyhole under the tower which I discovered when I was a boy. It gives a view into the vestry, so I crept in and watched them."

"And they never knew?"

"Not till I was clumsy enough to knock a stone over, and it fell with an almighty crash on the floor. Even then I was quite safe, they searched the church but couldn't find me."

"All the same you took a big risk."

"Only of looking an ass. What else?" She did not reply, and he added: "Anyhow it paid off. I couldn't hear everything they said, but I know at least what they're up to. It's the same story as in his old parish."

"Black magic?"

"Yes, and this midsummer fooling is part of it."

"Does it really matter if it's his hobby?"

"Not much of a hobby for the lambs, or that girl either."

"No, of course." She blushed: "I was forgetting."

"Have you forgotten too that your own name's in his book?"

She shook her head: "I try to, but I can't."

"I'm sorry, Kate." He leant towards her earnestly: "We've got to clear this up. Brink isn't just a credulous dabbler in superstitious thrills, he isn't a charlatan either; he's a learned man ruled by an obsession bordering on madness. I heard him

72

tell Albert, and there was no mistaking the excitement in his voice, about old Parson Amos who died in the Devil's Church-yard. The story is that he was carried off by the Devil while he celebrated the Black Mass."

"Surely you don't believe that?"

"No, I don't; but I believe in the crimes of which he was accused, including ritual murder. He sets a dangerous example if Brink takes him as his guru."

"I've never heard of this Parson Amos. Who was he?"

"The Reverend Amos Pounder, rector of this parish in the early seventeenth century and as unsavory a character as you're likely to find from that day to this. I've a book about him at home, I'll let you see it."

"He lived a long time ago, and people were very superstitious then. Things happened which couldn't today."

"Murders are still committed."

Her eyes were wide with fear: "You'll go to the police, Jim, won't you? Not just Harry Bracken but the serjeant. You said you'd report the loss of your lambs, you can tell him now what you know of Mr. Brink."

"Tell him I suspect the parson of black magic? He'd think that if anyone's fit for the madhouse it's not Brink, it's me."

"There's nothing mad in trying to catch a murderer."

"I've no evidence that he is. Listen, Kate, do be sensible. We can take precautions without making fools of ourselves. He's planning some devilry for next Sunday, there's to be a mystery play or something of the sort. Do you know he wants you to act in the principal part?"

"Yes, I do."

"Well, you're not to."

"Why not?"

"That should be obvious."

Her colour rose: "I ask you to report Mr. Brink and you won't. Why should I be expected to do whatever you tell me?"

"It's for your own good, to protect you from great danger."

"What about you? It's for your protection I want the police."

"But I'm not in danger, you are."

She shook her head unhappily: "I've got to decide for myself."

"I don't know what's come over you." Anxiety sharpened

his temper, he spoke roughly: "Don't you believe me when I tell you he wants you in this play for no good?" He received no reply, her silence stung him: "I suppose you think you'll enjoy it, bent over the altar like that girl while he celebrates Mass on your bottom."

"How can you?" Her cheeks flushed scarlet, she pushed her chair back, leapt to her feet: "I'm going, I must anyhow for the children's supper."

"There's more than half-an-hour, and it won't take us ten minutes."

"I need a good half-hour. I mean to walk."

"Hullo, Jim. I saw you across the room, but you and Kate seemed to have so much to say to each other I didn't like to intrude." Pearl, very elegant, stood beside him.

"Good evening." He rose, his expression was thunderous: "I'm just off, I'm driving Kate back to Saint Ursula's."

"You can't run away at once. I haven't seen you for so long."

"I'm sorry, that's how it is."

She glanced at her watch: "There's a bus in a few minutes from the corner of the Esplanade. If you hurry you'll catch it, Kate."

"She doesn't need to," he put in abruptly. "She's going in my car."

Pearl frowned: "I suppose you can spare time at least to tell me what your answer is to my note."

"Your note?"

"Yes, didn't you get it? I dropped it into your car as I couldn't see you."

"I found a note, but it wasn't from you." His voice was puzzled.

"Of course it was from me. How silly you are."

"Something about a sore arm and Doctor Buttle."

"If you think you're funny I don't. It was an invitation to lunch. You're impossible, Jim; if you can't be civil I'll leave you." She flounced back to her seat near the hearth where a sleek young man, partner in a firm of auctioneers, awaited her return with impatience and annoyance.

"Dear me," Jim exclaimed. "I seem to be offending everyone. Another rebuff and I'll weep. Come on, Kate, you're driving back to the school with me."

She accompanied him without demur, sat beside him in

74

the car. Her eyes were lowered, their long lashes veiled them. She said nothing, they drove in silence.

They reached the entrance to the school, and instead of turning in he drew up on the verge of the lane. Taken by surprise she glanced at him, his eyes held hers:

"Kate," he exclaimed, "before you go you've got to listen. I didn't mean what I said; it was just anxiety boiling up, making me want to hurt you. I don't expect you'll ever forgive me."

"But I do, Jim. I've been thinking. Perhaps it's true, and you were right to say it."

"Of course it isn't true."

"I hope not."

He took her in his arms and kissed her.

"Then you'll tell Brink to find someone else? You'll have nothing to do with him?"

She shook her head, disengaged herself, stepped out into the grass:

"I wish I could, but it's no use wishing. I can't help it."

She stood and watched as he drove reproachfully away. Through a chink of blue piercing the clouds a distant shaft of sunlight ensilvered, glittered on the sea at the end of the valley beyond the town.

She walked up the drive, entered the house and went to look for Mrs. Buttle to let her know that she was back. She found her with the children reading a story aloud.

"Good, Kate." She broke off and looked up: "You're very punctual. We aren't ready for supper yet."

"Then I'll change my dress, shall I?"

"No, don't; that suits you so well. Did you enjoy yourself at the Angel?"

"Very much, thank you."

"That reminds me. Mr. Brink rang up after you left. I told him you were having tea with Jim there, and if he rang the hotel he could get you."

"He didn't. Perhaps it wasn't important."

"Perhaps not." She hesitated: "He knows, doesn't he, you don't want to act in this play of his?"

"I've changed my mind, Mrs. Buttle. I think after all I will."

"Oh, Kate." Her tone held both reproach and dismay, then she glanced at the group of little girls clustered at her feet on the carpet, and she picked up her book again: "We'll talk about it later, I thought you agreed with me." She found her place and resumed the adventures of E. Nesbit's children in *The Amulet*.

Jim drove fast as soon as his car was out of the lane and on the main road from Easby. His mood craved for relief and found it in speed, and he could indulge it the more easily as there was little traffic at this hour following a wet Sunday afternoon. Mounting the long hill on to the moor he kept his foot on the throttle, still pressed it as the car bounded forward on the level over the summit. Near Kemsdale Wood the ground fell away steeply on his left, the road skirted the edge of a disused quarry. He had a clear view ahead to a distant rise on the skyline; the road was empty, flanked by open moor. He approached at headlong speed, faster and faster.

A figure sprang up out of the bracken on his right, leapt in his way gesticulating and dancing. He had no time to see who or what it was, he jammed on his brakes. The road was even greasier than he expected, the car skidded, and as he still braked desperately to avoid the living obstacle the skid became uncontrollable, wrenched him to the left. The post and rails guarding the quarry yielded under the impact, the car lurched over the cliff, bounced from crag to crag till it lay upside down far below in a rushy pool.

Chapter 5

Molly Corrington enjoyed her breakfast. She spread the butter thick on her scone, helped herself liberally to marmalade. Pearl watched her morosely and toyed with a thin slice of the patent bread sold for dieting.

"Did you have a good time, dear?" her mother asked.

"Deadly. I was thankful the Angel closes early on Sundays."

"You dined at the Angel, did you?"

"Yes, with Leslie Potts. I didn't want to, he made me."

"I'm sure he meant to be kind."

"He isn't my style at all, he's too common."

Her mother nodded: "What a pity Jim couldn't take you."

"Thank you, I'd rather not. When he isn't mucking about on the farm he's flirting with Kate Evans."

"Good gracious. With Kate?"

"Yes, brains and brawn, just the type for him, bookish, bucolic, outsize round the hips."

"You're horrid, Pearl, she's a sweet child and she's got a charming figure; but of course it's more chic to be slim, and that's what men admire, one's told." Observing the sarcasm in her daughter's expression she sighed: "Well, what's the use at my age? I'd only make my life a misery." She buttered a second scone with undiminished appetite.

Pearl reverted to her own concerns: "I can't understand Jim, he used to have such good manners. I suppose it's farming that's spoilt him."

"What's he done now? He's always polite when I meet him."

"I don't call it polite to leave an invitation unanswered and then insult me with a senseless joke."

"You look for insults, Pearl, where none are intended."

"I do nothing of the sort, Mother. I took the trouble when I couldn't find him after church to get a sheet of paper and an envelope from the newsagent at the foot of the steps, and I wrote him a note to ask him to lunch today. Hadn't I the right to expect an answer?"

"How could he, you goose? If you put it in the post it wasn't delivered till this morning."

"I didn't put it in the post. I left it on the seat of his car."

"Are you sure you did?"

"Quite sure. What do you take me for?"

"Well, I'm not blaming you, dear, I know you've a bad memory; But Mr. Brink gave you a note for me yesterday, and I never got it."

"The *billet doux*. Yes, of course." She laughed gruffly: "I'll go and fetch it."

"You needn't trouble. I've seen him since, and no harm's done."

Pearl was already on her feet: "It's yours, not mine. I

don't want it." She darted out into the hall, came back with her bag.

"Here's your precious letter, you can put it under your pillow." She extracted an envelope, stared at it in amazement: "No, it isn't. It's my own writing." She tore it open, glanced at the contents, burst into laughter: "No wonder Jim didn't thank me for inviting him to lunch. I must have mixed the notes up, he got the one asking Molly to wash Oswald's surplice."

"Whatever are you talking about?" Her mother spoke with unaccustomed asperity.

"Well, if that wasn't the message it was something of the sort."

"It wasn't, it was something very private, and I'm much distressed at its falling into Jim's hands."

Even Pearl was abashed by the vehemence of her tone: "I didn't do it on purpose," she replied sulkily. "I'll slip over to Kemsdale Farm in my car if you like, and ask Jim to give it me back."

"That's no use when he's read it. No, I'll have to talk to him myself, appeal to his better feelings. You've made such a muddle, Pearl, I don't know if I'm standing on my head or my feet. Is he coming to lunch or isn't he?"

"He doesn't know he's invited." She crunched the invitation into a ball and threw it into the wastepaper basket.

"I'd like him to come, I'd like to clear this up at once. You can get him on the telephone, can't you?"

"I'm more likely to get some moron, the old hag who keeps house for him or that fat slut of a girl who milks the cows, and after repeating the question six times I'll be told he's on the moor or in the wood gathering sheep or something, and not expected back till God knows when. He's an impossible man to ring up, or I'd have tried yesterday instead of writing that note."

"Try phoning him now. Do, please; you may be lucky."

Pearl shrugged her shoulders, gulped down the last of her coffee and left the room. Her mother pushing aside her empty plate reached across the table for the *Daily Express;* but after a glance at the headlines she let the paper fall into her lap, sat staring out of the window with an anxious frown.

The house was one of a terrace built at the foot of the west cliff. The principal rooms looked out across the harbour to the tiers of red roofs closely packed on the farther cliff, surmounted by the parish church and abbey ruins; but the dining room was at the back with a view only into the street, and the window was shut to exclude the noise of traffic. The sun, making up for its failure of the day before, shone cheerfully outside from a blue sky. Molly Corrington could not resist it; she raised the sash, leant out. As she did so she caught sight of a group of people gathered a short way off on the pavement, overflowing into the road. The policeman, Harry Bracken, who stood among them, did nothing to move them on or to direct the vehicles trying to pass; he himself was taking part in the conversation, seemed indeed to be the centre of interest.

Her curiosity was aroused; she was still watching them when Pearl came back into the room.

"Mother, they don't expect him to live."

The rotund amplitude of garish skirt blocking the window quivered, butted into the table as Molly swung round:

"Who are you talking about?"

"Jim, of course. He's had an accident. Concussion, I think; but the old woman was quite hysterical, and I never can understand her dialect anyhow."

"Dear me. There seem to be so many accidents on farms."

"It wasn't on the farm, it was last night on his way back from Easby in his car. As far as I could gather, they waited and waited and when he hadn't turned up after midnight the men went to look for him, and they fetched Harry Bracken from his cottage to help. It was Harry who found him; he was caught in some bushes halfway down a quarry, the car had skidded over the edge and was smashed up at the bottom. The bushes saved Jim's life."

"I thought you said it wasn't saved."

"How can I know?" she retorted irritably. "He's alive at the moment. These old crones love to pile on the gloom."

"If Harry Bracken found him he can tell us more than anyone."

"No doubt, but I haven't the least idea where he is."

"He's here, just outside the window." She pointed: "Look, on the pavement, with all those people round him. I expect he's giving them the news."

Pearl pushed the sash up higher and joined her.

"Shall we call him?" her mother asked.

"I don't suppose he'd hear. No, I'll slip on my coat and go out and talk to him."

"I'll come too." She scrambled back into the room.

"Like that?" Pearl eyed her severely: "How can you, Mother, in those slippers?" They were of pink flannel lined with rabbit fur frayed and scruffy from long service.

Molly gazed down at them regretfully: "They're so comfortable, and my outdoor shoes pinch so. All right, dear, you go without me; he's your boy, not mine. Come back as soon as you can and let me know what happened."

The crowd made way respectfully as Pearl approached.

"I've just heard of Mr. Tranmire's accident," she told the policeman, "when I rang up Kemsdale Farm."

"Yes, miss," he replied. "It's a shocking business."

"I didn't talk long on the telephone. I wonder if you can tell me more about it."

"You've come to the right man if you want information. It was me who found him."

"If it wasn't for Harry he'd be dead," a voice put in from the crowd.

Pearl nodded: "So they said. But he's not dead, you found him alive?"

"No more than alive." He spoke gravely: "He lay there like a corpse, and I thought he'd had it. His head was bleeding something cruel where he'd caught it on the rock; but it's the mercy of heaven he was driving an open car and was tipped out when it slewed over. If he'd still been inside at the bottom—I don't like to think."

"What happened when he fell out?"

"Well, it seems that the whin bushes caught him. There's a nice clump of them on a ledge not far from the top. Pricks enough to tear all the skin from your body; you wouldn't believe what a job it was to get him free, but I'll never look at a whin bush again without gratitude."

"Nor Mr. Tranmire, I'll be bound," an admirer exclaimed. "It takes some doing to climb down a steep drop like that, pick a man out of the whins and hoist him back up, ten foot and more. I wouldn't like to do it myself, I know the place well."

"Yes, he deserves a medal." Pearl's voice thrilled with appropriate praise.

Harry was silent, pleased but embarrassed. There was an awkward pause, and she changed the subject:

"Have you any idea what made the car skid? Mr. Tranmire's an experienced driver."

"He's as careful a driver, miss, as any in the county, but no one could hold a car on that road."

"Why?"

"It was a sheet of oil."

"From Mr. Tranmire's car?"

"No oil left his car till it fell in the quarry."

"Then how did it get on the road?"

"That's what I want to know, what we all want to know at the station."

"You mean someone spread it there on purpose to make his car skid and kill him? Whoever would?"

"I'm beat, miss. There's no one in the town who hasn't a good word for Mr. Tranmire."

"Except parson." The voice was from the back of the crowd.

"You keep your mouth shut, Tom." Harry turned on him angrily. "The law doesn't hold with slander. You'll get yourself into trouble."

A curt bark from the horn of a car interrupted him, restrained and dignified but loud enough to command attention. An elderly Daimler was creeping through the men blocking the thoroughfare. Doctor Buttle leant out of the window:

"Harry," he called. "If you're holding a public meeting I wish you'd choose a street farther from my surgery."

"Sorry, Doctor." He bustled forward, waved the crowd back with a gesture of professional authority.

Pearl stepped quickly to the car before it moved on: "Have you heard about Jim?" she asked.

"My dear, I've been with him ever since they sent for me in the early hours of the morning. I'm only just back from Kemsdale now to attend to my patients, if Harry can clear me a way to them."

"How is he? Jim, I mean. Will he live?"

"Yes, if all runs as it should and there's no relapse; but it's been touch and go, a severe shock to the system with concussion on top. At any rate he's recovered his senses, and his temperature was down when I left."

"Can I do anything for him? Would he like me to go and see him?"

"You know better than I do whether he'd like it, but I can tell you this, Pearl, you're not to. I've ordered complete quiet, as much sleep as he can get. If you're at a loose end perhaps you'll do something for me instead."

81

"Yes, what is it?" There was little eagerness in her tone.

"I'll be busy I don't know how long in the surgery, and I've a round of patients afterwards to visit. It could be late in the day before I'm home, and I'd like to have this book off my mind or I'm sure to forget it. Would you be kind enough to take it up to Saint Ursula's and give it to Kate?"

"To Kate Evans? Why to her?"

He smiled as he watched her expression: "All I know is that Jim asked me to see she got it."

"I thought he was at death's door, too ill to see anyone."

"He is, but while he was delirious he kept fretting about some Parson Amos, and the first thing he did when he came to was to ask me to go to the shelf and fetch him this book down."

He handed it to her, and she read the title aloud: *"The Godless Life and Diabolic Death of the Reverend Amos Pounder."* Her lip curled: "What's this? Light reading for her class of schoolgirls?"

"No, of course not." He frowned: "Helen wouldn't allow it, and Kate wouldn't dream of it any case. I don't suppose the book will mean anything to her, but Jim was so worked up I had to humour him for the sake of his peace of mind. So be a good girl, Pearl, and help me to fulfill my promise."

"You aren't firm enough, Doctor Buttle, you're too good-natured. All right, I'll take this load off your conscience."

"I'm much obliged to you." He drove on. Harry Bracken, ostentatiously alert, made haste to ensure him free passage.

Pearl went back into the house. She found her mother preparing to wash up the breakfast things.

"He's still in danger, but Doctor Buttle thinks he'll get over it."

"Oh, I'm so glad, dear. Easby could never be the same place without Jim. You saw Arthur, did you?"

"Yes, he was passing in his car. He'd been at the bedside all night."

"He's so kind. Jim couldn't be in better hands." She picked up the tin of detergent powder and slushed an avalanche into the water: "Take your coat off, Pearl, and help me, will you? There's a clean cloth over there, I'll soon have plates ready for you to dry."

Pearl glanced at the sink with distaste: "I'm sorry, Mother. He's given me an errand, to go up with this book to Saint Ursula's."

"What is it? Some medical textbook?" She wiped her hands and took the book from her daughter with curiosity: "How odd," she exclaimed as she read the title. "Whatever can Arthur want with it?"

"It isn't his, it's Jim's, and I'm to give it to Kate Evans."

"Well, I never. Still, it shows Jim can't be so bad, a dying man wouldn't send a girl a present." She turned the pages carelessly: "If you can call it a present, as dusty and dirty as it is."

"I don't suppose Kate will care or even notice."

"Why, I know this face, I'm sure I do." Molly was staring at the frontispiece, an engraving portraying a clergyman in old-fashioned gown and bands: "The clothes are odd of course, and the features aren't quite right; but there's no mistake about the eyes, they're Oswald Brink's."

Pearl peered over her shoulder: "These old fogies all look alike to me." She broke off, pointed to some words scrawled faintly in pencil underneath. She stooped to decipher them: "See page 64. It's Jim's handwriting."

She seized the book, flicked through it eagerly: "Page 64. Yes, here it is, and he's drawn a line against the paragraph." Then her face fell, there was disgust in her voice: "It's in a foreign language, probably Latin."

Her mother laughed: "I'm afraid I can't help you. You'll have to ask Kate what it means."

"Yes, and let her know I've been prying into her secrets. You've no sense, Mother."

"Perhaps not, dear, but I've got this washing-up on my mind. Can't you spare a few minutes to lend me a hand? It won't hurt Kate to wait for the book a little longer."

"No, I'm sure Doctor Buttle wanted me to go at once. I'm sorry, I can't help it, and I'd like to talk to Mrs. Buttle. She can tell me a lot of the things I didn't have time to ask him. She'll know of course when the message came and what was said."

She slipped out of the house before her mother could say more. The garage was across the street; she made haste to get the car out and drive to Saint Ursula's.

When Easby Hall was converted into a school extra accommodation was needed for classrooms, and these were provided by building a row of wooden huts painted green to match their surroundings in what was formerly the kitchen garden. Helen Buttle was coming from them, crossing the lawn to the front door when Pearl drew up.

"Hullo, Pearl," she greeted her. "You're out and about early."

"Doctor Buttle asked me to come with a book."

"Poor Arthur, he's had such a hard night; but he rang me up before he left the farm, and I'm delighted to know that Jim's a bit better. It was a terrible accident."

"From what Harry Bracken tells me, it wasn't an accident at all."

"Whatever do you mean?"

"The road was thick in oil so that the car couldn't help skidding. Somebody wanted to kill Jim."

"Nonsense. Who would? I don't wish to find fault with Harry Bracken. He behaved, from all I hear, with great energy and courage and saved Jim's life; but he suffers from a lurid imagination, he watches too many thrillers on TV."

"He seemed quite sure of what he said."

"He would be." Her tone dismissed the subject: "Did you say you've a book for Arthur? Put it in the hall, will you, that's a dear child."

"As a matter of fact it's for Kate. I gather that Jim was raving, quite delirious, and he insisted that she should have it."

"So he asked Arthur to be his messenger?"

"Doctor Buttle lets people get round him too easily. There aren't many who'd pay attention to what a patient says when he's out of his mind."

"Why not, if it made Jim happy? Anyhow you can give it her yourself if you like. She'll be out any minute now, it's the midmorning break."

Doors already slammed in the classrooms; girls streamed from the huts, raced across the grass to a side door into the house leading to a lobby where milk, fruit and bread and jam were provided. The teachers followed more slowly. Kate walked by herself; her face was pale and anxious, and she looked round startled when her name was called:

"Kate, come here please, I want you."

She hurried to obey the summons, glanced inquiringly at Mrs. Buttle and smiled at Pearl, who replied with a curt nod.

"Pearl has a book for you," Mrs. Buttle explained. "Jim sent it, and I thought you'd like to have it at once."

Kate took the book with a flush of surprise. She turned eagerly to Pearl:

"Have you just seen him? Is he any better?"

"I've no idea." Pearl spoke with irritation: "I'm only running an errand for Doctor Buttle. I saw him in the town, and he asked me to give you this as he's too busy himself."

Kate clutched the book, stared at it in bewilderment: "Why did Jim send it? Didn't he say?"

Helen Buttle laid her hand gently on her arm: "I expect when Arthur comes home this evening he'll be able to tell us. Anyhow it's a sign that Jim's better that he can spare a thought for things like this."

"I suppose so." Her eyes were still doubtful, she fixed them again on Pearl: "Doctor Buttle had nothing else to say, nothing about how the accident happened?"

"How could he? He wasn't there. Whatever I know comes from Harry Bracken."

"Harry Bracken? You've seen him?"

"Indeed I have." The interest shown gratified her: "He told me quite a lot."

"Wild theories," Helen Buttle put in. "We mustn't jump to conclusions."

"Well, he's been to the place, and we haven't." Pearl's voice rose defiantly: "He sticks to it that this was attempted murder."

"Murder?" Kate stared at her aghast.

"Yes, a deliberate attempt to kill Jim my spreading oil on the road so that his car would skid over the quarry."

Helen Buttle frowned disapproval: "We can't pass judgement till we've more evidence. What's certain is that he's still alive."

"For the present." Pearl added sourly.

Kate grasped the fence beside which they stood. Her head swam, she feared that she would faint. She controlled herself with an effort:

"I'll take this book up to my room. I've just time before my next class." Her voice trembled, she darted into the house.

Helen Buttle gazed after her with concern: "Why did you want to upset her?" she asked severely.

"I was only telling her the facts. She's got to face them like the rest of us. I'm as worried myself, but I don't make a fuss of my feelings. I've as good reason for them, haven't I, as she has?"

Alone in her room Kate threw herself on her face across the bed, burst into tears. "I must, I must," she whispered again and again as she sobbed. The repetition of the words seemed to comfort her, to inspire resolutions; her shoulders quivered no longer, the sobs died down. She sat up at last, groped for a handkerchief on the dressing table, and her fingers touched the book lying there where she had thrown it. She picked it up, glanced at the title. The name of Amos Pounder stirred her memory; she turned the pages, they opened at the frontispiece, and she stared at the face. Like Molly Corrington she was struck by the resemblance; it startled her, and as she examined it Jim's note scrawled underneath caught her eyes. She turned quickly to page 64.

The paragraph against which the line was drawn was written in simple Latin, and she read it without difficulty. It was part of a report of Pounder's trial in the Bishop's consistory court on charges including the ritual murder of a girl, Bess Atkins. The witness claimed to have been present at the rites; his description reminded Kate of that given her by Jim of the Black Mass in Brink's former parish, the girl's naked posture on the altar, the sacrament celebrated on her upturned seat. The official account proceeded:

Tum sacris impudenter consummatis sacerdos cultello tergum puellae inter costas percussit, cor confodit, sanguinem hausit, vinum sorbuit aeternae vitae.

"Then on conclusion of the shameful liturgy the priest stabbed the girl in the back between the ribs with his knife, pierced her heart, drew the blood, drank the wine of everlasting life."

Kate put the book down, buried her face in her hands, she felt very sick; but the clang of a bell reverberated through the passages. The midmorning break was over, the school summoned back to work. She leapt convulsively to her feet, ran to the basin and soused her face in cold water, dabbed some powder on, tugged the comb fiercely through her hair, fled downstairs to take the class awaiting her.

It was a class of older girls far enough advanced to read a Latin author, Ovid's lament for the death of Corinna's parrot. She had chosen the poem for them herself, hoping that the subject would amuse them; but it was all that she could do now to explain the meaning and correct their mistakes. She had no spirit to enjoy or encourage enjoyment of the poet's humour, was more inclined herself to weep than to laugh over the parrot's funeral. The polished couplets were confused in her mind with the jurisprudential Latin of the Bishop's court. The wine of everlasting life, her own blood; she pressed her hand to her heart.

The lesson came to an end at last, and she went out with Doris Wayworth to invigilate in the playing field. Then the bell rang for lunch, where her place was at the head of the table occupied by the youngest children. She was thankful for the noise that they made, drowning the terror that haunted her.

After lunch she was free for an hour or two. She changed her shoes, but as the day was fine and warm no other preparation was needed. As soon as she was done she hurried down, anxious to start before her courage failed.

Helen Buttle met her in the hall, she held a scarf of blue chiffon: "You aren't going into the town, are you, Kate?"

"No, I wasn't, Mrs. Buttle. Is there anything you want there?"

"Nothing urgent. Pearl left this when she was here this morning. It's her own fault for being so careless, she can wait to get it back."

"I thought of taking a walk on the hill towards the abbey. It's come out such a lovely afternoon." She blushed at her own lack of frankness.

"You're wise, it does you good to stretch your legs."

"If I happen to see Mr. Brink as I pass the rectory I'll tell him about Jim's accident."

"He's sure to have heard of it already in the town."

"As a matter of fact, there's something else." She could hold out no longer against her conscience: "I've thought carefully over everything you said, but I'm afraid I still want to act in this play. I shan't need any time off for it. Mr. Brink says he'll rehearse me separately if I come to him when I'm free."

"My dear child." She frowned: "If it were only a question of releasing you for rehearsals I've no doubt I could arrange it; but for your own sake I don't want to, I'm not happy about the idea at all."

"It's quite usual, isn't it, for a clergyman to get up things like this for the church?"

87

"No, Kate, not like this, and Mr. Brink isn't a usual clergyman. I don't want to say anything against him, but if you take my advice you won't have too much to do with him."

"Why not? Does he mean to do wrong?"

"No, no, of course not, or at any rate I hope not." The question put her out, her tone became colder: "I've no idea what he intends."

"Then oughtn't we to find out? Someone might be in danger."

"Who? Whatever are you talking about?"

Kate hesitated: "You heard what Pearl said. Isn't it better for me to do what he asks and see what he's up to, so that it can be stopped in time?"

"What nonsense. I never thought you were the hysterical type, Kate. You're worse than Pearl, or Harry Bracken either. At least they left the rector out of the melodrama."

"You said you weren't happy about him yourself."

"I don't regard him as a suitable companion for a young woman. There are many men of whom that can be said, and they aren't all dangerous criminals. If anyone's suspected of crime you can rely on the police to investigate, and there are wiser heads among them than Harry Bracken's, unlikely to waste time on wild accusations."

Kate was about to reply, checked herself and was silent.

Helen Buttle watched her with a frown: "You must make your own decision of course. You're old enough, and I've no power to interfere; but don't say I haven't warned you." Then her manner thawed, her voice held entreaty: "Do be careful, Kate. There's something about the man, I must admit, that turns my blood cold."

Kate nodded, the words made her shudder: "I shan't do anything silly, Mrs. Buttle, and I'm very grateful for your advice."

"But you don't take it."

"I wish I could."

"You're a strange girl. I don't understand you." She sighed and moved away.

It was indeed a lovely afternoon for a walk. A few fleecy clouds low in the distance over the hills were all that remained of the storm of the day before. Every colour seemed to be fresher after the rain, the green of the grass, the gold of buttercups on either side of the lane, the pale pink of wild roses, the creamy clusters of elder-blossom in the hedge.

There was a sweetness of flowering clover in the air, mingling with the salt tang of the breeze from the sea.

Despite herself Kate felt her spirits rise in the sunshine. As she passed Dinah's field she whistled, and the mare came cantering up, leant over the fence to nuzzle her skirt. She stroked the importunate nose:

"I'm sorry, Dinah. There's no chocolate today."

Charlie Bracken appeared from an outhouse: "Going for a ride, miss?"

She laughed: "Not in this dress."

"I wouldn't put it past you."

"Well, I'm afraid I'm not. I wish I were."

She reached the rectory. The sun shone as bright as ever, but as she turned in up the drive it was as if a sudden cloud extinguished all the light within her. Brink saw her from the window, came out to meet her at the door:

"Something told me this was my lucky afternoon. I consulted Virgil's prophetic tome for an omen, and it opened at the very words, *tibi candida Nais.*"

She ignored his greeting: "There's something I want to say. It won't take up much of your time."

"The longer it takes the better. Come in."

She hung back: "I can't stay. I'm on duty again very soon."

"Duty, duty, always duty. Mrs. Buttle works you too hard. She's a bit of a slavedriver, isn't she?"

"She's nothing of the sort. I've got to earn my salary."

He smiled, holding the door open, and she resigned herself to the inevitable and walked in past him. He followed her into the hall:

"Nothing this time to take off? No, you're down to bare essentials, I see, glad as I'd be to help you to shed them. Never mind, let's go into the study."

She kept her temper with an effort and obeyed him. The room had the window tightly shut and reeked of stale cigarette smoke. She was uncertain whether to be relieved or dismayed to find it occupied by Albert Dockin.

"Hullo, Miss Evans," he greeted her. "We'll soon be regular buddies." He held out his hand; but she left it ungrasped, and as it hung in the air he lowered it with a discomfited grin. The charred butt of a cigarette clung to his lip, he spat it out defiantly into the wastepaper basket.

Brink frowned at him: "Take a seat, Kate, and join us."

He drew up a chair: "We're in conference, Albert and I, to arrange the scenario."

She sat down, tugging her skirt angrily as it rucked back from her thighs: "That's what I've come about."

"So I supposed. You've come to tell me you accept the part?"

She checked with difficulty the impulse to contradict him: "Yes," she replied curtly. "I have."

"Second thoughts are always the wisest. I'm sure you'll enjoy it." His smile was affable, but it made her flesh creep.

"I'll hate it, but I can't refuse."

"Bravo, the willing victim. You feel that at whatever personal sacrifice you should support the work of the church?"

"You can put it like that if it pleases you."

"It does." He patted her knee, she wore no stockings, and his hand slid round under her bare thigh. She jerked her chair back out of his reach.

He betrayed no discomposure: "You'll need a copy of your part of course. Fetch it, Albert, will you? It's in that heap on the desk." He pointed to an untidy litter of documents.

"If I can find it in such a mess." Albert rose unwillingly, rummaged with impatient violence.

Brink turned again to Kate: "I hope that my version will reconcile you to the inner meaning of the legend." He broke off in annoyance: "Be careful, Albert, you'll have everything over."

He spoke too late. As Albert pushed the papers to and fro an accumulation cascaded on to the floor, dislodging and carrying with it a book that lay buried beneath. It fell by Kate's chair, and she picked it up, glanced at the title: *The Godless Life and Diabolic Death of the Reverend Amos Pounder.*

"Now by every saint in the calendar," Brink exclaimed. "I was hunting all over for that book yesterday in the vestry, and here it was the whole time." He reached out to take it from her.

She ignored the gesture, laid the book on her knees and opened it. He watched her with a troubled frown:

"A dull work, I don't recommend it. Mostly in Latin."

"It seems quite easy Latin."

"Forgive me, the charms of the flesh disguise the gifts of

the mind." The compliment slipped from him mechanically, his voice was uneasy.

She paid no attention, she enjoyed his discomfort. She was looking for page 64:

"It's rather fascinating. Is it very rare?"

"I know only of one other copy; it belonged to old Mr. Tranmire at Easby Hall. I often wonder whether his son has it still."

"Perhaps he sold it to raise money for death duties." She kept turning the pages casually till she found what she wanted: "Who was this Amos Pounder? Ought I to have heard of him?"

"No, my dear, he doesn't concern you at all, merely a former rector of this parish."

"He seems to have been in trouble with the Bishop."

"Yes, he was a trifle unorthodox even for the Church of England."

"I'm glad to know he isn't typical."

"Why? What are you reading?" Again he tried to recover the book; but she held on to it, put her finger on the paragraph, unmarked in this copy:

"About this girl, Bess Atkins."

He could restrain himself no longer, he snatched the book from her and closed it: "We mustn't waste time when you've so little to spare from your duties. Let's get down to serious business. Have you found her part yet, Albert?"

"It's here." He held out some sheets of typescript. As he handed them to Kate he winked: "You don't need to dig in old books for wrong 'uns. I could point to quite a few in this town today." He added with another wink and a leer: "That was a queer sort of accident to happen to Mr. Tranmire."

The colour drained from her face, and she nodded.

"I'm much relieved," Brink put in, "to hear that he's getting over it."

"Doctor Buttle hopes so, but he isn't certain yet."

"He'll have to be more careful in future. He isn't a cat, you know, with nine lives."

"One from nine leaves eight," Albert reminded her, "and one from eight leaves seven. A time may come when one from one leaves nought."

She sat silent, struggling with her fears, sustained only by her anger.

"When do we start rehearsals?" she asked at last. "I want to meet the rest of the cast."

"I'm sure you do, and I'm sure they're anxious to meet you." Brink's voice was full of regret: "Unfortunately they're able to rehearse only in the middle of the morning, and I doubt if Mrs. Buttle would consent to set you free."

"The middle of the morning?" Her face fell: "How can I when I'm working?"

"All work and no play? Never mind, there's a way to get over the difficulty. I suggested it yesterday, if you remember. I'll rehearse you myself in the evening whenever it suits you."

"Alone?"

"By all means bring a colleague to keep you company if you wish."

"Yes, I do wish; but that won't help me to get to know the other actors in the play. Won't I ever see them?"

"You'll meet them of course on Sunday at the great event."

"That's putting it off much too late. How can we act together if we're total strangers?"

"You're right, as usual. I'll have to do something about this. Perhaps I could arrange a dress rehearsal for all of you on Saturday evening. You could come then, I suppose?"

"Probably. But why not sooner?"

"There are wheels within wheels to fit in. Aren't there, Albert?"

"Proper stinkers, Mr. Brink."

"You see, Kate." He smiled blandly: "I'm doing the best I can, and it's up to you now to get your part quickly by heart. I'll rehearse you tomorrow evening at eight."

"That doesn't give me very long." She glanced with distaste at the typewritten sheets in her hand.

"You'll be word perfect, I'm sure."

His tone held a hint of dismissal, and she rose with alacrity, unwilling to protract the interview by argument. The atmosphere of the room stifled her with a nausea that was less of the body than of the spirit, as if she would never cleanse her thoughts and feelings of the smell. She cut short her leavetaking, turned her back on Albert without a word. Brink insisted on accompanying her into the hall, he opened the door for her. She fled past him into the sunlight and strode long-legged down the drive, aware but savagely heedless of his eyes fixed on her. She filled her lungs thankfully with fresh air.

Brink returned to the study rubbing his palms: "Providence favours our prayers."

Albert nodded: "We've power on our side."

"I hope so, I really believe that my little efforts to apply the teaching of the masters are bearing fruit."

"Tasty fruit." He smacked his lips, sketched voluptuous curves in the air with his forefinger: "Oh boy, I can't hold myself thinking of that girl turned up naked on the altar. You've an eye for peaches, Mr. Brink."

"I don't deny it, Albert, but you're wrong if you suppose that's the main purpose of this experiment."

"No, the main thing is that she's coming to a sticky end."

"You're wrong again. Her painful death is only the means, a regrettable necessity. I'd gladly dispense with it if I could."

"I wouldn't miss it for worlds, I'm looking forward to it. She deserves all she gets for treating me like dirt."

"Listen, Albert." He frowned sternly: "If you and I are to work together you'll have to understand me. This power of which you speak isn't to be trifled with. It's a privilege bought at the price of another's life blood, and a heavy vengeance falls on the adept who puts it to unworthy use."

"What, no fun?"

"You needn't upset yourself, I'm no spoilsport. Carnal licence is a traditional feature of the rite. The masters recommend it to stimulate suitable ecstasy."

"I should hope so. We aren't on a purity campaign."

"Not in regard to the flesh, but I warn you most solemnly against impurity of motive. Any trace of self-seeking or spite will bring disaster on our efforts, and on ourselves too."

"Who's to know?"

"He who reads your inmost heart."

Albert scowled, picked up the life of Amos Pounder from Kate's empty chair, stared at the frontispiece: "You're not going to tell me this old bird was a do-gooder."

"He wasn't. That's why his story ends as it did."

"You mean, the way he died?"

"The details aren't very pleasant, it's as well Kate didn't come across them." He smiled: "The book isn't suitable reading for her at all."

"She seemed to be getting the hang of it."

"Not fast enough, I was too quick for her; but it's unlucky

she hit the page about Bess Atkins, it might put ideas in her head."

"Who was Bess Atkins?"

"Her prototype, the victim whose fate she'll share."

Albert closed the book and laid it on the desk: "There's a lot here to study, but it's the other I'm interested in, the book I found for you in the wood with all the Reverend Pounder's secrets jotted in his own hand."

"His notebook? I'm thankful that wasn't what Kate got hold of. I've added her name to the list of victims at the end."

"It's a wonder she hasn't seen it by now, you're so untidy."

"We all have our failings, Albert, no one's perfect; but that book's put safely away up there on the top shelf." He pointed to the bookcase, and Albert gazed covetously:

"When are you going to teach me the words of power you promised? Don't you trust me after all I've done for you? Didn't I make a good job of mister bloody Tranmire last night?"

"As it happens, you did; but it was luck alone saved you from killing him."

"What do you mean? Don't you want him dead?"

"Use your brains if you've got any. What hold have we left on the girl with her lover in the grave no longer needing her protection?"

"I never thought of that." His tone was crestfallen: "It was too good a chance to miss to smash him into mincemeat in the quarry. I've a score or two to pay off on my own account."

"Another word, and I'll kick you out of the house." Brink sprang to his feet, his eyes blazed, he raised a brogued toe as if to carry out his threat. Tall and formidable he towered over Albert's chair: "Weren't you listening to what I said just now when I warned you against impure motives? Tranmire needs to be eliminated, his presence hinders the great work; but I'd rather a thousand times he lived to thwart me than let you indulge your petty spite, you contemptible worm. You defile the Holy of Holies."

Albert cowered, taken aback, intimidated by the violence of his anger: "I'm sorry, Mr. Brink. I'm sure I didn't mean to offend you. I respect the power just as you do. That's why I'm trying to help, I swear I've no other purpose."

"Good." He spoke curtly but more calmly, went back to

his chair and sat down: "You understand then? There'll be no more of this spite?"

"There won't, I swear. I'll do whatever you tell me."

"It isn't what I tell you, it's what the great spirits command." His voice was recovering something of its accustomed geniality. Albert's frightened submission mollified him:

"You're eager, you say, for instruction in the hidden arts. Well I'm going to take you into my confidence, tell you the course of events at the end of the week."

"The play, you mean?"

"That's eyewash. There'll be no play on Sunday, no goddess."

"But you were so keen on getting her to act. You've just given her her part to learn."

"An appalling screed in Wardour Street jargon. I wish her joy of it."

"Aren't you going to rehearse her?"

"Indeed I am, but not with the others. You heard me tell her they're only free in the morning?"

"I'll admit it puzzled me. They're on holiday, they can come any time."

"They'll come in fact late at night, not here but to the Devil's Churchyard."

"For rehearsal?"

"I prefer to call it initiation."

"What's it for, if there isn't to be a play on Sunday at all?"

"On Sunday all will be over except the inquest. The rite will be celebrated on the octave of Midsummer Eve. Kate Evans meets the cast on Saturday night."

"At the dress rehearsal?"

"The undress rehearsal, to be accurate, the first, last and only performance. She won't survive it."

"You're a masterpiece, Mr. Brink." Albert slapped his thigh. His recent discomfiture was forgotten, he relit a chewed cigarette: "I've got your idea, and it's as pretty a plan as you'd find anywhere. She's fallen for it too, you made her think you're fixing this jamboree on Saturday night to do her a favour."

"Yes, I rather pride myself on my success. I doubt if old Parson Amos could have planned it better."

"What about the police? Won't her death be awkward to explain, or aren't you worrying? You'll have the power of course, no one can touch you."

"It would be presumptuous to rely on supernatural power. I'm taking all reasonable precautions to ensure that the mystery remains unsolved."

"There'll be a hullabaloo in the town. Can you put the cops off the scent? Will no one suspect us?"

"No one will know why she went to the Devil's Church-yard. I'll say I rehearsed her at the rectory, and that was the last I saw of her."

"It sounds all right, it ought to go down, unless Tranmire gets nosy."

"Tranmire won't be able to nose if you do what I ask."

"I will, I swear I will, and if I do this for you, Mr. Brink, you won't disappoint me? You'll let me share?"

"Don't worry, I'll look after you." His tone was patronising, but intended to reassure. He pointed to the book-case: "If you care to get Parson Amos down I'll copy out the invocation, and you can start learning it at once. You'll need it when the time comes."

Albert rose eagerly, peered on tiptoe up at the shelf. The white vellum was easy to distinguish from its larger neighbors. He reached for the book and gave it to Brink, who took it with a curt nod:

"Let me hear no more complaints after this of my failure to provide instruction."

"Is it the bidding prayer, the mystery of mysteries?"

"It's a formula of the greatest sanctity. I warn you to treat it with reverence."

He drew his chair up to the desk, pushed the litter aside and laid the book there, open at the page required. Then on a sheet of foolscap he transcribed the crabbed characters into a handwriting whose neatness contrasted with the chaos surrounding him. Albert watched with rapt attention, leaning over his shoulder to peer through thick-lensed spectacles. Their rim touched Brink's ear, and he put down his pen with a grunt of irritation:

"You'll oblige me by keeping your distance instead of breathing down my neck. Your breath doesn't smell too sweet."

Albert retired to his chair, sat in silence till the document was complete. Brink held it out to him, and he clutched it greedily, crammed it into the pocket of his trousers: but his face was sullen, his voice morose as he took his leave.

Brink saw him out of the house and returned to the study moodily with a troubled frown. He restored the vellum-clad notebook to its place on the shelf and made room at its side for the bulkier volume, *The Ungodly Life and Diabolic Death of the Reverend Amos Pounder*. Then he lit his pipe and sat smoking; from time to time he hummed a tune, that of the hymn, *Jerusalem the Golden*.

At last he rose, put on his hat and went out himself, following the lane to its end at the abbey ruins and the church. A small group of tourists waited to pass through the abbey turnstile, but there was no one in the churchyard, no one in the church when he entered. He shut the door behind him, turned the key and shot the bolts, locked himself in.

Assured of solitude he stood for a moment with bowed head, then walked briskly up the nave to the pulpit and turned aside into the vestry. He emerged carrying a black cloth, advanced with it into the chancel with slow, measured steps, pausing before chosen carvings in the choir stalls and bowing reverently to each. When he reached the altar he spread the cloth and covered everything with it, pulling out the folds to hang evenly. There was a flap attached like a bag, which he used to drape the cross.

He stood back, surveyed his handiwork, an image of darkness, shrouded, shapeless, black, dominating the chancel. He prostrated himself before it on the chequered tiles within the altar rails.

He rose, returned to the vestry. When he came out his burden was a huge oval vessel of black earthenware, which he gripped by a handle at either end, holding it at arm's length, sustaining the weight without effort. He laid it on the draped altar in front of the draped cross.

A third task remained. He went to the ambry and unlocked it, removed the carcase of the lamb deposited there on Saturday afternoon. Close confinement for two days in such a place in high summer was conducive to rapid decomposition. He examined the remains with disgust, hesitated, then with a helpless shrug of his shoulders and no pause for ritual on the way he carried the offering to the altar and dropped it into the cauldron on to a heap of wooden kindlings, resin and other aromatic gums put ready inside. Taking a box of matches from his pocket he set fire to the holocaust. A column of black smoke soared to the roof, blotting out the crucifixion in the glass of the east window. He contemplated the effect with his hands raised in supplication:

"Hear me, great Archangel," he prayed. "Hear me, Mephistopheles, Baphomet, Ialdabaoth. Strengthen, instruct, inspire me to perform my destined task, not my will but yours. Expunge from my heart all base motives, all hatred and malice, all craving for the tinsel of earthly honour. May the glory of the purpose that I seek purge whatever is gross in the means to attain it, and defend me from the folly or treachery of this rascal on whose service I rely."

Smoke billowing from the burnt offering on the altar filled the chancel. Swathed in its pungent clouds he sank devoutly to his knees.

His prayers were interrupted by a clatter at the outer door, repeated and increasing in volume. At first he paid no attention, but when the noise persisted he rose to his feet and with a final genuflexion to the black vortex strode into the nave, frowning angrily. As he approached the door the handle twisted with convulsive movements; someone on the other side was trying to get in. He released the bolts, turned the key, opened just wide enough to admit his own body, stood blocking the aperture.

"What do you want?" he asked sternly.

A middle-aged couple waited in the porch; they had an air of solid comfort and respectability, ruffled by the inconvenience inflicted. There was injured dignity in the man's voice:

"You've no right to keep this church locked. It's a historic monument."

"There's a service going on."

"Very well, we'll attend it. We belong to the Church of England."

"The service is strictly private."

"Nonsense, the church exists for public worship, and for the education too of members of the public interested like myself in antiquities. Let me tell you, sir, we've driven eighty miles, the wife and I, to visit this town, and your church is starred in the guide book. I'm not going home till I've seen it."

"If you come tomorrow you'll find it open."

"We're only here for the day."

"Percy." His wife clutched his arm: "What's that extraordinary smell?" The smoke from the chancel wafted down the nave was seeping into the porch through the chink of the door.

"Incense, madam," Brink told her. "We observe the Anglo-Catholic tradition here in Easby."

The visitors eyed him askance. Their own sympathies were Evangelical.

"It smells to me of rank Popery," Percy growled.

His wife was unable to speak. The fumes poured thicker and thicker out of the building. She succumbed to a paroxysm of coughing, buried her face in her handkerchief and retreated into the fresh air to breathe. Percy followed her solicitously, glad himself to escape from the stench. Brink at once pulled the door to, locked and bolted it.

The couple walked away disconsolately across the churchyard. "If that's what they mean by high church," the man declared, "I want nothing to do with it, Ethel. The incense would suffocate me."

She nodded: "The smell reminds me of the time when I was roasting the joint and forgot to turn down the oven."

"I'd be sorry to eat what's cooking there."

Chapter 6

Kemsdale Farm lay higher up the Rune than the Devil's Churchyard; but the valley widened here, transformed from a gorge between ridges of bare moorland into a fertile basin of cultivated fields with a belt of trees at the bottom lining the watercourse and others scattered in the hedgerows on either slope. Most of the land was under grass, all the greener in contrast to the heather of the surrounding hills. The farmstead itself was set on a shelf of high ground at the lower end, overlooking the point where the river plunged into its narrow cleft through the moors. The stone-built house faced south, sheltered from the prevailing southwesterly wind by a clump of oak.

Doctor Buttle, having assured himself over the telephone that his patient was following his treatment and making good progress, allowed a day to pass before his next visit, and it was Wednesday morning when he drove again into the yard. Fan barked vociferously, a vigorous convalescent, then as he got out of the car she recognised him and bounded up wagging her tail, till Flossie, the land girl, called her off in tones of shrill authority, and he went on unimpeded into the kitchen.

A gaunt old woman was busy there, the housekeeper, Jane Torgill, who bore the burden of the cooking and housework.

"Now, Jane," he greeted her. "That smells good whatever you've got in the pot."

"It's for Master James's dinner." There was a note in her voice that implied that no one else should touch it.

"I'm sure it'll do him good. How is he?"

"He's quick yet, laid there in his bed, and that's more than I thought when they carried him in on Sunday night."

"He'll pull round, don't you worry, he's young and strong."

"It's no thanks to those murdering hikers he isn't laid in his grave."

"Hikers? Who do you mean?"

"You ask Harry Bracken. He can tell you a thing or two, Doctor."

"Well, I've more urgent business at the moment. I've come to see my patient."

He walked through into the passage. As on many hill farms it was a large house with the farmer's own quarters separated from the rest; he passed through the connecting door, climbed the front stairs to the bedroom.

Jim was sitting up in bed reading a newspaper. Except for the bandage round his head he showed little trace of his accident. He greeted his visitor with a smile:

"Good morning, Doctor Buttle."

"Good morning, Jim, and a fine morning it is, especially for those with any hay out."

"Ours is all in, thank God, or you wouldn't catch me malingering here in bed."

"You'd be little use in the hayfield or anywhere else with a raging temperature."

"My temperature's normal, I'm sure."

"It wouldn't be if you'd been fool enough to go out. Let's have those bandages off and look at the damage."

He examined the wound on his head, then those on other parts of his body, pressed them with a grunt of satisfaction:

"Very nice. You'll earn no sympathy, Jim. You look much too healthy for an invalid."

"Does that mean I can get up?"

"Yes, I don't see why not, but stay indoors."

"Indoors?" He frowned: "It wouldn't hurt, would it, just to slip into Easby?"

"It most certainly would. Anyhow, your car's at the bottom of the quarry."

"There's the Land-Rover."

"My dear man, only the day before yesterday we all thought you were dying, and now you want to drive into Easby. It's madness." He hesitated, stroked his beard: "I'm not poking my nose into your affairs, but if there's anything to be done in which I can help you've only to tell me."

"You're very kind, but . . . Did you give that book to Kate?"

"I did, at least I gave it to Pearl to give her."

"Pearl?"

"Yes, I met her on the way to the surgery, and as I'd a busy day before me I thought Kate would get it quicker if I sent Pearl up to the school as my messenger."

"I hope she did what she was told."

"I've no doubt she did, it gave her a chance to gossip about your accident with Helen. I ought to have asked Helen when I got home, but what with one thing and another I forgot."

"I expect it's all right." He tried to make his voice sound casual: "Do you happen to know if Kate means to act in these theatricals of Brink's on Sunday?"

"She insists on doing so, much against Helen's will. Kate can be very stubborn."

"Yes, I know she can. Has she begun rehearsing?"

"I gather the rehearsals are in the morning to suit the rest of the cast. Lord knows why, as they all seem to be holiday-makers. Anyhow Kate can't be spared then, so Brink rehearses her at the rectory alone."

"She's alone with him?"

"No, I don't mean that. She's the only performer, but

101

she takes Doris to keep her company, one of the other teachers."

"Yes, I know Miss Wayworth by sight. I suppose she's a reliable escort?"

"You think Kate needs one?"

Jim laughed bitterly: "It sounds odd, doesn't it? There can't be many parishes where a girl needs protection from the rector."

"I hope not. Have you found out anything more about the man, anything to support the gossip one hears?"

"A little, but not enough. This accident hasn't helped."

"No, it's put you out of the hunt for the time being. You know of course that according to Harry Bracken it wasn't an accident at all?"

"You mean his story about a pool of oil? It could have come from a lorry with a leaking sump, or anything. The blame lies, I'm afraid, on my own bad driving."

"To judge from his description, no one could have held a car to the road in the state it was in."

"Well, I couldn't, not when I had to brake. It threw her into a skid, and I'd had it."

"Why did you brake?"

Jim fingered the bedclothes, spoke with embarrassment: "You won't believe this, but I thought I saw someone dancing in the middle of the road blocking the way."

"Have you told Harry Bracken?"

"It would put him in an awkward position. He'd suspect me of driving under the influence of drink; but in fact I'd only been having tea at the Angel, and the bar wasn't even open."

"You've no theories of your own about this dancer?"

"None, but there'd be plenty, I'm sure, if the news got round. The press is on the scent already. Have you seen yesterday's *Gazette?*" He picked up the paper lying on the bed, found the place and indicated a paragraph under the headline *NEAR TRAGEDY AT EASBY.*

Doctor Buttle took it and read:

"Mr. James Tranmire J.P., prominent landowner and farmer, had a narrow escape from death on Sunday evening when his car plunged over the cliff of a deep quarry on the road to his farm at Kemsdale. Mr. Tranmire owes his life to the fact that he was driving an open convertible and was thrown out on the verge into a clump of gorse before the car

102

fell to its doom. He was found there by P.C. Bracken, who rescued him from his dangerous plight. Local wiseacres point out that the accident occurred near the spot known as the Devil's Churchyard, an ill-omened and legend-haunted circle of ancient stones associated with gruesome traditions of satanic rites in the past."

"Well?" Jim asked: "What do you make of it?"

"Spooks? They're not much in my line nor, I think, in yours either."

"They aren't. So what are we left with? Hallucination?"

"No, Jim, you're not the sort to imagine things. I'd like to get to the bottom of this."

"So would I, and I mean to, if you let me out of prison."

"Not today." He shook his head firmly: "Not for all the spooks in the halls of Pandemonium. You're not going straight from a sickbed to the Devil's Churchyard, or anywhere else out of doors."

"What about the sheep?" Jim grumbled. "I'm the shepherd here. I've told Flossie to keep an eye on them, she means well, but she's scatter-brained."

"She's a good girl, conscientious. Leave the sheep to her, and the spooks till later in the week. You need a long rest after that touch of concussion."

"A long rest looks like turning into utter boredom."

Doctor Buttle smiled: "It occurs to me that when Kate finishes with her class this afternoon she'll want to exercise that mare of hers. Shall I suggest Kemsdale as a destination?"

"You've a genius for prescribing the right tonic. Oh, and if you meet Pearl again, and she asks how I am, you can tell her you've ordered a long rest with no visitors."

As Doctor Buttle went out through the kitchen Jane Torgill intercepted him:

"How is he, Doctor? Will he live?"

"He'll outlive you and me too, Jane, and as soon as that stew of yours is ready I'm sure he'll do it justice."

"So he should. I've seasoned it with marjoram the way he likes."

"He can get up to eat it, but he's not to go out and not to be troubled with anything, remember."

"If anyone tries I'll make them sorry, man or woman."

"That reminds me. If a young lady comes on horseback let her in, but if she's in a car keep her out. You won't make any mistake?"

"Get away with you, Doctor. Do you think I don't know the difference between a car and a horse?"

He left her cackling with laughter at her own wit.

On his return to Easby he drove to his surgery to replenish his bag for the remaining visits on his list. He took the opportunity to ring up Saint Ursula's and give Helen the message for Kate.

"I'll tell her," she replied, "and I hope it'll cheer her up. She's been very much in the dumps these last two days."

"About Jim's accident or the rehearsals with Brink?"

"I've no idea, and it's useless arguing with her. She's a strange girl, I don't know what to make of her."

"Jim seems to know."

"Yes, it's beginning to look quite a case. I'm sorry for Pearl, but I always suspected there was more wishful thinking on her part than encouragement on his."

"Poor girl. I hope it won't break her heart."

"Don't be silly, Arthur. She'll console herself with Leslie Potts."

"You're a human crustacean, Helen, a soft core encased in the hardest of common sense."

He rang off.

Helen Buttle gave Kate the message before lunch, and gloom lifted from the table occupied by the youngest children. A smiling face presided once again, a cheerful voice ready to join gaily in the conversation. Kate was content to forget impending troubles; her heart glowed with the prospect of riding to see Jim, knowing that he had asked for her.

When lunch was over the teachers retired to the common room for coffee. Kate drew Doris Wayworth to a sofa:

"I needn't bother you this afternoon, Doris. I'm not going to the rectory after all."

"Oh, Kate." Her face fell: "You're not giving the part up, are you?"

"No, nothing so drastic. It's just that I've been neglecting Dinah, and I really ought to take her for a ride to exercise her."

"How extraordinary you are. If I were acting in a play like this with its fascinating symbolism I'd have no thought to spare for anything else, least of all for a horse."

"I wish you were. It's much more in your line than mine."

Doris indeed had a passion for the esoteric. Even in school hours she wore a bead necklace and bracelets of copper charms, and the tortoiseshell clasp matching her spectacles that held the coils of her fair hair in place bore the shape of a pentacle.

She shook her head sadly: "I'm sure Mr. Brink wouldn't say so. He chose you because you look like a spirit of mid-summer conjured out of the woods, mine only haunts books."

"It's no compliment to be chosen by him, Doris. I can't explain, but his ideas aren't as romantic as you imagine."

"He's a man of great learning, he knows such a lot about ancient lore, and those lines he's given you to speak are so wonderful, pure poetry."

"Pure yes, surprisingly so considering the author; but if that sort of rant's poetry, all that 'lady's bane' and 'lovelorn swain,' give me something nice and prosaic, fatstock prices or quadratic equations, which I can recite without feeling a perfect fool."

"You don't mean what you say. You aren't really such a Philistine."

"Anyhow I mean to go through with it." She glanced at her watch: "Look Doris, I tried to ring him just now to put off the rehearsal till tomorrow; but there was no reply, I expect he's out. If I write a note, would it be a nuisance to slip it in the rectory door? You haven't a class, have you?"

"Yes, of course I'll take it. I haven't a class till three."

"Mine's waiting. There's probably all hell let loose by now."

She darted to the writing table, bent over it to grab a sheet of paper and an envelope, scribble a note and lick it up. She handed it to Doris:

"You're an angel. No Midsummer Goddess is a patch on you." Then she fled downstairs.

Doris put the letter in her bag, rose more slowly herself to follow. She paused before the mirror on the wall and examined her neat features reflected there. She sighed dejectedly.

Shortly afterwards, having changed her shoes, she set forth on her errand. As she came out on to the drive she saw Pearl approaching, who called to her:

"Hullo, Doris. I've come for my scarf. Do you know where it is?"

"Scarf?"

"Yes, I left it when I was here on Monday. Mrs. Buttle rang me up to tell me."

"I'll ask Mrs. Buttle. Come in, won't you?" She turned back, and they entered the house together.

"Am I interrupting anything urgent?" Pearl asked.

"No, I'm only taking a note to the rectory."

"Ah, Kate's rehearsal for the church pantomime? I hear you're her chaperone."

"I keep her company; it's for my own sake, I enjoy watching and listening. Anyhow, she isn't rehearsing today, she's going for a ride."

Helen Buttle appeared from her room, hearing their voices:

"Are you looking for your scarf, Pearl?"

"Yes, and if I'd known Kate was going riding I might have saved myself the fag. She could just as well put that pony of hers to some use."

"She's riding over to Kemsdale, not to Easby."

"To Kemsdale? If she thinks she'll see Jim she can think again. I met your husband just now in the town, and his orders are still complete rest, no visitors."

Helen Buttle frowned: "Kate knows her own business. I'm her employer, not her nurse."

"She needs one, a nurse I mean, to put some sense in her head. She'll get what's coming to her if she isn't careful with that parson. Mother won't hear a word against him; but I know the type, and it's not the sort any decent girl should want to associate with."

"Doris." Helen Buttle turned to her quickly: "Would you be kind enough to fetch Pearl's scarf from my room? You'll find it on the filing cabinet." She spoke sternly when she and Pearl were alone: "I can't have you talking like that in front of my staff. It's bound to make mischief."

"It's all right, Mrs. Buttle, it's only Doris Wayworth. She was probably dreaming as usual, paying no attention."

"She was attending to everything you said about Mr. Brink. I mayn't always see eye to eye with him myself, but I don't approve of irresponsible attacks on his character. Whatever his failings, his office deserves respect."

"I'm sorry." Her tone belied the words: "I'll try to remember."

Doris returned with the scarf and handed it over. Pearl took it with a curt nod:

"Well, I'd better be off, I'm supposed to be playing tennis with Leslie. He'll be there at the court already kicking his heels. It won't hurt the man, I've got to change first."

106

She moved towards the door, paused as she opened it: "I might drive over to Kemsdale afterwards myself. It's only civil to call and ask how Jim is."

"You can do what you please, Pearl," Helen Buttle turned away: "It doesn't concern me."

Doris lingered in the hall till Pearl's car was out of sight, then she set off herself on foot. She neither expected nor wished to be offered a lift.

It was a long afternoon for Kate, she was at work till teatime; but at last the sound of the bell set her free. It was not her turn to invigilate at the children's meal, and she was too impatient to wait for her own. She ran straight to her room, changed into a blouse and jeans, then hurried out of the house to Dinah's field. Much to her relief, old Charlie Bracken was not about; she caught and saddled Dinah more quickly without his help and conversation. She mounted, trotted out into the lane. Doctor Buttle's car was turning into the entrance as she passed Saint Ursula's; he waved cheerfully, and she smiled and waved back.

The road crossed the Rune over a stone bridge, just beyond which a gate on the left led to the bridle path, the short cut to Kemsdale. As she leant to release the snick a voice called behind her:

"All right, miss. Wait a moment."

Albert Dockin was approaching. She recognised him with a frown of displeasure, but sat still gathering her reins while he opened the gate for her.

"You'll be at the rectory again this evening?" he asked. She shook her head: "I can't today."

"Nothing wrong, I hope?"

"Nothing, but I've other things to do."

"You'd be wiser to put them aside. You know what happened Sunday night. I warned you, didn't I?"

"Yes, and I took your warning. You were there, you heard me agree to do what Mr. Brink wants. I'm not going back on my word, I'll rehearse tomorrow."

"I'm glad of that. I'll tell him."

"You needn't bother. I've sent him a message."

"I'll be seeing him anyhow. If you aren't rehearsing we'll get on with other business."

She stared at him doubtfully: "You're very much in with him, aren't you?"

"What's the harm if I am? What's wrong with being a buddy of the parson's? You're not suggesting, are you, he fixed up that car smash?"

"Who did, then?"

"Isn't that what we're trying to find out? That's why you're joining in the play-acting. Stick to it and you'll know a lot more, perhaps more than you like."

He turned away into the road and slouched off, leaving the gate open. She shut it herself, replacing the snick; then she rode on puzzled and frightened along the fields. She was on the verge of tears, deprived brutally of the glow of happiness in which she started; but the weather was making amends for the rain and thunder of the weekend, the sun shone in a clear sky, the air was full of the sweetness of clover from the mown meadow already springing up into aftermath that she skirted. Her spirits were unable long to resist the coaxing of the summer afternoon. Even Dinah seemed to respond to it, or to the relief of soft turf underfoot after the metalled road; she forgot that she was sluggish, soft from a diet of fresh grass, broke into an eager canter.

Kate encouraged her joyfully. The gathering speed carried her forward into light, outdistancing with every stride the spectres that beckoned behind her.

The path rejoined the main road near the top of the long hill on to the moor. There was a fresh smell here, that of high ground, the tang of peat, a sweetness no longer of clover but of clumps of flowering gorse. Few cars either met or passed her, there was little traffic on a weekday afternoon. She seemed to have the hilltop to herself and yielded to its spell with rapture. A glimpse of trees on the skyline ahead, heralding Kemsdale Wood, recalled her first meeting with Jim in the old intake at the bottom. She kept her mind resolutely detached from the Devil's Churchyard.

Her intention was to ride quickly past the quarry, not to dwell on its painful associations; but as she approached the spot she saw a car drawn up there and two policemen walking in the road, the serjeant from Easby and Harry Bracken. They moved to and fro, examining the surface, then the serjeant went to his car, got in and drove away. Harry lifted his bicycle out of the heather; he stood holding it as Kate trotted up. He knew who she was, knew Dinah even better, having often seen her grazing in his father's field.

"Good day, miss." He saluted: "Come to visit the scene of the accident?"

"No, I don't want to look down. It's dreadful even to think of it. I'm going to Kemsdale."

"You'll find him a lot better, so they tell me. It's a bad business, but it might have been much worse."

"It might indeed, without you. I heard how splendid you were, all that you did to rescue him."

"Thank you, miss." He smiled, well pleased: "I'd have done more than that to help Mr. Tranmire. You couldn't find a nicer gentleman anywhere if you looked from here to world's end. What beats me is who could have it in for him, why they should do it."

"You mean the oil on the road? Do you really think it was spread there on purpose?"

"I was sure of it from the start, and now I've the evidence. That's what I had the serjeant here for, to prove to him it couldn't have been chance, the stuff was put there by someone who knew very well what he was up to."

She stared down at the road. There was a large patch in front of her, discoloured from curb to curb, clearly distinguished from the rest of the surface by its paleness.

"We had to shift the oil of course," he explained. "We couldn't leave it to cause more accidents; but I took care with the detergent to keep it to the same pattern, to show where the oil had been."

"There must have been an awful lot of it."

"There was, miss. Fifteen gallons."

"You mean that was the exact amount? How do you know?"

"I found three empty five-gallon drums in the quarry, and they weren't Mr. Tranmire's, he knew nothing about them. They all had a mark stamped on them, you wouldn't notice it if you didn't look carefully; but I'd seen it before, they were from stocks belonging to Snooker's Garage at Freeborough."

"That's quite a way off, isn't it?"

"Not more than ten miles. Well, I talked to them at the garage, and it seems they're open on a Sunday all day, and a young chap came in the afternoon after the rain stopped and bought three five-gallon drums. The man who served him offered to help to load the stuff; but the youth wouldn't have that, said his car was parked in a side street, and he

109

went off with the drums himself one by one, making three trips of it. They all thought him daft. The garage is in the marketplace; but it's quiet enough there on Sundays, and he could just as well have driven his car round. Still, he'd paid for the oil, it was no business of theirs."

"What did the young man look like?"

"That's where I'm beat, miss. No one could remember enough to be of use, except that he was short and skinny, with glasses and a hat pulled down over his face. It's a description that would fit quite a number, but there's one in particular I've in mind."

She nodded: "Albert Dockin."

"You know him, miss?" He glanced at her in surprise.

"I've seen him at the rectory, and Mr. Tranmire told me about him. Didn't you catch him in Kemsdale Wood on Saturday night?"

"I did, and he was up to no good there, I'll swear, with Mr. Tranmire's lambs. He's a tricky customer, this Albert Dockin. I can prove nothing against him, neither the lambs nor this business of the oil; but I'm keeping my eye on him, he'll be sorry before I've done with him. Attempted murder, that's what he's guilty of, and I shan't rest till he's charged with it in court."

"There isn't much to go on. It might be someone else after all."

"That's what the court will say unless I can prove it; but I need no proof for myself, I feel it in my bones. You've only to look at him to know what sort he is."

She did not argue, she was too inclined to agree.

As she rode on towards Kemsdale his eyes followed her with approval. He felt some doubt whether he had not said too much, none at all that he had enjoyed the conversation.

Flossie appeared from the byre as Kate entered the yard at Kemsdale Farm. She put down the pail that she was carrying and ran into the house:

"Right-o, Mrs. Torgill. It's a lass on a mare."

Kate stared after her in surprise, dismounted, led Dinah to a ring in the wall to tie her up.

"I've come to see Mr. Tranmire," she explained as Flossie returned. "He's expecting me."

"That's right, miss." Flossie's freckled face wore a grin: "Go straight in. I'll take the mare; there's a stall free in the byre, she'll be easier there."

110

"Yes, much better. Thank you very much." She gave her the rein and went indoors.

She paused in the kitchen, uncertain where to go next. Then she saw Jane Torgill holding the door open into the passage: "Good afternoon," she greeted her shyly.

"Straight through, miss, and on to the end. It's the door facing you."

The tone was laconic but friendly, the passage quite dark as Kate entered except for a glimmer from the open door behind her. She had the feeling of a welcoming strangeness, an unknown that expected her, like Psyche ushered by mystery into Cupid's enchanted palace.

She knocked on the door indicated, and Jim's voice called sharply: "Come in."

"Good Lord, Kate," he exclaimed when he saw who it was. "Why didn't they tell me you were here? I'm afraid old Jane Torgill hasn't the right manners for a butler."

His head was still bandaged; but standing dressed and spruce to receive her he looked anything but an invalid. It was a comfortable room, the walls were lined with bookshelves, above which hung framed engravings, local views of moor and sea. The table was littered with papers almost as untidy as Brink's, the windowsill with an axe, a billhook and an assortment of veterinary oddments.

Fan rose from the rug in front of the empty hearth, wagged her tail, licked Kate's hand.

Jim watched with satisfaction: "She'd have barked her head off for anyone else."

"She looks very well." Kate rubbed her under the chin: "Very different from four days ago."

"Four days? It seems a lifetime since your epiphany through the hedge, and you're looking just as you did then."

"With my face muddy and scratched?"

"And the repair outfit stuck fast in the pocket of your pants. No, you needn't delve there today. You might have stepped out of an advert for skin-cream."

"I wish you looked less in need of repair yourself."

"I shall tomorrow." He fingered the bandage: "Doctor Buttle or no Doctor Buttle, this is coming off." He drew up a chair: "Sit down, Kate. I want to talk seriously."

She removed a pair of shears from the cushion, sat in their place.

"You got that book I sent?" he asked.

111

She nodded.

"That's good. I was worried when I heard from Doctor Buttle he'd used Pearl as his messenger."

"She brought it to the school and gave it to me. Why shouldn't she?"

"I don't know, except that her mother seems to be up to something with Brink."

"Nothing wrong, I'm sure. Mrs. Corrington's a dear."

"She may be, but I happen to know she shares a secret with him."

She laughed: "I can guess what it is. She'd love to be Mrs. Brink."

"Every man to his taste, every woman too. Well, to get back to this book, did you read the paragraph I marked?"

"Yes, I did. It was horrible."

"So you understand now why I don't want you to play the goddess in Brink's charade."

"I do, Jim, but you've got to understand too why I'm still going to, why I must. It was no accident when your car fell into the quarry; someone meant to kill you."

"You mean the oil on the road? You've been talking to Harry Bracken?"

"Yes, I have, and he's found out a lot more. The oil was bought from a garage in Freeborough on Sunday afternoon by a young man whose description seems to fit Albert Dockin."

"What was Albert doing in Freeborough? How did he get there?"

"This young man had a car."

"Albert hasn't, as far as I know; only a bike."

"He could have borrowed Mr. Brink's, I suppose, he probably knows how to drive. He was very cagey about the car, it seems, parked it in a side street and insisted on carrying the oil drums there himself, so that no one would see the car and be able to recognise it."

He frowned: "I wouldn't put anything of the sort beyond Albert, but there are too many loose ends. How could he be sure I'd drive past the quarry when he laid the trap?"

"I've been thinking, and I've remembered something. Mrs. Buttle said that soon after we left for the Angel for tea Mr. Brink rang up to speak to me, and she told him where we'd gone. I don't know what he wanted; he said nothing about it yesterday when I rehearsed with him, and I forgot to ask."

"If the call was a pretext he made a lucky guess. Why should he suppose I was at Saint Ursula's?"

"Perhaps he didn't, but when Mrs. Buttle told him it put ideas in his head. Albert had plenty of time to drive to Freeborough, buy the oil and smear the road, and if he wanted to make sure you were still in Easby he'd only to go to the Angel car park and see your car there."

"It could be. It helps to explain my dancing ghost."

"What was that?"

He described the apparition which made him brake and the car skid.

"It's a relief at least," he concluded wryly, "to know I'm not suffering from delusions."

"It was Albert," she declared. "I'm sure it was, it's just his line." She frowned, perplexed: "All the same, if he's trying to kill you, why should he be so keen to warn me you're in danger?"

"Albert did?"

"More than once."

"Who did he warn you against? Brink?"

"No, he refused to name anyone. He was terribly mysterious, full of sinister hints; but he suggested that if I acted in the play I'd be in a good position to keep watch."

"Oh, Kate, and you fell for that?"

"It's true, isn't it? I don't care what his motives are, his advice makes sense."

"It makes nothing of the sort. Look, Kate, I lost my temper at the Angel, and I don't want to again now; but we've got to have this clear, I'm perfectly capable of looking after myself. You've already saved my life once. That ought to be enough for you."

"How did I save your life?"

"By making me take the hood down when we left Saint Ursula's. If the car hadn't been opened I'd have been trapped inside when it crashed on the rocks."

"Oh, Jim, I'm so glad. How lucky we both love fresh air."

"Yes, we agreed on that. Can't we agree on this too? Tell Brink you've changed your mind."

"I can't. It's too late."

"It isn't too late at all. If you're thinking of the inconvenience you're being ridiculous. You read in that book what the purpose of the rite is, and how it ends. Can you seriously call it inconsiderate of the victim if she upsets the programme by resigning before the climax?"

"No, of course not, but if I back out now Albert will know I suspect something, and he'll make haste to do what he wants quickly before it comes out. I'm sure he means to try again."

"If he does the police will get him."

"They weren't able to stop him at the quarry. They need someone to tell them what to expect."

"You mean, they need Kate Evans? I doubt if the serjeant would share the view."

"He ought to, if he has any sense. The police can do nothing without evidence, and they haven't enough yet, Harry Bracken told me so. If I can keep the game going, Albert and Mr. Brink happy, it gives time to search round, till the case can be proved and the police arrest them."

"That's as likely as not what Bess Atkins thought. It didn't help her when they bent her over the altar and Parson Amos held the knife."

"Don't." She covered her face with her hands.

"I'm sorry, Kate. I only want you to see reason, to save you from these abominations."

"You couldn't want it more than I do. I'm a dreadful coward really, and I'm taking no risks. The rehearsals couldn't be more respectable; I recite a lot of third-rate verse, and Doris sits beside me and applauds."

"The girl in beads? You can depend on her?"

"Absolutely."

"What about the rest of the cast?"

"I'll meet them at the dress rehearsal on Saturday. That's when I hope to find out what the plans are. They'll all be there together, Mr. Brink, Albert Dockin, the whole crew, and if I watch and keep my ears open I'm sure to pick up something useful."

"You've a touching faith, Kate, in your own skill as a sleuth. What happens if you pick up nothing?"

She hesitated: "He can't bring things to a climax till the performance is over, and that's on Sunday evening in church."

"The church won't deter him. I told you what happened to the girl in his last parish."

"Yes, but here at Easby the church will be full, he expects a big congregation, much too public for the Black Mass."

114

He shook his head gloomily: "Well, I don't know how he means to do it, but I'm sure from what I heard him say to Albert that there's devilry behind it all, he believes himself a reincarnation of Parson Amos."

"Perhaps we'll know more after the dress rehearsal."

"I don't like it, not a bit, least of all this fantastic idea that you've got to run into danger to protect me. I've told you, I can take care of myself. If Albert tries any tricks again he'll be sorry."

"There's more to it than just ourselves." She frowned: "Don't you see, we've got to stop this man if he's as mad as you say. It's no use my backing out; he'll still have his Black Mass, he'll find some other girl to be his victim."

"Let him, as long as it isn't you on the altar."

"You know you wouldn't think so if he killed a girl and drank her blood. It's just as horrible, whether or not the blood's mine."

"There's no need to make sure it's yours."

"It needn't be anyone's. I'm not a fool, I've too much regard for my own skin; but there's no harm, there can't be in rehearsing, and I've a feeling something will happen at the dress rehearsal that will give me all the evidence I want."

"What do you mean, something will happen?"

"I don't know. It's a hunch. Anyhow that leaves plenty of time to collect every policeman in the county and arrest him before the event."

"I'm no great believer in hunches." He spoke reluctantly: "Still, if the rehearsals are as you describe, I suppose there's no harm in your going on with them. Up to the dress rehearsal, but no longer. You've got to promise me this, Kate, that if you've still no clue to his plans after meeting them all on Saturday you'll chuck the whole thing up, either tell Brink you've resigned or, better still, just fail to appear when the play begins."

"I'll tell him of course. It wouldn't be fair not to."

"All right. That's agreed. He'll either have to cancel the play or find another goddess."

"I hope not." She shuddered: "I'd never forgive myself."

"Don't worry. He's much more likely to call the show off; but even if he finds you an understudy I'll have an eye on him, and Harry too, and we'll intervene in time. The girl won't be hurt; all the same I'd rather it wasn't you serving to bait the trap."

"You don't suppose I want to?"

"Then promise me you won't."

She nodded: "I'll attend the dress rehearsal, and if I find out enough there won't be any play on Sunday, the police can stop it; but in any case I promise not to take part in it."

"Good girl."

"Yes, and you're to be good too and see that Harry Bracken guards you well. Remember, Jim, no more quarries." There was relief in her voice however, and she broke off, pointed to a tin standing on one of the bookcases: "Are there biscuits in it? I'm rather hungry."

"Why, of course." He opened it and brought it to her: "They're probably loathsome, they've been there for ages. I ought to have ordered tea when you came. I deserve to be kicked."

"It was so late when I got here you thought I must have had tea already." She took a biscuit and munched it: "Anyone sensible would."

"But you hadn't?"

She blushed: "I was in a hurry."

"You put me to shame." He leapt to his feet, went to the door and shouted into the passage: "A pot of tea, Jane, and as many of those hot cakes as are ready. I can smell them baking."

Her head appeared from the kitchen: "They're ready and more than ready, Master James, and if the tea's stewed you've no one to blame but yourself. I've been waiting this past half-hour and more for you to call. The young lady won't thank you, to bring her riding all this way and keep her fasting."

The tea was very strong, but in consequence the more reviving; the cakes were crisp, hot from the oven. Kate left the biscuit unfinished, turned gladly to the heaped dish on the tray.

"I'd a snack myself earlier in the afternoon," Jim admitted, "and I've done nothing but sit indoors. I've no right to eat now."

He helped himself to a cake nevertheless, even took a second. Kate went on with undiminished appetite till the dish was empty.

He offered her a cigarette, and they sat smoking, contentedly replete, when Fan sprang up suddenly from the rug, stood at the door barking vociferously. At the same time

116

there was a clamour in the distance, voices raised in shrill dispute, among which Jane Torgill's was the most penetrating, most easily distinguishable:

"Doctor said so, I tell you," she screamed. "If you come in against his orders it's over my dead body."

The window of Jim's room looked south across the fields sloping to the river, bounded by the hill beyond. No glimpse was afforded of the yard on the other side of the house.

"What's happening?" Kate asked. "Ought we to go and see?"

He shook his head and grinned: "Leave it to old Jane. She's coping very well without us."

The noise persisted, Fan's frenzied barking within, volleys of acrimonious argument from somewhere beyond the kitchen.

"Be quiet, Fan," he hissed. "I'm trying to listen."

Fan paid no attention, she was beside herself.

"All right." He went to her: "Have your own way. You'll do more good there than here, the more the merrier." He opened the door, she bolted out, and he pulled it quickly to again.

"Charge of gallant reserves completes the discomfiture of the enemy." He winked at Kate, seated himself on the arm of her chair.

"Won't she bite someone?"

"I hope so."

Soon after Fan's departure the noise subsided. When all was quiet he rose, looked out into the passage:

"Who was that, Jane?"

"She in the car."

"What on earth do you mean?"

"Doctor said if she came in a car to send her packing."

He came back to Kate, laughing: "Doctor Buttle's a genius. He deserves to end up in Harley Street."

"I still don't know who it was."

"Can't you guess? Pearl."

When Kate herself left she refused to let him accompany her out of the house to see her off:

"Doctor Buttle said you're to stay indoors."

"I warn you, if we say goodbye here, I'll kiss you."

"You must obey a doctor who's practically a Harley Street specialist."

"Then I will, and you take the consequences."

She was held too tight, kissed too often to answer.

She came out into the yard to find Jane Torgill and Flossie in anxious consultation. Still dazed by the recent leavetaking, she paid them little attention and was walking past to fetch Dinah from the byre when old Jane stopped her:

"We're in a rare fix. Could we ask you to help us out, miss?"

"Yes, of course. What is it?"

"It's like this. Since Master James got his accident Flossie's had charge of the sheep, and now she's just taken a count and she's three ewes short. They've as like as not strayed into the wood, and they'll be struck there, that's certain sure, rotten with maggots."

"Mr. Tranmire won't half carry on," Flossie wailed.

"Master James won't know nothing about it, not till he's well. He's not to be upset, that's doctor's orders; but meantime we've the ewes to fetch back, and Flossie won't go into the wood alone, not if it was ever so, I can make nothing of her."

"Not if you were to beg me on bended knee, Mrs. Torgill." Flossie's jaw set stubbornly: "I've had enough of the wood and its goings-on. It's not for nothing they call it the Devil's Churchyard."

"What happened to you there?" Kate's eyes rested on her with interest.

She was silent, Jane Torgill replied on her behalf: "I keep telling her it's just her ideas, but she won't have it. Yesterday evening it was, and what was she doing in the wood you'd best not ask. We'd all the sheep nicely penned in the long pasture."

"I went to make up the fence." Flossie glared sulkily.

"Maybe you thought Ron Smith would be coming to help you. I saw his motor-bike left here in the lane."

"Well, he didn't find me."

"No." She chuckled: "If it had been him you'd have let him catch you all right." She turned to Kate: "She's got it into her head there was someone after her. From the way she came haring and screaming back to the farm it might have been our Guernsey bull."

"I'd sooner the bull," Flossie retorted, "than a spook."

"You see how it is, miss." Jane Torgill wore a troubled frown: "She's taken against the place, and here we are with these ewes to find and no one else to send. My man's up in

118

the high intake cleaning gutters with the lad, and they've got their teas with them and won't be back till dark. I'd go myself, spooks or no spooks, but I can't leave Master James as he is."

Kate began to see light: "You'd like me to go and look for the ewes?"

"Not alone, you wouldn't know where to look; but Flossie doesn't mind going if you keep her company."

Flossie nodded reluctantly: "We'll be two to one if anything jumps out."

"Yes." Kate smiled, pressing her hands to her hips: "And both of us pretty solid."

"That's right." Mrs. Torgill surveyed with her approval: "You're no wisp of a lass. You give as good as you get, I'll be bound. Well, I'm much obliged." She turned and went back into the house.

Flossie whistled to Fan, who came bounding up:

"She'll be handy. It's luck she's here when she's wanted. She's been moping all day in Mr. Tranmire's room."

"He let her out. She made such a noise barking at your visitor."

"Her in the car?" Flossie grinned: "My word, didn't she scuttle."

"Fan didn't bite her, did she?"

"No fear, she wouldn't; but she chivvied her into her car the way she chivvies the hens. Squawking, clucking. You never heard the like." Flossie shook with laughter.

"Who was it? Miss Corrington?"

"Could have been the name, I didn't rightly catch it. I told her it was doctor's orders, no one to see Mr. Tranmire, and she wasn't pleased. Out she gets all hoity-toity, struts round the yard as if the place belonged to her. I'd left the byre door open to give the mare some air, and she peeked in. My word, she turned real nasty, looked as if she'd clout me if she dared, then off she stalks to the house to have it out with Mrs. Torgill."

"I wonder why."

"Maybe she knew the mare." She caught Kate's eye, and both laughed. Kate was too happy, she could not help herself.

"I gave the mare a drink," Flossie added, "and a feed of corn."

"Thank you so much." She went into the byre, patted Dinah, saw that she was comfortable: "She settles in easily, she'll be quite content till we come back."

They crossed the fields with Fan at their heels.

"What did you see yesterday?" Kate asked: "Can you describe it?"

Flossie shook her head: "I'd soonest not talk of it, not if I've got to go in there again."

Kate did not press her. The day was drawing in, and as they followed the path downstream a spur of the hill cut off the westering sun. The light was not yet too dim while they walked in the open, but under the trees in the wood it was almost dusk.

Kate stared into the shadows: "The sheep won't be easy to see."

"It'll soon be dark, I don't like it." Flossie's voice trembled, she clung to Kate's side.

The track winding to avoid the tangles of the thicket was the same that Kate had travelled with Jim after their adventures in the Devil's Churchyard. Fan ran on ahead, stopped suddenly; branches rustled, feet scuttled, shorn backs glimmered through a dusky screen of leaves.

Flossie whistled to Fan, who raced forward.

"It's them. Two of them, maybe all three." She spoke in triumph and excitement, forgetting her fears in her relief, the prospect of a successful end to the quest.

Her hope was premature. The sheep vanished again into the gloom; Fan lost them, struggled in vain through the brambles. The two girls, however, pressed on undiscouraged, sure now of their direction, convinced that at any moment they would catch another glimpse of the strays. They were on ground that Kate recognised, not far from the Devil's Churchyard. They passed the spot where she found Dinah among the trampled remains of the goat mask. Behind those dark trees lay the river and the grassy headland that had held the pool of lamb's blood, Fan beaten almost to death.

Whether or not Fan remembered the place, she turned away from it, and they let her guide them. The track became fainter, barely distinguishable. Branches encroached, impeding their way; they crept underneath on hands and knees. It was all familiar to Kate, strange only in the darkness enshrouding them. She was ready for the bog when they came

120

to it, leapt across from tuft to tuft of rushes without wetting her feet.

The ground rose steeply; Fan scrambled to the crest, and they followed. Suddenly she turned, rushed back with her tail between her legs, cowered beside them, growling or whining, the sound was a mixture of both. They peered out through the bushes at the open sward of the knoll.

"Oh," Flossie gasped. Her voice died in a gurgle as Kate clapped her hand over her mouth.

With her other hand Kate grabbed Fan by the collar. She lost her own balance, slipped backwards, sat down with a bump in a patch of nettles. Not daring to move, she sat still.

"Be quiet," she hissed. "He hasn't seen us."

Flossie edged towards her, where the nettles left room: "It's him, it's the Devil."

"It isn't. It's just a man wearing a mask."

They spoke in whispers, heads close together. Kate's long hair tickled Flossie's neck. She pushed it aside with a giggle; she was getting her spirit back, reassured by her companion's presence, her words.

"A man you say? Flesh and blood, you mean?" She quivered with suppressed laughter: "Look at him. Look at his—"

"Yes, I'm not blind. He leaves nothing to the imagination."

The evening light glowed on the knoll, on the circle of upright stones and the altar-stone pale and flat in the centre, on which a figure stood with arms raised in prayer, tall, erect, stark naked. From feet to neck the figure was a man's, the head a goat's.

Flossie was about to say more, but Kate frowned and pursed her lips. The man was looking in their direction almost as if he suspected something; but if he did the silence reassured him, he turned to face the cromlech and began to chant. They could distinguish neither words nor tune, only the rise and fall of a voice, monotonous, unmelodious, blood-curdling.

"Are you sure it's just a man?" Flossie whispered. Her confidence was ebbing.

"Quite sure. Wait."

Figures were emerging from the cromlech, a small group of men as naked as their leader on the altar. Their heads were horned, their faces black masks with slits for eyes. Two dragged a burden between them, trailing it along the ground.

121

As it approached it became clear what it was, a sheep's carcase.

Flossie was unable to restrain her indignation: "That's one of our ewes, the murderers, the nasty, ugly, sneaking jelly-bellies. Look at them, showing all they've got, as if they'd reason to be proud of it. A girl only needs one peek to see they're no use to her."

"Do be quiet." Kate nudged her with her elbow: "Do you want them to catch us?"

The men lifted the sheep, laid it on the altar at the priest's feet; but he paid no attention, absorbed in his interminable chant, droning on and on as if hypnotized by his own cacophony. His acolytes grouped themselves on either side, waiting. Kate wondered which, if any, was Albert; there were several whose puny frame resembled his. They shivered without their clothes; the sun was low, a chill wind rising. Still the priest chanted, time without end.

Kate wriggled, whispered: "I can't sit here any longer. I'll have to move."

"What's wrong?"

"The nettles. They sting my behind."

Flossie giggled: "I've known when I liked having my bottom tickled."

"It's all very well to laugh. Mine smarts, my pants are too thin."

She rose cautiously on her knees, gripping a protruding root with one hand to steady herself, applied the other vigorously to rub her itching seat. To do so she had to let go of Fan's collar. The movement, the sudden release aroused Fan from dazed and trembling submission; she stood up, threw back her head, vented her pent emotion in a lugubrious howl, which blended and vied in penetrating discord with the voice from the altar.

Kate and Flossie did not wait to learn what effect the interruption produced in the Devil's Churchyard. They leapt up, fled into the wood, with Fan bounding at their heels. They lost the track, plunged through the bushes, stumbled, fell sprawling, picked themselves up and ran on again. A hue and cry behind spurred them on, shouts, curses, crackling branches.

They had the advantage that they were well-shod, while their naked pursuers trod barefoot on twigs, stones, thorns and briars. The dismay that this provoked was evident from

122

their yells of pain, growing fainter as the girls advanced, dwindling behind them into the distance. Flossie who knew her way in the wood found the track again, the going became easier. They ran freely, even felt secure enough to pause for breath. At last when light glinted between the trunks ahead they slackened pace to a walk, came out safe into the field.

They returned to the farm in silence, too exhausted to talk. Flossie brooded downcast, remorseful, not looking forward to the confession that lay ahead, that she had failed to recover the ewes, that one of them was dead. Kate's thoughts were less occupied with the loss than with the purpose for which the slaughter was intended.

Flossie helped her to saddle Dinah. She led her out into the yard, and Kate mounted.

"Will you tell Mr. Tranmire about this?" she asked.

"As soon as he's well."

"I suppose you must, but I wish you didn't have to."

"You couldn't wish it more than me."

The glow of sunset was fading from the sky as Kate rode home; but the moon little diminished in its third quarter shone in front of her, lighting the way, ensilvering the film of mist on the heather as Dinah plodded up the hill and over the crest on to the high moor. She broke into a trot on the level, and Kate let her choose her own pace; she herself was absorbed in her thoughts, trying to make order of the turmoil, to sort out anxiety and terror from joy.

Kemsdale Wood loomed ahead impenetrably dark on the right. As she approached she listened apprehensively for unholy echoes from the depths, but there was no sound except the whirr of wings, angry croak of a cock grouse whose sleep she disturbed in the deep heather beyond the gutter. Dinah too eyed the trees askance, as if infected with fear; more than once she would have shied if Kate had not been ready for it. Then suddenly her body stiffened, she laid her ears back flat on her mane; she broke from a trot into a canter, from a canter into a gallop, grabbed the bit between her teeth and bolted, swerving away from the wood up the bank on the left of the road, gathering herself at the top and leaping the low wall on to the moor.

Kate gripped tight with her knees, recovered her balance; but she had no power to hold the mare, no wish either. She was as one with her in her terror of the unseen pursuer, the

123

wild huntsman urging on after her the hounds of hell. Across the high moor through the moonlight night horse and rider fled, over heather and bracken, ditches and watercourses, up to the crest of the ridge and still faster, faster along it, silhouetted against the sky, the girl's hair streaming in the wind, the mare's white flanks phantom-pale. A tradesman's van passed on the road; the driver pulled up, stared in astonishment, superstitious dread. His story, suitably embellished, earned him attentive hearing for days afterwards. Some accused him of drinking, others recalled the legend of an ancient goddess of the hills.

Chapter 7

Above the bridge at Easby the harbour narrowed, and at low tide only a shallow stream of water was left between sloping shelves of mud. None of the fishing craft whose home port this was ever came up so far; but one or two dinghies rocked at buoys in the channel, and derelict hulks rotted on the foreshore. This was the poorer end of the town. The houses on the right bank dwindled to steep woods, over whose crest lay Saint Ursula's; the left bank held the railway station and drab terraces built for the railwaymen.

Brink was walking in one of these streets on Thursday morning when Doctor Buttle emerged suddenly from a door, nearly knocked him over.

"Sorry, Brink," he exclaimed. "I'm always in too much of a hurry."

"The cure of the body calls for more urgency than the cure of souls."

"You're right. A split second may lie between life and death, seldom between heaven and hell."

"Fortunately for me. My work leaves me time for my hobbies."

"Ah yes, folklore, you mean?" He hesitated, stroked his beard: "It's an interesting study, no doubt, but I feel I should warn you, Brink, against too much of it here at Easby. Not everyone sees eye to eye with you about your innovations."

"Some people must have a grievance, if it's only about the smell in church. You wouldn't believe how many have complained of it in the past two days. It's probably a dead rat under the boards, I can't see that it matters on a weekday. I'll have a good search made before Sunday comes."

"I'm not talking of a smell in church but of people's feelings, their prejudices if you like. They've old-fashioned ideas, and if you'll forgive my saying so it shocks them to hear broad jokes from a man of your cloth."

"My tongue runs away with me at times, but there's no harm in it."

"I can't agree."

"You're thinking of my *bon mot* on Sunday, I suppose, the treatment I prescribed for Kate Evans. Why shouldn't I call her callipygous, when the word suits her? Who in Easby knows what it means?"

"Jim Tranmire did."

"So I gathered. Let me put this to you, Doctor, as a question of professional etiquette. How would you like it if a layman claimed the right to interfere in your work?"

"I claim no right, I'm only speaking as your friend."

"Not you, I mean Tranmire. He thinks because he's patron of the living that any incumbent he presents should behave as he chooses. He shows his ignorance of the law relating to advowsons. His rights cease with his signature of the deed of presentation."

"Jim didn't put me up to say this, I can assure you. He's in no fit condition, he's had a narrow escape for his life."

"So I heard, but he's better now, they tell me."

"He's still an invalid, confined to the house."

"All right, Doctor, I'll take care not to upset him. My tongue will be under strict control when Kate comes this evening to rehearse."

"There'll be no rehearsal, I fear."

"You don't mean to say that she wants to shirk again?"

"I'd know better what she wants if I knew what's happened to her. She went out riding yesterday, and we haven't seen her since."

"She never came back?"

"Apparently not. She'd a key to the door, all the teachers have so that they can stay out as late as they please. We'd no reason to be anxious, we went to bed as usual; but in the morning her room was empty, her bed hadn't been slept in."

"Not so odd perhaps as you think. She was riding to Kemsdale Farm, wasn't she?"

"Yes. How do you know?"

"A little bird told me, someone who saw her setting off in that direction. It wasn't hard to guess what the urgent business was, why she sent me a message to cry off yesterday's rehearsal. Well, Doctor, I can solve your mystery for you. It seems that Tranmire has recovered his health and strength sooner than you expected."

"If you're hinting that she spent the night there you're quite wrong. My wife rang the farm up at once, it was the first thing she did. She spoke to Mrs. Torgill, the housekeeper. Kate left just before dark, and it shouldn't have taken her more than an hour to ride home."

"Has Tranmire himself any suggestions?"

"My wife was anxious not to worry Jim, she asked Mrs. Torgill not to tell him. We're doing all we can, we've informed the police, and Harry Bracken's out on the road now, looking for Kate and asking if anyone's seen her."

"A chance for Harry to earn fresh laurels. He'll be an expert soon in scaling the cliffs of that quarry."

Doctor Buttle frowned at the levity of tone: "The quarry has nothing to do with it. Kate wouldn't go near the edge, and she'd be in no danger if she were to. She can manage a horse better than anyone I know."

They were standing on the pavement with their backs to the road and did not see Harry Bracken on his bicycle till he drew level with them.

"Excuse me, Doctor." He dismounted, saluted.

"What is it, Harry. Have you found her?"

"I'm afraid not, and there's more trouble come on top. Mrs. Buttle said I'd find you here, as like as not, at old Mother Agg's."

"Yes, I've just been visiting her. What's happened?"

"It's Mr. Tranmire, Doctor. They didn't mean to tell him about the young lady; but when that girl, Flossie Daw, heard she took on so they could do nothing with her. Off she goes to Mr. Tranmire and blurts out some story about the sheep in the wood. I couldn't make head or tail of it myself, except that Miss Evans was with her, and they both had to run for their lives. Anyhow, what with one thing and another, Mr. Tranmire got it all out of her, that Miss Evans set off home in the dark and hasn't turned up. There was no stopping him when he heard it; he would have it she was in the wood still, and he went off to look for her himself."

"Sheer madness in his state of health. Why should she be in the wood at all?"

"I don't know, Doctor. They tried to argue with him, but he wouldn't listen; so Alf Torgill went with him, and Flossie too, they wouldn't let him go alone. It was a good job they didn't, he hadn't got far on his way before he was took real bad, fell dizzy and fainted. Alf and Flossie carried him home between them."

"Delirious, I suppose?"

"That's about the look of it; but they didn't know where to get you on the phone, so I thought I'd fetch you myself. I'd got to slip back on my bike into Easby anyhow to see the serjeant about some information I've picked up."

"I'll drive straight to Kemsdale now. What's this clue of yours? Anything hopeful?"

"I wouldn't say it was or it wasn't, but it's worth looking into. I stopped a lorry on the road, I've been stopping anything likely to be passing to and fro. This chap had seen nothing himself; but he'd had a cup of tea, he told me, at that transport café, the Flying Saucer they call it, a mile or so short of Freeborough, and there was some talk there about a tale they heard last night from a traveller with a van. He was sober enough, they said, but he swore he'd seen a ghost on the moor."

"What sort of ghost?"

"That's the point. It was a horse, and the rider had long hair streaming behind."

"If it was a ghost it was an odd coincidence."

Harry nodded: "There was a lot of nonsense added, that the horse shone like the moon and galloped up into the sky; but the van was a long way off, it seems, and a man can be speaking truth for part of the time and inventing for the rest."

"At any rate, the horse very evidently was white."

"I saw heaven opened," Brink quoted, "and behold a white

horse, and he that sat upon him was called Faithful and True."

Harry, who had ignored him hitherto, turned to address him: "I hardly think it was a man, sir. The hair sounds more like a girl's."

"So what are you going to do about it?" Doctor Buttle asked.

"Well, I thought if Miss Evans was crossing the moor, on the rigg-top maybe from this talk of the sky, they might know something about her in one of the farms on the other side, and it wouldn't take Serjeant Cleaver long in his car to go round to them and make inquiries."

"It's quite an idea. She might have been galloping on the moor, I wouldn't put it past her. If the serjeant's doubtful, Harry, tell him I think you're right."

Harry departed on his bicycle.

"The white horse of the Apocalypse." Brink nodded thoughtfully: "Yes, a goddess clothed with the moon, with a vesture dipped in blood."

"I've no idea what you're talking about." There was a sharp edge to Doctor Buttle's voice: "I must be off and see what's the matter with Jim. I told him to keep quiet. A relapse can be dangerous." He moved towards his car drawn up against the curb: "He's a fool, but I suppose one can't blame him. We're all fond of Kate." His last words were addressed less to Brink than himself.

Brink, left alone, walked on to the end of the street. It was a blind alley; progress was barred by a stone wall except where a gate in the corner gave access to a patch of waste ground, coarse grass and weeds sloping down to the mud of the foreshore and bounded at the top by the railway. A notice on the gate announced that camping was permitted. Already in early summer there was an agglomeration of cars, motor bicycles and caravans.

Brink entered the field, picked his way through the litter. Inquisitive eyes peered at him from caravans. A small boy naked except for a pair of drawers, who was playing in a puddle of slops, pointed his finger and shouted:

"Look, Ma, look at that man. Why's he all in black? Is someone dead?"

His sister, even smaller and more lightly clad than himself, came to the top of the steps, stared and burst into tearful screams:

"Nasty man. Don't like him. Take him away."

The noise abated for a moment as a plump woman in an orange bikini stooped and picked her up:

"He won't hurt you, Maureen. It's only a parson."

"Bloody parson," the boy yelled, inspiring Maureen to renewed efforts. His mother smacked him, and a concert of wails pursued Brink as he strode hurriedly past.

Farther on he found refuge among familiar faces. The party of adolescents who frequented the rectory inhabited two caravans on the outskirts of the site. A willowy girl with sharp features and rolls of peroxide-blond curls called to him:

"Are you looking for Albert?" She pointed to a tent pitched alone under the hedge.

Albert crawled out as Brink approached: "Hullo," he greeted him. "Come to visit me in my stately home?" He held the flap back with a gesture of hospitality.

"Thank you." Brink shook his head.

"What's wrong with it? I keep my things a bloody sight tidier than you do."

"No doubt, but I prefer my own effluvia to yours." He sat down on the grass, and Albert, scowling resentfully, chose a place beside him.

Brink paid no heed to his mood, sat silent, engrossed in his own thoughts. When at last he spoke his voice held reproof:

"That was a bad business last night. The proceedings of course were only a prelude; but all these rites have sanctity, the least of them deserves respect."

"We did what you told us, and a nice job we had too, catching and killing the sheep."

"I'm not finding fault, but I'm unhappy about the interruption."

"That bloody dog, you mean? What more could we do, chasing through a tangle black as hell, treading on thorns with no shoes or even socks on? My feet are as sore as pincushions. You'd know if you hadn't been too careful of your own skin to help."

"I couldn't risk damage to the sacred mask. It's my only one left. I'd an accident with the other."

"You could have taken it off."

"I'm not anxious to reveal my identity."

"To a dog?"

"It wasn't alone."

"No, that's what most of the chaps thought. They swore there was someone with it, and I'd like to know who."

"I can tell you. Kate Evans and Tranmire's land-girl."

"How do you know?"

"Lucky chance, a few words overheard."

"So I was right, she was riding to Kemsdale, and you said she'd be safe in the house holding Tranmire's hand."

"I'm not infallible. I wish I were. To add to the confusion, it seems that she's disappeared, no one knows why or where."

Albert smirked: "I could put them wise."

"What do you mean? Did you have a part in this?"

"It was just a lark, Mr. Brink. I was coming through the wood after we packed up, and I saw her riding on the road. So I thought to myself I'd practise the words of power I've learnt, and hey presto, they worked like an H-bomb. Not on the girl but the gee. The beast went crazy."

"Was she thrown?"

"No, she stuck to the saddle, I'll say that for her. She took the wall like a bird, and off helter-skelter across the moor. That was the last I saw of her."

"The last anyone's seen. Your invocation had such power, Albert, she's vanished into thin air."

"I've the knack. I'll soon be an adept."

"You've a knack for making a fool of yourself. How can I perform the rite of the goddess if she's lying with a broken neck under some god-forsaken crag?"

"We'll find another as good."

"We won't."

Albert stared at him, crest-fallen: "You told me to think up some useful trick."

"Not on the girl but the man, on Tranmire himself."

"So I did too, didn't I, when his car took the high dive? He'd have had it if he'd kept the hood on. Is it my fault he's one of these fresh-air fiends?"

"Thank goodness he is. I want him out of the way; but I've told you, not killed. Not yet."

"You're hard to please, aren't you? Whatever I do, it's wrong."

"All right, Albert, you needn't look so aggrieved. If it comforts you, there's some advantage come even of your blunder with the girl. Tranmire was so upset by her disappearance he went to hunt for her himself, and the result is he's had a dangerous relapse."

"So I've nobbled him after all? He won't be able to meddle with us?"

"He wouldn't, if there was anything to meddle with; but without a victim the sacrifice is off."

"Have a heart, Mr. Brink. There are other girls. What about her high-mightiness, Lady Curlywig? She'd give style to the part."

"Who the hell do you mean?"

"I don't know her name, but you're thick as thieves with her mother."

"Pearl Corrington? What do you take me for? Am I capable of such sacrilege, to offer scrag-end on the altar of the great ones?"

"She's all right in her clothes."

"The goddess wears none. We need Kate Evans."

He sank into glum silence. Albert watched him apprehensively, not daring to break it.

"Has the place been tidied up?" Brink asked at last. "After this land-girl's stories they'll be ferreting every hole in the wood."

"I've seen to that." Albert's confidence returned, he was conscious of merit: "I sent Aidan early this morning."

"Aidan? Yes, yes, I remember. Tall, fair, might be a scoutmaster."

"That's the lad. He's keen too; there's only one thing the matter with him, he's a queer."

"What if he is?"

"No harm of course, if you like it. Lots of parsons are that way, I know."

"Well, I'm not; but I can't see for the life of me that it matters where Aidan's fancy roams."

"Last night it didn't, we were all boys together; but when the big show comes I'm not sure how he'll take it. We'll be a mixed party."

"That problem can wait till we know if there's going to be a big show at all."

"Must it be a wench? Wouldn't a chap do as well?"

Brink shook his head: "Not even to please Aidan."

Albert was staring across the field, he pointed with his finger: "Here he is. You can talk to him yourself."

131

A youth in khaki shorts came in through the gate, skirted the caravans and approached them. He raised his arm to Brink in a gesture not unlike a Fascist salute:

"I was just coming up to the rectory to report, sir."

"I've saved you a journey." He smiled at him: "Have you left everything tidy?"

"Yes, sir. I buried what I could and carried the rest into the bushes."

"You met no one from the farm?"

"Not in the wood, only in the field as I was coming away. The girl who works there, Flossie Daw, was gathering the sheep, and I passed the time of day with her."

"She wasn't suspicious?"

"No, she'd never seen me before."

Albert grinned: "She had, Aidan; but not your face, and I don't suppose you were showing what she'd recognise."

"Flossie was in the wood last night," Brink explained, "she and another girl. They were responsible for the noise that disturbed us."

Aidan blushed to the roots of his hair.

"You'll have to get used to mixed company," Albert warned him.

"It's all very well for you." His voice was peevish: "I'm not keen on girls, I can't help it."

"Did you talk to Flossie Daw?" Brink put in.

"Yes, sir, we'd quite a chat."

Albert winked slyly: "Take care, Aidan. She'll have a yen on you."

Aidan paid no attention: "I thought it my duty to get into conversation with her, to find out how the land lay."

"Very wise of you." Brink nodded: "What did you hear from her? Did she tell you of her own adventure in the wood?"

"Not a word. She talked of Mr. Tranmire's illness. She was upset, she kept on and on about it."

"She'll have it on her conscience that she was to blame for his relapse."

"She didn't say so. She put all the blame on his accident. She doesn't believe it was an accident at all."

"What was it then? Attempted suicide?"

"According to her, it was attempted murder. She's been talking to the policeman."

132

"Harry Bracken?" Brink caught Albert's eye: "The hero of the occasion, and he doesn't let anyone forget it. He found oil or something spilt on the road, didn't he?"

"Yes, and he's got a clue now, he knows where it came from."

"What on earth do you mean?"

"It's only what Flossie says, sir, what the policeman told her. He traced the oil to a garage in Freeborough."

"All oil looks alike. Don't tell me the garage has identified it as theirs."

"I can't see how; but they did, and they described the customer."

"Does the busy know who it is?" Albert asked anxiously.

Brink frowned at him: "All right, Albert. Leave this to me." He turned again to Aidan, who replied:

"Not yet, but he's making inquiries. The description was rather vague. He'll have more to go on if he finds the car."

"What's this about a car?" Albert checked himself in obedience to a glance of angry warning.

"There was a car, was there?" Brink asked. "The nefarious customer didn't come on foot?"

"As a matter of fact, he did. He parked the car round the corner, bought three drums and carried them to it himself. The garage people thought it funny."

"They well might; but I don't understand, if they never saw the car, what clue it can offer."

"A woman noticed it parked in front of her door. It was a light-blue Cortina."

"And the registration number?"

"She didn't take it."

"Not very bright of her. There are plenty of light-blue Cortinas about." He laughed: "I own one myself."

Aidan laughed too: "The police won't waste time on you, sir."

"I hope not, I expect I've an alibi. Thank you, Aidan, you've done very well. Our rites interest you, don't they?"

"I've known nothing like them." His voice quivered with fervour: "They take me out of myself, put me in touch with the cosmic."

"That's the right spirit. Stick to it. Don't let anything deter you."

"I won't, sir." He departed, saluting with the same gesture as before.

133

Brink frowned when they were alone: "This isn't your lucky day, Albert. Thanks to you, our victim has vanished, and the police are hot on our track."

"I was as careful as could be. It beats me how they traced me to the garage."

"What concerns me more is that they traced you to my car. I wish with all my heart I'd never let you use it."

"They don't know whose car it was."

"Not yet, but blue Cortinas aren't as common here as I made out to Aidan." He paused, asked sharply: "How much has that boy been told?"

"No more than's good for him. He isn't ready for strong meat."

"So I gathered."

"Don't worry, he'll be all right when I've had time to work on him. Step by step, that's my motto."

"Are they all like that in your gang?"

"No, the others are the couldn't-care-less sort, they'll do anything for the kick of it; but Aidan's different, he takes things seriously."

"So much the better. He's the type I want."

"Yes, he's worth taking trouble with, he's a born medium. Orgasm, that's all he needs to cure him of scruples."

Brink rose to his feet, dusted his trousers, picking off shreds of paper and other debris adhering to them:

"Well, I leave him to you. I've a visit to pay on a lady who's usually a mine of information and will be able, I hope, to relieve my mind."

"Hoity-toity's ma?"

"I'd rather you referred to her in my presence as Mrs. Corrington."

He strode briskly back by a short cut beside the railway past the station into a busy shopping street, dodged through the crowds, passed the approach to the bridge and continued on along the quay by the main harbour. At this hour late in the morning tourists flocked there, strolling, dawdling in chattering groups, leaning over the railings to admire the view of the cliff opposite with its patchwork of red-tiled roofs, crowned with the church and abbey ruins. A family party stopped him to ask the way up to the church, an elderly American to assure him that this was the quaintest old fishing port in all England. Absorbed in his own thoughts, he answered curtly and at random, pressed on unheeding,

134

leaving those who addressed him to stare after him in surprise, some offended, others amused, numbering among the town's curiosities an eccentric parson.

Farther on, the street swung away from the harbour behind an intervening cluster of little dwellings, spick-and-span like dolls' houses. He turned in at one of these, rang the bell. Molly Corrington opened the door:

"Why, Oswald. What a nice surprise. I'm afraid everything's rather untidy, but do come in."

He smiled: "I hope I don't disturb you at a busy time."

"Of course not. I'm never too busy to see my friends. Pearl keeps on at me to start cooking lunch, but she'll have to wait for it. I'll make you a cup of coffee first."

"No, I'm sure it's too late. Haven't you had yours already?"

"I'll not be sorry for another."

She ushered him into the drawing room. Pearl sat on the sofa smoking a cigarette. The face that she turned to the visitor was unwelcoming.

"You'll have to play hostess for a few minutes, Pearl," her mother told her, "while I boil up the kettle."

"What for?" Pearl frowned: "Coffee? Its nearly lunchtime. I'm sure Mr. Brink doesn't want us to live the day backwards."

"Well, I want a cup, and he'll drink one to keep me company. You can do as you like." She bustled out of the room.

Brink sat down in an armchair. Traces of the litter from the caravan site, still clinging to his clothes, soiled the gay cretonne.

"Have you had any news from Saint Ursula's?" he asked.

"News?" Pearl raised her trimly plucked eyebrows: "Oh, this fuss, you mean, about Kate Evans? Mother's been in such a state she let everything else go to pot. She's done nothing all morning but ring up Mrs. Buttle."

"It's a bad business, it looks as if the poor girl has suffered some harm."

"If she had it's what she's asking for, showing herself off on that pony with a glad eye for anyone who comes her way; but she hasn't of course, it's just as I said to Mother from the moment we heard of it. The Devil looks after his own."

"How do you know she hasn't?" His eyes glinted.

"Mrs. Buttle rang up just before you came, she's had a message from the police. While everyone's been scouring the

135

country for Kate Evans she's lying tucked up cosy in bed at a farm."

Molly Corrington entered with a tray of cups and a coffeepot.

"You're talking about Kate?" she exclaimed. "Isn't it wonderful, Oswald? They've found her."

"I'm delighted." He spoke with sincere fervour, rubbing his hands: "Have you any details of what happened?"

"Very few, except that her horse ran away with her, and it caught its foot in a rabbit hole or something, and they both came down among the rocks. I don't know if Kate was hurt or just fainted; but it seems that she lay there most of the night till a shepherd found her, and he took her to a farm in Golstondale. It's ever so lonely a spot, right in the heart of the moors, and they aren't on the telephone, so they couldn't let anyone know where she was."

"They could very well," Pearl interrupted, "if they'd tried. Even if they haven't a car they must have legs."

"There was probably good reason," her mother replied. "We'll hear later. The main thing is that she's safe."

"And none the worse, I hope," Brink added.

"It doesn't seem so. Helen's driving over to fetch her."

"Then I'll call at Saint Ursula's this afternoon to inquire."

"How thoughtful you are, Oswald. I'm sure Kate will be touched." She poured out his coffee, turned to Pearl with the pot poised in her hand.

"Not for me." Pearl shook her head: "I've more respect for my figure than to keep on swilling the stuff."

Her mother laughed: "I like coffee, and my figure deserves no respect." She filled her own cup, glanced coyly at Brink.

"Don't worry, Molly," he assured her. "It suits Pearl to be slim, it wouldn't suit you."

"That's what my Ernest used to say. My buxom belle, he called me." She took her handkerchief from her bag and wiped her eyes: "It was his pet name for me, I can hear him still."

Pearl smiled sourly: "Father preferred quantity to quality. He'd a knee to spare for any woman with plenty to sit on. I've heard you tell him so, Mother."

"Poor Ernest." She sighed: "He was so susceptible."

"That's the excuse they all make, all men of his type. It's

a waste of time to appeal to their higher instincts; they've no taste except for flesh."

Brink listened, puzzled and disconcerted. Molly Corrington explained:

"Pearl's rather upset. She'd a most disagreeable experience yesterday at Kemsdale Farm."

"With Tranmire?"

"No." Pearl exclaimed: "Not with Jim. I can't believe he meant to insult me. I know who's to blame, and I shan't forget it." She hesitated, eyeing Brink doubtfully: "If I tell you this I don't want it put in a sermon or anything of that sort."

"It shan't be. I'll treat it as if under the seal of confession."

"Confession indeed? I've nothing to be ashamed of, unlike some girls I could name, the sort Jim runs after."

"You jump to conclusions too fast, Pearl," her mother protested. "There mayn't have been anything wrong."

"There never is, Mother, in your eyes. There wouldn't be if you stood looking on while they undressed."

"Oh, Pearl, you shouldn't say things like that."

"All right, Mr. Brink can judge whether I'm being fanciful. A parson can't be so ignorant of the facts of life."

"I've had opportunities," he agreed, "to study them during my years of service to the Church."

"Listen then. I drove to Kemsdale yesterday evening to ask how Jim was getting on. I knew he wasn't really well enough for visitors, Doctor Buttle warned me beforehand; but I thought as Kate Evans had gone over earlier in the day I'd be allowed just a minute or two with him. That half-witted land-girl, Flossie Daw, was in the yard, and she put my back up at once; she has no manners, she isn't fit to work on a gentleman's farm. All the same I didn't argue, I turned the car to drive home. Then what do you think? I couldn't help seeing into a shed, the door was wide open, and there her pony was standing as pert as you please."

"Whose? Kate's?"

"Whose else would it be, a white brute with a long mane?"

"It's a sweet little thing, so pretty," her mother exclaimed.

"More vicious than sweet, from the look of it. I don't like horses, but I'd like very much to know what the rider was doing in the house while I was kept out."

"Didn't Flossie say?" Brink spoke with tactful sympathy.

137

"Flossie? I got nothing but a flood of coarse abuse when I asked her, most of it luckily unintelligible in her awful dialect. Flossie, it's the right name for her; she's the very type of a floozey, and that old hag, Mrs. Torgill, isn't any better, cackling and screeching at me. I've never known such a household, I was thankful to escape from it."

Her mother shook her head: "I can't understand it. They're so civil when I call. There must have been some mistake."

"There's no mistaking what Kate Evans was there for."

"No, Pearl, I won't have it, I don't believe it."

Brink laughed soothingly: "I don't believe it either, from what I'm told of Tranmire's health. He's in no fit state for such pastimes."

"You needn't be so crude," Pearl reproved him. "How do you know what Jim's fit for or isn't?"

"I know this, he's just had a dangerous relapse. I met Doctor Buttle in the town and was with him when he got the message."

"Oh, poor Jim," Molly Corrington exclaimed. "I'm surprised Helen said nothing about it when she rang, but I expect she was too much taken up with Kate."

"As a matter of fact, there's a connection between the events. When he heard that Kate was missing he insisted on going to look for her himself, and this is the result."

"What a fool he is." Pearl shrugged her shoulders: "He might have known she'd turn up like a bad penny."

Her mother sighed: "I think you're being very unkind when he's so ill."

"We hope he won't be ill for long." Brink smiled: "I can guess what's in Pearl's mind, and I'm inclined to agree." He turned to her: "You feel, don't you, that a young man in Tranmire's position ought to marry a girl from a well-to-do background, accustomed to the life money can buy and able to take her place in local society?"

"Yes, I do. That's what he needs, but not just an idler, of course. I've a job of my own like anyone else."

"Pearl works hard," her mother explained, "at her little boutique at the Angel, selling face cream and things like that."

"Not face cream, Mother. You make it sound so vulgar. I keep nothing that hasn't a French name, *esprit de Pompadoure, rêve de bon ton.*"

138

"I've heard of your venture," Brink assured her, "and I mean to become one of your customers when I want a gift for parishioners of the fair sex."

"Come when you like, but I don't promise you'll find me there. I only open the place when I'm in the mood."

"How delightfully amateur." He laughed genially: "She shows the right spirit, doesn't she, Molly, one of the world's workers and yet unsoiled by commerce?"

Molly nodded: "There's nothing unladylike in Pearl's work."

"Quite so. A very suitable occupation for the future Mrs. Tranmire."

"I'd be better pleased," Pearl complained, "if Jim thought so too."

"Don't worry." He put his coffee cup down on the table and patted her shoulder as he passed to resume his seat: "He will, he must, it's for his own good. We've a duty to help him, you and I. Will you join me in a crusade to save him from himself?"

"Not to mince words, from a shameless hussy."

"I don't care what you say," her mother protested. "She's sweet."

"Of course she is, Molly," he agreed. "I'm as fond of her as you are, she's charming. It's for her sake as much as his that I deplore so unsuitable a match. I foresee too clearly how it would end, I've known too many broken marriages."

"Yes, I understand what you mean. It makes me cry to read of them in the papers. I don't pretend Ernest was perfect; but I always remembered our happiness at the beginning, and it helped me to bear with his faults. How could I let it end in an ugly law-suit?"

"You were too weak with Father," Pearl told her, "a rich man like him. You could have stung him for thumping alimony."

"Anyhow," Brink interposed, "that's what we want to prevent at Kemsdale Farm."

Molly Corrington shook her head: "Jim isn't that sort, I'm sure, and Kate wouldn't want to take advantage of it if he were."

"Neither will be put to the test if Pearl and I can help it."

"Can we?" Pearl asked. "What can we do?"

He rose to his feet: "Much can be done by friendly neighbours with a Christian sense of duty, especially when one of them is the most elegant young lady in the town."

She grasped his outstretched hand with unaccustomed goodwill.

Molly accompanied him from the room to exchange a few parting words in the hall:

"How good you were with Pearl. She was in such a difficult mood when you came."

"I can see she's upset about her reception at Kemsdale yesterday."

"Yes, it does seem odd, and so unlike Jim; but there may have been more to it than Pearl told us. She can be rather brusque sometimes, and neither Flossie nor Mrs. Torgill would like that. It was a pity too she saw Kate's little mare, she's jealous enough of her already. She's devoted to Jim and can't bear him to look at anyone else."

"They aren't engaged, are they?"

"Oh dear, no. In fact I'm not sure that he feels that way about her at all; but she's set her heart on it, and I do think they'd be very well suited."

"I'm sure they would. I told her so just now, in so many words."

"Yes, you did, and it pleased her; but you mustn't encourage her too much, it would make it all the more painful if she's disappointed."

"She won't be, if we go about things the right way. Listen, Molly, I wasn't merely flattering her, I honestly believe she's the right wife for Jim Tranmire; but I've another reason too for wanting to bring them together. You remember what I told you on Sunday about a group of misguided people in my former parish who dabbled in black magic, and how I suspect that something of the sort will be tried at Easby?"

"Indeed I do, Oswald. How could I forget it? You thought that Jim might be, not mixed up in it of course, but in danger from them."

"Well, he has been in danger, hasn't he?"

"His accident with the car? You don't mean to say—"

"Why not?"

"I heard that the police weren't satisfied and were investigating."

"You didn't put two and two together, connect it with this business in the wood?"

"I'm afraid not. There were stories about oil on the road and a garage in Freeborough, but nothing to do with black magic."

"The police have a single-track mind, it runs on oil. They've learnt that a man bought some at this garage, and that's enough to convince them he's a criminal."

"Have they arrested him?"

"They haven't caught him yet. All they know is that he was driving a blue Cortina. If suspicion falls on anyone owning that make of car I'll have to be careful, or I'll be arrested myself."

"How ridiculous. Not even Harry Bracken could be so silly."

"Nothing's too ridiculous to be believed if trouble enough is taken to propagate calumny. There are people it would suit very well to make me their whipping boy."

"I wish we knew who they are."

"So do I, but you'll understand why I'm so anxious meanwhile for Pearl to keep an eye on Tranmire."

"I don't see the connection. I'm afraid I'm too stupid."

"Let me explain more clearly. He needs someone to protect and distract him from these dark influences. What antidote could he find better than Pearl? She's so chic, so sophisticated, she'll draw him out of himself. If I may use the expression, she'll exorcise the shadows of Erebus."

"It sounds a nice compliment; but I can't help feeling sorry for Kate. Do you really think she's wrong for him?"

"I'm afraid so. She wears the aura of Proserpine."

"You do talk in riddles." She laughed: "You forget that I haven't your brains."

"Never mind, Molly. I count on your good sense."

He opened the gate, stepped out into the street, and she stood gazing affectionately after him.

He crossed the bridge, climbed the steps to the church, walked on past to the rectory. He lived alone there; but old Charlie Bracken's wife, his nearest neighbour, came in for a couple of hours of housework and to cook his lunch. She was waiting for him, a stout woman with a firm but pleasant face, an air of stolid dignity.

"You're late," she told him, "but I've kept the cutlets hot. If they're dried to a cinder you've no one to thank but yourself."

"I'm sorry, Mrs. Bracken. There's always so much to do in a parish like this."

She nodded: "If you're on about that smell in church it's

141

high time something was done. I was in there yesterday cleaning, and it's as bad as ever, fit to knock you over."

"Yes, it's rather pungent. It's probably a dead rat, or something."

"All the rats in town, if you ask me, boiled up into broth."

He laughed: "You've a picturesque way of putting things, Mrs. Bracken."

"Well, it's your business, not mine; but if it's still like this come Sunday you won't find many willing to sit through the service."

"I'll have a good search made before then, even take up the boards in the pews."

"Would you like our Harry to help? He's handy at such-like jobs, and he's here now, he came across with me. He can wait of course till you've eaten your dinner."

"Thank you, I can manage very well alone. Why did Harry come with you to the rectory? Does he want to see me?"

"He said not to trouble you. It's just a piece of routine they've set him on to." There was a note of embarrassment in her voice, her eyes were fixed on the window at the back of the hall where they stood. It looked out on to a shed used as a garage, from which Harry at this moment emerged and crossed the yard.

"What the hell?" Brink muttered. He opened the window, leaned out: "Hullo, Harry. Taking a stroll?"

Harry approached unwillingly: "I beg pardon, sir, I didn't want to trouble you. It's just a check we're making on all cars."

"All Cortinas, you mean. I hope mine's been given a clean bill of health?"

"I'm only carrying out orders, sir."

"It's his duty," his mother put in. "He can't go against the serjeant."

"All right, I'm not denying it." Brink turned to her testily: "He can spend the day in my garage, for all I care."

"Thank you, sir," Harry replied. "I've got what I want." His tone was respectful but formal, he avoided Brink's eyes.

Mrs. Bracken glanced from one to the other: "Dear me, I don't know what's come over me, dawdling here. I'll fetch your dinner and set it on the table. It's been in the oven long enough already." She hurried off to the kitchen. Harry hesitated, then turned to move away.

"Harry," Brink called him back: "You were looking for Miss Evans when I saw you last. I hear your hunch was right, they found her in Golstondale."

"Yes, thanks be." The relief in his voice was inspired as much by the change of subject as by Kate's reappearance: "At Rowantree Farm. It's a lost sort of place up on the moor, but Serjeant Cleaver thought it worth trying, and there she was."

"No bones broken, I hope?"

"He didn't see her himself; but the people at the farm thought she'd taken little harm, more shock than anything else. They said she was coming round nicely."

"I wonder they didn't send word to let Mrs. Buttle know."

"They'd no idea where she came from. The lad found her on the hill, he was out early shepherding, and it seems she was either unconscious or in no state to talk; then when they got her to the farm they put her to bed, and she fell asleep and they didn't like to wake her."

"A tame ending, the White Goddess transformed into the Sleeping Beauty."

Harry stared at him uncomprehendingly.

"All right, Harry, only a joke of mine; but there's a lesson for you in this, that real life seldom follows the pattern of a thriller on TV."

"It's a good job it doesn't, sir. We've enough work in the force without that."

"I'm sure you have, with all these cars to check. Don't let me keep you."

Harry departed. Brink went into the dining room where the cutlets awaited him, dressed with new potatoes and peas. Mrs. Bracken looked in while he was eating them:

"The coffee's keeping hot on the range. If there's nothing more you want I'll be off home."

"Nothing, thank you, Mrs. Bracken. I'll do very well by myself."

After lunch he retired to his study, took down Amos Pounder's notebook from its shelf, fingering the vellum binding caressingly, licking his finger to rub off any stains left by the nettlebed in the Devil's Churchyard. For a long time he sat poring over the crabbed handwriting; his lips moved as he committed words to memory, reciting them to himself. Then he turned to the list of names at the end, and his eyes gleamed as they rested on the last entry. He rose, drew the curtains across the window, lit a candle, clearing a space for it among the papers on the table. It was short and thick, of black wax, gave off aromatic smoke as it burnt. He sank to his knees in prayer:

"Thank you, thank you, thank you, great Archangel. How could I be doubtful of your promise? How could I show less faith than the patriarch Abraham? God will provide himself a lamb for a burnt offering. The altar stands ready, the holy rites have been performed. Neither heaven nor earth can deny me the chosen victim."

He knelt with bowed head in silence for several minutes, then again he prayed aloud:

"I vow myself, Lord, to your service with all my heart and mind, soul and spirit. May the victim's blood be a draught of everlasting life and power to do your will, but of confusion and damnation to all whose motives are unworthy."

He stood up, folded his hands, recited in Latin the version of the Lord's Prayer:

"Pater noster qui eras in caelo."

Then with a final genuflexion he blew out the candle, pulled back the curtains, opened the window to let out the smoke. The light of the summer afternoon flooded into the room.

It was nearly six when he paid his call at Saint Ursula's. By that hour, as he knew, most of the day's work at the school was over, the atmosphere relaxed, Helen Buttle more at leisure to attend to him. Nevertheless she frowned as she saw him coming up the drive. She was with her husband in their private sitting room.

"What's the matter, Helen?" he asked.

She pointed to the window: "Mr. Brink. He'll be coming to ask after Kate."

"An innocent purpose, surely?"

She shook her head: "He'll want to see her, and she's had quite enough already without him to worry her."

"We've all had enough, you especially. I'll tell him she's to ill to be seen."

"That's not much use when she's sitting there in full view on the lawn, talking to Doris."

He laughed: "Unless I take care I'm going to lose my reputation. You say Pearl can't forgive me for prescribing selective company for Jim?"

"So Molly told me when she rang up. She said Pearl was furious."

"And if I offend Brink I'll have Molly furious too."

"Poor Molly. I love her dearly, but her taste is quite appalling, in men as much as in clothes. Think of Ernest."

"It's better not to, if we aren't to think ill of the dead."

Helen's eyes were on the lawn: "Oh dear, he's seen her already. There's nothing we can do about it. I was hoping to make her accident an excuse to get her off his midsummer follies."

"If your plot depends on presenting Kate as a frail invalid it hasn't a chance."

"No." She sighed: "She looks provokingly blooming. How she can I can't think, after spending the night out on the moor half-stunned."

"Youth and a healthy body are magicians with whom no doctor can compete."

"All the same, she was lucky. It must have been a nasty fall."

"Yes, she hit her head against something pretty hard, a rock probably, that knocked her out, but I can find no serious injury. What did her more good than anything was the long sleep at the farm. Those people deserve a medal for leaving her in peace to sleep the shock off."

"I suppose so; but I didn't feel much like awarding it when I went to fetch her, thinking how much anxiety we'd have been spared if we'd known sooner what had happened. It was especially hard on Jim."

He nodded: "I was really worried about him this morning, but both my patients have responded to more effective treatment than mine. Jim's temperature fell with a plop when he got the news that Kate was found. It only goes to show how much illness is psychosomatic."

"You're too fond of that catchword, Arthur."

His attention was on the group outside the window: "I'll need a lot more beginning with psycho before we've done with this parson."

Brink had drawn up one of the canvas chairs, seated himself beside the two girls on the lawn. He smiled benevolently at Kate:

"I came to ask after the invalid, but the answer stares me reassuringly in the face."

"Yes, I'm quite well again, thank you." Her voice was polite, but her eyes were averted, fixed expectantly on his chair.

"My only regret is that I'm too late for the part of Prince Charming."

"Excuse me, Mr. Brink," Doris interrupted nervously; but a glance from Kate restrained her, and she relapsed into silence.

He looked at Kate, waited.

"Why Prince Charming?" The blood rose to her face from the effort to control her muscles.

"To kiss the Sleeping Beauty awake. You ask for it, Kate, you blush so prettily."

Her eyes gleamed, she pressed her hand to her mouth.

"Oh dear," Doris exclaimed. "I thought so."

The frayed canvas of his chair split beneath him with rending, jarring eructation. His rump sank through the hole, hung suspended, the wooden struts gripped him tightly by the hips. Doris sprang to her feet in dismay, grasped his arms to help him up, wrestled to extricate his trousers from the splintered frame. Kate sat watching, unable, no longer even trying to suppress her laughter.

"I'm sorry," she sobbed. "I can't help it, you look so funny."

Erect at last and free from encumberance, he glared at her: "You did that on purpose."

"How could I? You chose the chair yourself."

"You wouldn't listen," Doris protested. "I wanted to warn you it's unsafe."

He mastered his temper, laughed gruffly: "From the sublime to the ridiculous, from your accident to mine. I suppose I must forgive you, Kate, but I beg you to keep your sense of humour in check on Sunday, not to turn a mystery play into a farce."

"I'm not likely to, am I? There's nothing comic about the part I play."

"Of course not. It's allegorical, symbolic, a fairy story with esoteric meaning."

"That's just what I felt," Doris assured him, "when Kate was reciting her lines."

Kate's eyes mocked him: "Doris is a great admirer of your literary style."

"From which I gather that you yourself aren't."

146

"Perhaps I'll be more impressed by the action."

He glanced at her sharply; but he dropped his eyes, meeting hers.

"When are you coming for another rehearsal?" he asked. "You've only had one so far, and it's Thursday already."

"I'll spout the lines now if you like. We've quite a good audience."

He turned to look. A party of little girls stood congregated on the lawn, watching them.

"Does Mrs. Buttle allow them here in the garden?" He regarded them with disapproval.

"Why not? They're very good, and they'll love to see me making a fool of myself, even if the performance isn't up to the standard of yours when you sat through the chair."

"Oh, I don't think they saw that." Doris smiled at him soothingly: "They've just come."

"They saw everything," Kate retorted. "They were climbing in the beech tree."

He frowned: "In any case, I'm sure Doctor Buttle would blame me for overtiring you so soon after your ordeal. We'll make it tomorrow at the rectory."

"If you want to please Doctor Buttle you'll do without a Midsummer Goddess."

"Don't tell me you're crying off. Oh no, Kate, I don't believe it. A fall from a horse and a night out on the moor are nothing to a plucky girl like you. I'll let you off tomorrow, you can complete your recovery; but you must appear at the dress rehearsal on Saturday. No excuse can be accepted."

"I'll come to the dress rehearsal, I promise; but I may be rather late."

"Why should you be late? Don't tell me that fresh complications have arisen."

"Nothing serious. It's just that on Saturday afternoon I'm going over to Golstondale to collect Dinah and ride her back."

"That damned mare? Excuse my language, but I thought she'd fallen over a crag or something and broken her neck."

"She didn't even break a leg, though she well might have. She caught her foot in a hole and came down on top of me. It wasn't her fault. I'm sorry to disappoint you, Mr. Brink, but there's nothing wrong with Dinah. Mr. Alsyke at Rowantree Farm says she isn't lame at all, and he's looking after her till Saturday when I call for her."

147

"Can't she stay there a day or two longer?"

"No, she can't."

"It's important, this dress rehearsal, your first chance to meet and act with the rest of the cast."

"Yes, I know, and I don't intend to miss it; but it's quite a long ride from Glostondale. If I'm late you'll just have to wait for me."

"We can't start without you." He hesitated, frowning; but the eyes of the children staring at him, their muffled giggles and whispers disconcerted him. He took his leave and departed.

"Poor man." Doris spoke reproachfully: "You were very rude to him, Kate. I never thought you had it in you to behave like that."

"I never thought so myself till I met Mr. Brink."

"Why have you taken against him? He's quite fallen for you, that's plain enough. You ought to be flattered."

"You wouldn't be, Doris, if you knew what he wants to do."

"You don't mean?"

"No I don't. Something much more alarming."

Doris waited, sympathetic and curious, for further details, but none were forthcoming. She sighed, took off her spectacles and wiped them:

"I like him myself; he's such a character, so eccentric and amusing, much better company than other clergymen I've met, and at the same time I respect him for his learning. It's hard to believe any wrong of him."

"Yes, I felt like that at first."

"Do tell me, Kate, what the trouble is. Do let me help you. If you dislike him so much, why don't you refuse to act in his play?"

"I wish I could, but I can't."

"Why not?"

Kate did not reply, and Doris sat in silence, rebuffed.

Doctor Buttle came out of the house and crossed the lawn towards them: "Kate," he called, "you're wanted on the phone."

"Me?" She jumped to her feet in surprise.

"It's Jim, and before you take the call I'd better reveal what I've been keeping dark. This morning when he heard you were lost he insisted on going to look for you himself,

148

and the result was what anyone might have known, a nasty relapse."

She stared at him in dismay.

"It's all right," he assured her. "I can tell you now because it's over. When I saw him this afternoon he was recovering by leaps and bounds, thanks to an incomparable tonic."

"And a clever doctor."

"He owed the tonic to Doctor Kate."

"You mean, he owed his relapse to me."

"No, I mean the tonic, the news that you aren't lost after all. No drug in the pharmacopoeia could have acted more quickly."

She blushed: "He really is better?"

"He won't be for long if you keep him dawdling at the telephone. It's sure to be in some draughty passage."

She fled.

He turned to Doris: "What were you two girls doing to the parson just now? Practising judo?"

She laughed nervously: "It was an accident. He sat in the wonky chair, and it gave way; but he wasn't hurt."

"Except on the tenderest spot of all?"

"Oh no, Doctor Buttle, he didn't touch the ground."

"I meant, his dignity."

She laughed again, more to please him than from amusement.

He looked at his watch: "I must hurry, I'm late for my evening surgery."

Kate took the call on the extension in the common room. She was alone.

"Perfectly well, thank you," she replied into the receiver. "But what about you? Doctor Buttle's only just told me."

"Perfectly well, thank you." His voice teased her, and she laughed.

"It was stupid of you, Jim. You might have known I wasn't in the wood."

"It seemed only too likely when I heard Flossie's story."

"She said she wouldn't tell you till you were well."

"I am well, quite well enough to hear your story too. What sent you galloping off across the moor? I don't believe Dinah ran away and you couldn't stop her."

"I didn't want her to stop."

"Tell me what frightened you."

"Not now, it would take too long. Doctor Buttle said I wasn't to keep you in a draught."

"Damn Doctor Buttle."

"He's very wise."

"All right, if I can't have your story you shan't have mine, the important news I rang you up about."

"No, that's not fair. I'll tell you everything when we meet."

"Tomorrow?"

"I can't come to Kemsdale tomorrow. I'm a bad bargain for the school as it is, paid all day today for doing nothing."

"Stick to your work then. I'll leave mine to come to Easby."

"Oh no, Jim, I'm sure Doctor Buttle wouldn't approve."

"I'll travel in luxury as passenger, with Flossie at the wheel of the Land-Rover."

"Can Flossie drive?"

"She calls it driving, but she's more at home on the tractor. Anyhow, we'll come well armed with L-plates."

"I do think you ought to stay quiet."

"I do think you oughtn't to keep me here in a draught while you waste time with futile objections; but I'll forgive you, I'll tell you my news. I've just had Harry Bracken to see me. He's examined Brink's car, and he found an oily label in the boot, marked Snooker's Garage, Freeborough."

"Where did it come from?"

"Use your intelligence. From one of Albert's drums, of course. Goodbye, darling."

He rang off.

Chapter 8

Friday morning was heavily overcast. Clouds scudded, driven by a chill wind, and as Albert and Aidan climbed the church steps they looked down over the twin moles of the harbour on a steely-grey sea flecked with white horses, barely relieved in the distance by a shaft of light from a narrow patch of blue sky on the horizon. Albert shivered:

"If it's like this tomorrow night I've a good mind to pack up."

"You're joking?" Aidan glanced at him anxiously: "You wouldn't really let Mr. Brink down."

"It would bloody well serve him right if I did, the way he treats me."

"You're so touchy, Albert. He means no harm, it's only his fun."

"Poor fun for me. If he isn't sneering he's shouting at me, telling me off for something that doesn't suit him; but when it comes to any awkward job, any hint of danger, it's me he turns to. I get the kicks while his lordship sits cosy with his books."

"He needs to read a lot. We depend on his learning."

"What about my own? I'll soon know as much as he does."

"I'm sure you will, and I admire you for it, I do honestly: but Mr. Brink has more experience, and a single mistake can have dreadful results in an invocation of this sort."

"Don't I know." Albert nodded: "We're invoking power, and it's not to be trifled with. I hope you'll bear that in mind when the time comes, Aidan my boy."

"I've learnt all the words he taught me. I keep repeating them to myself in my head to make sure I haven't forgotten any."

"You need more than the right words, it's the right behaviour that matters. Nothing else can save you when power answers the call."

"What will happen when it does?" His voice quivered: "The others think this is just play, but I know it's the real thing, powerful magic. Can't you tell me what to expect?"

They were at the top of the steps. Albert paused, his eyes glittered through his spectacles:

"No, Aidan, I can't. If you read the old books you'd learn that it's forbidden to divulge the mysteries. You must do your part and ask no questions, lay the goddess on the altar, leave everything else to the adepts, Mr. Brink and me."

"The goddess? That girl we saw on Sunday at the rectory?"

"That's the wench. She's agreed, I thought she would."

"Do we really need a girl in the show at all?"

"We've cut out any others, haven't we, to please you?"

"You'd no choice. In mixed company we'd have to wear slips."

"Well, we've saved your modesty, Aidan. We'll be all boys together except for the goddess, and she'll be in no position to look."

"I'm glad to hear it. All the same, I wish we could have done without her. I know what girls are, they chatter. She'll be talking about it afterwards to all her friends."

Albert shook his head: "She'll say nothing."

They walked on past the church.

"Look, Aidan." Albert laid his hand on his arm: "You're not just one of the gang; you're an initiate, you play an important part in the rite. I chose you because I can see you've the right spirit, you're in earnest."

"I am, I certainly am. This means more to me than anything I've known. I've tried different sorts of religion, Plymouth Brethren, Jehovah's Witnesses, even the Catholics, but I got nothing out of it till I met Mr. Brink. He's opened my eyes, put me in touch with something big, something cosmic."

"You'll go far, my lad. You've the makings of an adept."

Aidan's lips parted rapturously: "You think so?"

"Your chance will come tomorrow night, you'll be put to the test. Remember that the first lesson is to have faith in the wisdom of the masters, your duty to obey, say nothing, hear nothing, see nothing while the Saviour receives the sacrament."

"The Saviour? You mean Mr. Brink?"

"Don't ask more than it's good for you to know. The name could be Albert Dockin."

Aidan stared at him in wonder, not daring to speak. They walked on in silence to the rectory.

Brink opened the door to them: "You got my message?" he asked.

Albert nodded: "I'm glad she's turned up. So the show goes ahead, I suppose?"

"It does, if we can avoid more blunders."

"Was it a blunder to get Tranmire so het up that he's back in bed out of our way, on the doctor's danger list?"

"I shouldn't be too sure of that. The roundsman who brought my groceries just now had been over earlier to Kemsdale, and he told me that Tranmire's up and about, seemingly little the worse."

"That doctor's too smart with his pills."

"The cure, if you ask me, owes more to an errant nymph." He smiled at their incomprehension: "The goddess who presides over our rites."

"I haven't your learning." Albert's tone was resentful: "But you find me useful, don't you? Very well, I'll try again. Third time lucky."

"No, you can leave him to me now. I've a plan of my own."

"Just as you please. I shan't be sorry."

Aidan stood listening, embarrassed and puzzled. Brink glanced at him sharply, spoke with forced geniality:

"I've more important work to occupy my trusted lieutenant. I depend on your help, Albert, for the success of the great rite." He led the way into the study, and they followed, Aidan reassured, Albert mollified.

"Sit down," Brink invited them. "We've much to discuss. I want you both to understand what's expected of you at the supreme moment, the mystery of mysteries, when the moon rises in the Devil's Churchyard."

"Not till moonrise?" Albert asked. "We'll have to wait quite a time. It's a waning moon, in the third quarter."

"So much the better. The place is haunted."

"By woman wailing for her demon lover?"

"Bravo, you're more at home with Coleridge than Ovid."

"He's a scholar," Aidan put in eagerly. "You should see his room where he lives, books everywhere."

"I'm no dunce," Albert agreed.

"No fool either, I hope." There was reproof in Brink's voice: "This is a rite that calls for humility. We invoke a power able to destroy as well as reward."

"I've explained that to Aidan. I've warned him to do what he's told whatever happens."

"Yes sir, and I'm well prepared," Aidan assured him. "I've got all the words by heart. I know how much depends on it."

"Good." Brink nodded: "Every formula must be word-perfect, that goes without saying; but the words themselves aren't enough unless they're reinforced by the spirit. We must worship not only with our lips but with all our being."

"Yes, sir." Aidan's face glowed with devotion.

"Listen, both of you." Brink glanced from one to the other: "I can't repeat this warning too solemnly. Those who officiate, the hierophants, you two and myself, expose our-

153

selves to appalling danger, as my predecessor, Amos Pounder, learnt to his cost. The force that will respond to our invocation is a devouring fire; our only shield is the holiness of our motives, without which nothing can save us from the everlasting flames. There's still time to withdraw if either of you shrinks from the ordeal."

"I'm not afraid," Albert declared.

"And you, Aidan?"

"I'll go on, sir. I'll do my best."

"Very well. Perhaps you'll both kneel and join me in a prayer for strength."

They rose, turned and knelt on the carpet with their heads bowed over their chairs. Brink stood, joined his hands and raised them; his voice thrilled with earnest supplication:

"Great Archangel—"

The loud peal of a bell interrupted him; he broke off angrily, strode to the window. Harry Bracken stood at the front door, already putting his finger to the bell-push to ring again. It was a bell with a penetrating note; the clangour jarred every nerve in the study.

"Quick," Brink exclaimed. "Skedaddle, before I let him in. Across the hall, through the kitchen and out by the back door."

Albert hesitated: "What about Mrs. Bracken?"

"She hasn't come yet. Make haste, scoot. Oh and, Albert." He drew him aside: "I'd like to see you later in the day, alone."

He waited till they were out of the hall, then opened the door to the policeman.

"Are you looking for your mother?" he asked. "She isn't here, it's too early."

"No, sir, Mum's at home, I know that. It's you I want to see if you can spare the time."

"I'm rather busy. I've a lot of work for the festival on Sunday. Is your business urgent?"

"Yes, sir, in a manner of speaking it is; but it won't take long if you'll be good enough to answer my questions."

"I will, in so far as I can." He stood fast in the doorway, leaving Harry to fidget with one foot on the step.

"It's just this, Mr. Brink. Were you anywhere out in your car on Sunday afternoon?"

"Of course not. As you know, it was Midsummer Day, and I was planning to revive some of the traditional customs

154

here in the rectory garden. The rain washed the programme out, and I've put it off till this coming Sunday; but I had to stay in the house all the same in case people came unaware."

"Had anyone permission to use the car without you?"

"I make it a rule never to lend my car. I don't want it smashed up."

Harry coughed, fumbled in his pocket, brought out a dirty piece of paper: "Do you know anything about this label?"

"Snooker's Garage, Freeborough. I know the place, I've had dealings there from time to time. What do you want me to say about your unsavoury exhibit? Claim it as a long lost treasure?"

"It's your property, Mr. Brink. It was found in the boot of your car."

"A lot of rubbish accumulates there, some of it years old, I'm afraid."

"This isn't so old. It's got the current year and month on the stamp."

"Very likely. I've been in Freeborough once or twice since the beginning of June."

"Buying oil in five-gallon drums?"

"Why shouldn't I buy in bulk, if it's more convenient?"

"There's no reason at all, sir, why you shouldn't; but as a matter of routine I'd like to check that it's your ordinary custom. Perhaps you'd be good enough to show me some of the empties."

"Look here, Harry, what are you getting at? Are you suggesting that I was the criminal who bought oil in Freeborough to smear on the road, so that Mr. Tranmire's car skidded into the quarry?"

"I'm only doing my duty, making inquiries."

"Perhaps I can help you then. You say that this label was found in my car. Someone, a police officer, I suppose, must have been rummaging there to come on it, which goes to show how easy it is for any Tom, Dick or Harry to gain access without my knowledge."

"It's true, it's not so hard." Harry was red in the face.

"Anyone might," Brink insisted. "These young people from the camping site, for instance. They come up here to see me, and I encourage it, I take my pastoral work seriously; but I can't always keep an eye on them. They're often messing about round my garage."

"You think one of them stole a trip in your car on Sunday to drive to Freeborough?"

"All I'm saying is it's not impossible, but it's more likely you're barking up the wrong tree."

He broke off, and both looked round as a car approached along the drive. It drew up, and Molly Corrington got out, carrying a brown-paper parcel under her arm. Pearl remained sitting at the wheel.

"Oh dear," Molly exclaimed. "Is anything wrong? Has there been a burglary, or something?"

Brink smiled at her: "You've a vivid imagination, Molly. You see a policeman, and your mind jumps to crime; but it's nothing sensational at all, merely that Harry suspects me of attempted murder and wonders if he oughtn't to arrest me."

"No, Mr. Brink." Harry spoke reproachfully: "You know that isn't correct."

"Of course it isn't, Harry," Molly assured him. "The rector likes to have his joke. It's just his way."

"Don't you worry, m'm." His tone was soothing but non-committal. He turned to Brink: "Well, I'll be going, sir, unless there's any more you've to say."

"That's all, Harry. You can follow up that tip of mine, if you like."

Harry did not reply; he raised his bicycle from the wall against which it rested, mounted and rode away.

"What is it?" Molly asked anxiously. "Why did he come?"

Brink laughed: "I wasn't romancing too much when I spoke just now. I told you there are mischief-makers doing their best to blacken my character."

"Surely Harry wouldn't believe them? He doesn't come to church as often as he should perhaps, but his father and mother are so regular."

"Things aren't what they were, Molly. Our ideas are out of date. Modern youth, I fear, has no proper respect for the cloth."

Pearl left the car and joined them: "What an age you're taking, Mother, just to give Mr. Brink a parcel."

"I can't help it, Pearl. There was Harry Bracken. I had to speak to him."

"Yes, I saw. Has he nothing to do all day but chatter?"

"Poor Harry. It must be a dull life, a country policeman's."

156

Brink smiled: "We shouldn't grudge him a mare's nest or two to liven things up."

Pearl shrugged her shoulders: "He thinks he's Sherlock Holmes since he pulled Jim out of the quarry."

"He saved Jim's life," her mother declared. "He deserves a medal." She turned to Brink: "Well, I mustn't keep Pearl waiting. She's meeting Leslie at the Angel, and she's anxious, I know, not to be late."

"I couldn't care less," Pearl retorted, "but I don't enjoy standing shivering here in this wind."

"Come indoors," Brink exclaimed. "Forgive me, my wits are wool-gathering, and my manners with them."

Molly glanced at Pearl, received a discouraging frown. She spoke regretfully: "I'm afraid we haven't time, Oswald. I only came to bring you this parcel; it's not to be opened till tomorrow, your birthday."

He took it in surprise: "My birthday. How did you know?"

"Don't you remember the little picture you gave me on Saturday in the vestry, the green man, and what was written on the back? You don't suppose I haven't kept it?"

"Molly, I'm really touched; you're too sweet for words." He slipped his arm through hers: "No, I'll take no refusal, I insist; I'm going to open my present at once under the eyes of my fairy godmother."

She accompanied him into the house without reluctance. Pearl followed with an air of disapproval.

"In any case," he added in the hall, "I owe you a cup of coffee. I'll see if Mrs. Bracken's arrived yet. If not I'll make it myself." He passed on into the kitchen: "Ah, Mrs. Bracken, just the right minute. As soon as you've taken off your coat and hat I want coffee made. I've two visitors, Mrs. and Miss Corrington."

Pearl and her mother waited in the study.

"Phew," Pearl gasped. "It reeks of cigarette smoke, like a railway carriage full of workmen."

"Perhaps he's had company. Your father's study used to smell like this when his racing friends came to see him."

"If you thought more what Father was like you wouldn't be in such a hurry to replace him. I don't want to be disagreeable, Mother, but it's outrageous the way you make up to Mr. Brink. I'm only thankful this morning that I'm here to chaperone you."

"Don't be silly, Pearl. At my age."

"There's no fool like an old fool."

"I'd rather age made me foolish than turned me sour."

Brink joined them, looking put out: "I'm sorry to have been so long. I wanted a word or two with her about Harry."

"To tell her he'd been?" Molly asked.

"She knew already. She met him on her way here." His frown betrayed disquiet, but he pulled himself together, spoke cheerfully: "Anyhow she'll have coffee for us in a few minutes, and meanwhile I'm looking forward to my birthday treat, to unwrap the mystery." The parcel was still in his hand; he laid it on the table on top of the papers, fumbled with the string to unknot it.

Molly approached, unable to restrain her eagerness: "Shall I help? I've nimble fingers."

"No, we'll follow the example set by Alexander the Great." He reached for a knife lying on the chimney piece; it had a long blade tapering to a fine point, the handle was of bronze, chased with intricate emblems.

"What an odd knife," she exclaimed. "Is it very old and valuable?"

"Yes, it came from the East. It was a priest's knife used in sacrificial rites."

The blade, razor-sharp, cut the string through like butter. He replaced it on the shelf beside his pipe.

Molly had already lost interest in it. All her attention was occupied in watching him as he removed the brown paper, laid bare a cardboard box and lifted the lid. A dressing gown was revealed of crimson silk; he took it out and held it up. The colour was so bright that it dazzled; the cuffs and collar, in irreconcilable conflict, were of an equally garish pea-green.

"It was my last present for Ernest." she explained tearfully. "He never wore it, he died on his birthday before night."

"Whereas I fully intend to survive over mine." He patted her hand comfortingly: "It's a magnificent garment, Molly, but I can't deprive you of a relic so precious to you, associated so poignantly with your husband."

"I'd much rather associate it with you, I would really. Look, it's yours already." She showed him the breast pocket on which an emblem was embroidered in green, not the green of cuffs and collar but a hue nearer that of boiled

158

sweets. "Don't you recognise it?" she asked. "The green man."

He examined it: "Is this your own work?" The likeness was crude, but not incompetent.

"Yes, I copied it from your little picture. You told me the green man was a favourite of yours. You will wear it, won't you, Oswald?"

"I will indeed. To show my appreciation I'll wear it as my robe of honour at the midsummer festival."

"At the play on Sunday, you mean?"

"It deserves an even more solemn occasion."

Pearl, left superfluous, was wandering round the book-shelves, taking out volumes and glancing at them without much interest. Suddenly she turned with a book in her hand, raised her voice in surprise:

"Why, this is the book Doctor Buttle asked me to give Kate. I didn't know it was yours, Mr. Brink." She held it out for him to see, *The Godless Life and Diabolic Death of the Reverend Amos Pounder*.

He seized it from her abruptly: "Of course it's my book. What has Doctor Buttle to do with it?"

"I've told you. He sent me with it to Saint Ursula's, as if I'd nothing better to do than carry messages to Kate Evans. He did, didn't he, Mother?"

"That book?" She peered at it: "Yes, I remember it well. There's a portrait inside that reminds me so oddly of you, Oswald."

He opened it, stared at the frontispiece: "You see a like-ness, do you? I'm not sure that I'm flattered, but you're probably right." He closed the book with a snap: "At the moment I'm more interested in the puzzle how it ever got into Doctor Buttle's hands."

"There's no puzzle at all," Pearl replied. "He got it from Jim when he was at Kemsdale after the accident."

"From Tranmire, to give to Kate? She received it, did she?"

"I gave it to her myself. Why the fuss? You've got it back again."

"Or perhaps it was another copy of the same book," her mother suggested.

"Yes, Molly." He nodded: "With your usual commonsense you've solved the mystery. It's a rare book, but I believe there was a copy at Easby Hall in the old days, and it prob-ably went to Kemsdale."

159

"So you're making a fuss about nothing," Pearl declared. "You've got your copy, Kate hers."

"Not exactly about nothing. When did you give it her?"

"Monday morning. I went straight to Saint Ursula's after seeing Doctor Buttle."

"Yet when Kate was here on Monday afternoon she saw this book lying about and picked it up and talked as if it were entirely new to her."

"She'd probably forgotten," Molly declared. "I don't suppose she even looked at it when Pearl gave it to her. It's not the sort of book to interest a girl."

Mrs. Bracken's arrival with the coffee saved him from the need to reply.

"Good morning, Mrs. Bracken," Molly greeted her. "I saw Harry just now. He seems very busy."

"There's always work for them in the force, m'm, and Harry isn't one to neglect his duty."

"I'm sure he isn't, he's a credit to the police. Everyone's full of his praises in Easby for his courage after Mr. Tranmire's accident."

"If it was an accident." Mrs. Bracken's mouth set firmly.

"Yes, I heard something about oil on the road, and that someone put it there on purpose. It's hard to believe anyone could be so wicked."

"There's more wickedness in the world than you'd guess. Those in Harry's position have reason to know."

"All the same," Brink put in, "we needn't look for evil where an innocent explanation would suffice."

"That's not Harry's way at all, sir; but he sees what stares him in the face, and Mr. Tranmire himself says he's right."

"Is Mr. Tranmire well enough to be consulted? I was told he'd had a relapse."

"He was taken bad yesterday when he went to look for the young lady; but she's turned up, it seems, and he's picked up wonderful. Harry was with him earlier this morning and found him quite himself, up and about on the farm."

"I'm so glad," Molly exclaimed.

Pearl nodded: "I must go and see him. He needs cheering up, I expect. Don't you think so, Mrs. Bracken?"

"I'm sure I couldn't say, miss." She left the room.

Brink waited till the door shut behind her, then he addressed Pearl: "If you want to do him a good turn, ask him out to dinner tomorrow evening."

"Why then, more than any other time?"

He smiled at her: "Saturday night, the traditional scene for courtship."

"You're teasing her," Molly exclaimed. "You've a better reason that that, I know."

"Wheels within wheels, there always are." He stood up abruptly, removed his coat: "Now I'm going to try on my dressing gown." He took it from the table, draped himself in crimson finery.

Molly stared, enraptured: "Oh, Oswald, how it suits you. It makes you look so romantic, like a high priest out of the Bible."

"Not a priest of Astarte, I hope?"

"Of course not. She sounds improper."

"Come on, Mother," Pearl interrupted. "The whole morning will be gone by the time you two have done talking about all the tarts in the Bible."

Brink nodded: "A fascinating subject, but one of inordinate length, and meanwhile Leslie Potts is kicking his heels in the Angel."

"Him? I've more important things to think about."

"Preparations for tomorrow night?"

She did not reply, but her expression was not displeased.

Molly finished her cup and rose: "We're keeping you from your work too, Oswald. I never meant to stay so long."

"For me it's been time well spent, not only for this magnificent birthday present but also for the interest of your conversation."

"You're making fun of me."

"Honestly, I'm not. You've added to my knowledge."

Pearl drove her mother home.

"You don't want to come to the Angel to see Leslie?"

"No, dear. I'd only be in the way."

"You'll have plenty to do in the house if we're giving this dinner party for Jim tomorrow."

"It's to be a party, is it?"

"Yes, four of us. We'll need another man. I might ask Leslie to make up for keeping him waiting so long."

"Poor man. Is he expecting you to coffee?"

"He was, but it's too late now, and I don't want any more. It'll have to be lunch instead."

"Well, he knows his own business best, but I'd have thought

161

a young man like that would be better employed in his office than dawdling all the morning in a hotel lounge."

"He does what he pleases. His father's senior partner, and he'll make Leslie his heir."

"Then Leslie should take more interest in the firm."

"He's interested in nothing but cars. He hasn't any brains, but when his father dies he'll be worth several hundred thousand."

Her mother sighed: "Wealth isn't everything, dear."

"I know it isn't. Class means a lot more. I'll throw Leslie over without a tear if Jim comes up to scratch."

Having put her mother down at the door, she turned the car to drive to the Angel. It was midday, and the centre of the town heavily congested with traffic. As she passed the turning leading to the bridge a Land-Rover emerged from it. The lights were in her favour, and she kept on; so too did the other driver. Neither vehicle was moving very fast, no one was hurt; but the glossy nearside wing of her car crumpled under the impact.

"You're a public danger," she shouted. "Do you never pay attention to the traffic lights?" She sprang out into the road, stared in disgust at the damage, then at the offender: "Good Lord, it's Flossie. No wonder."

She was too full of her grievance to observe that the Land-Rover had a passenger till Jim stood beside her. His face wore an apologetic grin, his hand groped beneath the rucked metal.

"It doesn't look very elegant, Pearl, but it's clear of the wheel, I think. Wait a sec while Flossie and I bend it straight."

"I didn't see you were there, Jim." She smiled frostily: "Really Flossie isn't fit to be in charge of a car."

"She means well. Don't you, Flossie? Come on, help me to fettle this."

They grasped the wing, Flossie with a vigour that nearly wrenched it off altogether; then when the wheel had sufficient clearance they pushed the car up against the pavement, so that traffic was able to flow again. Harry Bracken, arriving to sort out the confusion, came across to them.

"Hullo," Jim greeted him: "Another accident for you, Harry; but this time we're aggressors, not victims."

"No personal injuries, are there, sir?" He took out his notebook.

"Not as far as we're concerned. What about you, Pearl?"

"Injuries?" She turned to Harry, pointed to the mangled metalwork: "Isn't that enough for you? A new car too."

"That's not personal injury, miss," he explained patiently. "Where there's nothing more serious than damage to vehicles it's in order for the parties to exchange addresses. You know Mr. Tranmire's address, and he knows yours, so that's all there is to it."

"All indeed?" Pearl exclaimed. "It's your duty to bring Flossie into court for dangerous driving."

Flossie's eyes filled with tears: "No, Harry, I did my best, I couldn't stop. I pressed my foot down right hard. Didn't I, Mr. Tranmire?"

He smiled: "You did, but on the wrong pedal. I'm sorry, Pearl, it was entirely our fault, we haven't a leg to stand on. It'll save your no-claim bonus if the insurance isn't involved. Have the car put right and send me the bill."

"Thank you, Jim. I don't blame you at all; but I do think Flossie should be punished, to teach her a lesson. You hear me, Harry?"

"Yes, miss, and I heard Mr. Tranmire too. I'll report when I get back to the station that compensation's been offered." He went up to Jim, lowered his voice: "I'd a word with him just now, sir. He thinks it might have been one of those types at the camp, who took his car without permission."

"Albert Dockin?"

"As like as not."

"I thought they were hand in glove."

"What's this?" Pearl demanded. "What are you whispering about? I've as much right as anyone to know. I suppose I'll be called as a witness."

"It's all right, miss. You won't be troubled." Harry replaced his notebook and buttoned the pocket.

Flossie giggled as he walked away: "He'd have had words at home if he'd put me into court. Maggie's a good wife to him; but she stands up for her own, and her brother Ron's my boy. She knows he's sweet on me."

"What's the use of police at all," Pearl complained, "if they're as slack as Harry Bracken."

"There was nothing slack about Harry on Sunday night," Jim reminded her.

She suppressed her ill-humour, put on a sympathetic smile: "No, of course we're all tremendously grateful to him

163

for the way he behaved then. It's odd, Jim, I was just saying to Mother that I wondered how you're getting on. I meant to drive over to Kemsdale this afternoon to ask."

"Instead of which, the invalid himself bumps into you."

"I'm sure you oughtn't to be going about so soon. You were too ill to see anyone at all when I called on Wednesday. So Flossie told me."

Flossie met her eyes unabashed: "Those were Doctor Buttle's orders. No visitors."

"Except for a nurse? Is it usual for them to arrive on horseback?"

"There's nothing more boring than illness," Jim put in quickly. "Do let's choose a more cheerful subject."

"Yes, I'm sure you need cheering up." She seized eagerly on the phrase: Mother suggested I should ask you to dinner tomorrow."

"Tomorrow?" He hesitated.

"Don't tell me you've doctor's orders to stay at home."

He laughed: "If I have you see how well I obey them."

"So we can really expect you, can we? There was a muddle, if you remember, last time."

"So there was. You sent me the wrong letter, something about a sore arm."

"It doesn't matter. I've forgiven you."

"You're being very magnanimous, especially when I've just made a hideous dent in your car." He stooped, examined the wheels again: "I hope it hasn't affected the steering. Where are you going? Can't we give you a lift?"

"Yes, I'm going to the Angel to have lunch with Leslie Potts. Why don't you join us?"

He shook his head: "I'm afraid I can't take you myself, I've too much to do in the town; but the Land-Rover's at your service, Flossie can drive you."

"Flossie? Thank you, I'll go in my own car, whatever the steering's like."

"As a matter of fact, I'm pretty sure it's all right."

He opened the door, she got in and started the engine: "See you," she called, "tomorrow evening at eight."

The car moved smoothly away under unimpaired control, damaged only in dignity.

Flossie stared after it with her hands in the pockets of her jeans: "They won't half look down their noses, those toffs at the Angel, when they see what a bash she's taken."

164

"It's all very well to jeer, you ought to be whacked."
His voice belied the threat, and she grinned:

"I didn't mean to do it, but if it had to be I chose the right one."

"Well, don't choose any more victims if I leave you now to find a parking place by yourself. We're unpopular here." It was a busy crossroads, the parked Land-Rover provoked angry comments.

"There'd be room for us among the waggons in the goods yard."*

"Yes, and Ron works there, doesn't he?"

She had the grace to blush: "It's his dinner hour, he'll be hanging about."

"Perfect, and it isn't far. You can make the journey in a low gear to be safe. I'll pick the old bus up there when I want it. I've an errand in the early afternoon."

"Will you want me to drive you, sir?"

"Thank you, Flossie, I'm so much recovered I think I'll drive myself. I'll leave you to entertain Ron till I get back."

"He'll be called to work at the stroke of one, but if he knows I'm around he won't be all that tied to the job."

Jim had business at an agricultural emporium, then at the bank, and a visit to pay at the local office of the farmer's union. Feeling hungry, he peeped in at a restaurant; but it was packed with tourists queuing for tables, driven from the beach cafés into the town by a grey sky and cold wind. He withdrew, walked on down to the harbour to a small public-house, the Merry Mermaid, where he lunched on bread and cheese and beer in the bar-parlour. He finished his meal, and with a glance at his watch he strode briskly to the railway station, found the Land-Rover without difficulty in the goods yard. A squeal, muffled giggles from behind a pile of timber hinted at Flossie's employment. He was careful not to investigate.

When he drove up to Saint Ursula's there were children playing round the buildings, running races on the lawn. He congratulated himself on his timing. Lunch was over, the afternoon classes had not yet begun. The teachers were still in the common room.

Kate saw him from the window. Her eyes had in fact

---

* Freight siding.

been fixed on it ever since she came upstairs. She ran down to join him in the drive.

"Oh, how nice," she exclaimed. "You're looking so much better."

"You don't look like fading away yourself."

"I'm not; my accident was nothing, not like yours."

"I refuse to argue which of us is star invalid. I warn you, Kate, that illness is a forbidden subject, I'm sick of it."

"Yes, but where's Flossie? You promised you'd bring her to drive you."

"She drove me from the farm to the town. My nerves for the moment are enjoying a well-earned rest."

"I thought she'd be such a steady driver."

"A steady twenty miles an hour on the open road. The spurts were reserved for heavy traffic when she mistook the accelerator for the brake."

"It's easy to make mistakes when you're flustered." She glanced at the Land-Rover: "Anyhow you've arrived intact."

"The dinosaur usually does when anything gets in its way. Ask Pearl."

"Pearl Corrington? What happened?"

"Flossie butted her nearside wing, and what's left would disgrace a scrap heap."

"Was she very cross?"

"She wasn't too pleased. Harry Bracken came up, and she wanted Flossie charged."

"Poor Flossie. He won't, will he?"

"Harry and I understand each other, and in any case Ron Smith, his brother-in-law, seems to have fallen for Flossie's charms. So she gets off all right, it's I who am punished. I couldn't in decency refuse when Pearl asked me to dinner tomorrow night."

"It was nice of her, wasn't it, after your running into her car?"

"Yes, Kate, it was very nice of her, and I'm an ungrateful brute. All the same, I'd love to ring her up and say I forgot I'd already asked you to dine with me, so I can't come."

She shook her head: "It would be horribly rude, and anyhow I can't. I'll be rehearsing at the rectory, and it's the dress rehearsal, the important one."

"That damned play. You haven't forgotten our compact, Kate?"

"I'm not likely to, not after reading about Bess Atkins; but I must at least attend the dress rehearsal. There can't be any danger there, and it's my great chance to meet the rest of the gang and find out what they're up to."

"I'd like a answer to some questions myself," he agreed, "especially whether Brink and Albert are working quite as smoothly as we thought in double harness. I told you, didn't I, that Harry found a label off one of those oil drums in Brink's car? Well, he went to see Brink, and this morning in the middle of Flossie's drama he told me the result. He couldn't say much because Pearl was there; but I gather that Brink wants to lay the blame on Albert, who took the car, he says, without his knowledge."

"I can believe anything of Albert."

"So can I, except when it cleans the slate for Brink. It wasn't Albert we saw in the Devil's Churchyard on Saturday afternoon."

"Or whom Flossie and I saw there on Wednesday evening. He was wearing a goat's mask again, but he spared us nothing else. I don't generally think what a clergyman would look like naked; but I did then, there couldn't be any doubt."

"A clerical Apollo Belvedere?"

"Apollo with a paunch."

He grinned: "Flossie described it when she told me of your adventure."

"Has she guessed who the man was?"

"No, she's coming to believe it was the Devil after all, and by the time she's finished spreading the story there'll be few people bold enough to go near the place."

"They might if they're dared to."

"I doubt it, not even the most sophisticated. Tradition sinks in deep, especially with a character behind it like Parson Amos."

She shuddered: "It wouldn't be surprising if something evil lived on in the wood after the dreadful things he did there. Dinah certainly thought so, and I did too."

"Was that why you went galloping over the moor? You haven't told me the reason yet."

"Dinah suddenly shied and jumped the wall. Perhaps there was nothing more to it, horses can be easily frightened."

"Is Dinah the sort to be?"

"No, she isn't, she's sensible, and if there was nothing to be afraid of I'm as much to blame myself. I know there was something behind us, Jim, something evil chasing us, and if Dinah hadn't flown like the wind we'd have been caught; but then she stumbled in a hole and came down, and after that I was sprawling on my face and the evil was leaning right over me. At least I thought so, but it was probably a dream. I hit my head against something hard that knocked me out."

"You must have lain there for hours before the shepherd found you."

"Centuries it seemed, and most of the time I wasn't on the moor at all, I was Bess Atkins lying on the altar in the Devil's Churchyard, and the portrait of Parson Amos came to life and stepped out of the book with a knife in his hand, and I waited for him to drink my blood. Then suddenly I was back on the hill again, terribly cold but safe, and I could hear Dinah munching in the heather. It was an enormous relief while it lasted, but I knew Parson Amos would soon be ready for another attempt."

"There's someone who's going to pay for this, someone more substantial than a ghost."

"If you mean Mr. Brink the police can't arrest him for what he did to me in my nightmare. It's over, and I'm all right, and Dinah's safe at Rowantree Farm. I'm going there tomorrow afternoon to fetch her and ride her back. It won't hurt them to wait if it makes me late for rehearsal at the rectory."

"How will you get to Golstondale?"

"Doris is lending me her bike. I'm afraid I can't bring it home with me on Dinah; but I'll ask the Alsyke boy to ride it one evening as far as the signpost, and I'll walk there and pick it up."

"You'll do nothing of the sort. You'll drive over tomorrow in the Land-Rover."

"With Flossie as chauffeur?"

"No, with me, and I warn you, Kate, if you tell me I'm too much of an invalid I'll lift up the back of that miniskirt, take down your pants and spank you in front of the school."

The bell clanged, summoning the children to work.

"Gosh," she exclaimed. "I've left their exercise books in the common room." She raised her fingers to her lips, blew him a kiss, raced off across the lawn."

"Tomorrow after lunch," he called.

She looked back over her shoulder: "Invalid, invalid, you hear me, I dare you to try."

She vanished into the house.

He drove the Land-Rover back to the goods yard to find Flossie. As she was nowhere to be seen he parked it between two cattle waggons, sat in it smoking a cigarette. The vehicles on either side engulfed his own, hid it from view. Neither Brink nor Albert was aware of his presence as they paused there, following the short cut that led beside the railway to the camping field. They spoke in tones clearly audible, believing that they had the place to themselves.

"So it's settled," Brink was saying. "You leave it to Aidan."

"Don't you trust me?" Albert's voice was sulky.

"You've only your own carelessness to blame. You're a bad risk, the police have their eyes on you."

"Was that what the busy told you?"

"In so many words."

"You aren't trying to pull a fast one, are you, leave me to carry the can, while the reverend marches off without a stain on his character?"

"Don't be a fool, Albert. When we celebrate the great rite your part will be second only to mine. We've both much to gain from its success, and I rely on you not to hinder it. There are difficulties enough without your tantrums."

"The police, you mean? They can't make much of a case out of an old label."

"I don't mean only the police. You know that book I showed you, the report on the life of Parson Amos? Well, it seems that Kate Evans has a copy, it's been in her hands since Monday."

"Monday? She was at the rectory with us that afternoon, and she picked the book up, if you remember, as innocent as you please."

"That's why I'm sure she suspects us. Otherwise she'd have said she'd seen it before."

"The sly bitch. It'll serve her right to come to a sticky end."

"Yes, there's justice in her fate, and it relieves me of scruples. She was abominably rude yesterday when I paid a call."

"What did she do?"

"I know what I'd like to do to her."

"There'll be nothing to stop you." He smacked his lips.

169

"An enticing prospect, Albert, for all of us but herself. It puzzles me what makes her so cheeky."

"Does she think she can doublecross us?"

"She won't find it too easy. There's an important piece of information hidden even from clever Miss Kate."

"Zero hour?"

"Exactly. She hasn't guessed it. She'll walk into the trap."

"I'll bait it for her nicely if you'll give me the job. Do let me, Mr. Brink. I've a knack, I've proved it, haven't I, for leading her up the garden path."

"Leading her out of the picture."

"What do you mean?"

"Never mind. I don't want to go into all that again. We've decided that Aidan fits the part better than you."

"Because I'm wanted by the police?"

"Yes, but also because she knows you. Aidan's a stranger."

"He's a mixed-up kid, I warn you, a bit of a Holy Willie under the skin. You won't get him helping anyone to take a header over a cliff."

"I don't want him to. I leave that sort of thing to the expert, Albert Dockin."

"So I still have my uses, have I?"

"Of course you have, and Aidan has his too. We'll go on to the camp, and I'll have a talk to him."

"You can have it at once, if you like. There he is, isn't he, coming along the street? It looks the way he walks, arms swinging like a serjeant major."

The man at whom he pointed was still some way off outside the station grounds. As he reached the entrance he turned in.

"Yes," Brink agreed. "It's Aidan all right, and it seems he's making for the footpath. I'll catch him on the way."

"Do you want me too?"

"No, thank you." He strode off across the yard to meet Aidan as he approached. Albert hesitated, then turned in the other direction, took the path beside the railway to the camp.

Jim heard every word of the conversation, and he had a good view of them in the driving mirror as they stood talking; but when they moved away both were hidden by the vehicles hemming him in. He stepped to the ground, peered out cautiously from behind a cattle waggon, saw Brink cross-

170

ing a metalled track but no one else. There were too many obstacles blocking the line of vision.

Then Brink himself passed out of sight behind a shed. Jim darted across to a neighbouring woodpile, but the change of position brought no reward. He was about to return frustrated to the Land-Rover when Flossie arrived, panting and contrite:

"I'm sorry, sir. I never thought it that late. I couldn't believe it when Ron told me the time by his watch."

He smiled: "Time flies in the goods yard. Were you helping Ron to load a truck?"

"I'd have better than let him court me on a heap of lime."

"Lime?"

"I didn't see it there till I sat up, and it was all over my pants."

He stared at her. The khaki jeans in which she set out were replaced by a man's navy-blue trousers, many sizes too small for her.

"Ron said he'd a clean pair," she explained pointing to the shed behind which Brink had vanished. "The men keep their things there, if they want to change after work. So we went in, and Ron found me these. Slacks he calls them." She clasped her hips and surveyed her legs doubtfully.

Jim grinned: "If those are slacks I'd like to know what you call tights."

"They took a bit of getting into," she admitted. "I made Ron wait outside, but I was such a time he would have it at last he must come in and help. No you don't, says I. What would folks think if they found us? But it was no use, you can't argue with Ron, and there he was in the shed with me when I heard someone coming, and I put my eye to the keyhole and it was the parson. We dursen't scarce breathe."

"How long ago was this?"

"Not above a minute gone. I waited for parson and his pal to move on, then I scooted."

"There was someone with him, was there? Could you see who it was?"

"Yes, the same chap who was in the pasture field yesterday morning, just when we were all flustered about the lass, the young lady, I mean, on the mare. I've never seen him before or since, but I couldn't forget him."

"Can you describe him?"

"Yes, all of a twitter, couldn't look a girl in the face if he was paid for it."

"You don't help me much. Do you know his name?"

"Parson called him Aidan."

They approached the Land-Rover. "Do you want me to drive, sir?" she asked.

"No, thank you, Flossie. You'll need all your attention to sit down without disaster in Ron's slacks."

She took the passenger's seat without demur and with appropriate caution.

As he backed out into the yard and drove off, threading his way through the litter, he glanced keenly from side to side; but he saw no one till, near the exit, Flossie leant out and waved cheerfully.

"Who was that?" he asked.

"Ron."

"Oh, of course. No sign of Aidan?"

"You wouldn't catch me waving to the likes of him."

"No, that would be too much to ask; but I want you to keep an eye out for him, and if you see him on the farm you can point him out to me. You understand, Flossie?"

"I do, sir. I doubt he's up to no good."

Chapter 9

Jim came out early before breakfast on Saturday morning for a walk round the fields where the sheep grazed. It was his custom at this time of year when the lambs were young, but since his accident the task had been deputed to Flossie. He resumed it with satisfaction, thankful to be his own man again, able to enjoy the freedom of health.

As he passed the open door of the byre Flossie's voice rose above the rattle of milk into the pail.

"Mind, Harry, don't you forget. You can tell Ron I'll be alone here."

Harry's reply, deeper in tone, was inaudible, but it provoked her to a shrill peal of laughter:

"Get along with you. He'll find me working, he can lend a hand."

"One of these days, my lass, you'll find yourself in the dock, charged with dangerous driving. Twelve months hard you'll get, and no boys to gallivant with."

Jim looked in. Flossie sat milking, while the policeman leant against the rudstake at the cow's head, grinning at his own wit. When he saw Jim he came to the door:

"Good-morning, sir. I'm going on duty. I thought I'd look in."

"Quite right. I want to see you."

"They walked across the yard out of earshot of Alf Torgill and the lad, his nephew, who were fuelling the tractor.

Harry sniffed the air: "This summer can't make up its mind, cold enough to starve a man yesterday, and today we'll be sweating in shirt sleeves."

They leant over the gate, looking down the valley to the gorge where the river entered the hills, flanked by open moor on one side, on the other by the summer-green foliage of the wood. The sun peering over the trees rose through gilded flakes of cloud; haze shrouded the watercourse, the fields glistened with dew.

"Yes, it'll turn into a scorcher," Jim agreed.

"If it holds up tomorrow it'll suit the parson. He'll get in his show after all, the one the rain washed out Sunday last."

"I want to talk about that, Harry, but first you can tell me a bit more of your interivew with him yesterday. We hadn't much chance when we met; the corner of Bridge Street isn't the best spot for a conference in the middle of the morning, with Flossie making chaos of the traffic."

"There was Miss Corrington too, sir. I didn't like to say much in front of her."

"You were right; it's better not. What's this about the rector trying to lay the blame on Albert?"

"If I understood rightly his case is that Albert took the car without his permission or knowledge and did the job on his own. It could be the truth."

Jim shook his head: "It isn't, I've reason to know."

"Is it best then I let Albert be?"

"No, Harry, keep on at him, chivvy him. He's up to the neck in it all right, even if he isn't the mastermind."

"There's an idea I've had. I could ask someone at the garage to take a look at him, see if he identifies him."

"How do you propose to get Albert to Freeborough?"

"There's no need. They're a good sort at the garage, willing to help. If I show them how matters lie they'll send a van over to Easby driven by one of those who were on duty Sunday afternoon."

"Yes, it's a bright idea, if you know where to find Albert when the driver comes."

"We'll find him, never fear. I've had my eye on him, and I know his haunts."

"How soon can you do this? Before tomorrow?"

"I'll get the garage on the phone as soon as I'm at the station. If they can spare the man they'll send him this morning."

Jim hesitated: "You wonder perhaps why I'm in such a hurry about it?"

"You've reason, sir. He tried to kill you, and he'll try again unless we stop him."

"Yes, but there's more to it than that. I'm as sure as can be there's dirty work planned for tomorrow threatening other lives, not just my own. I've no evidence yet that carries weight, but I ask you to take my word for it."

"That I do, sir. I know you aren't one for fancies. This Albert's mixed up in it, is he?"

"I'll be happier if he's out of the way tomorrow, where he can do no harm."

"You don't mean we should arrest him?"

"Why not, if the garage man recognises him?"

"I'd need a warrant."

"Well, I'm on the bench, I can sign it."

"That's so." His tone however was doubtful: "I'll have to talk to the serjeant and see what he says."

"Yes, talk to him and try to persuade him; but the first thing is to make sure we've got Albert identified."

"I'll tell the garage it's urgent. I'll do my best."

"I'm sure you will, and I'll be in Easby myself in the early afternoon. I'll look in at the station to hear the news and sign the warrant, if need be."

"Very good, sir. I'll inform Serjeant Cleaver." He took his

174

arms from the gate, raised himself to move away, but Jim recalled him:

"There's another thing, Harry. I want a close eye kept on Mr. Brink, especially tomorrow during his midsummer jollities."

"The rector?" he asked nervously. "You don't want him arrested too?"

"Not at this stage. Don't be alarmed, we'll take our fences as they come." He himself was still leaning on the gate, staring down the valley. He pointed to the wood: "What a picture it makes, all in leaf."

"Yes, it's bonny in summer."

"Too bonny to believe any ill of."

"Have you been losing more lambs, sir?"

"I wasn't thinking only of sheep-stealing. There are worse goings-on, if Flossie's right."

"There's nothing she likes better, that Flossie, than wagging her tongue, and she's got a lot of folks scared; but I wouldn't put it past her to be making a good part up."

"Miss Evans was with her at the time."

"Does the young lady confirm what Flossie says?"

"I'll know better this afternoon. I'm driving her over to Golstondale to pick up her mare."

"I was real glad, sir, the serjeant found her safe there. It would have been a sad day if anything had happened to her."

"I couldn't agree with you more." He opened the gate and passed through: "So long, Harry. Keep your nose to the scent."

Harry retrieved his bicycle from the yard, wheeled it up the hill on to the moor; then he mounted, pedalled vigorously till he reached the brow of the long incline into Easby, down which he plunged at a speed that overtook even some of the motorists. When he dismounted at the police station he glanced at his watch, noted with pride that he had beaten his own record over the course.

Having reported to the serjeant, he put a call through to Snooker's Garage at Freeborough. He was in luck; a van was about to set off for Easby to collect a consignment of tyres from the local agent. It was agreed to choose a driver who was on duty on Sunday afternoon and had served the mysterious customer with drums of oil.

Brink rose late. He had a long day ahead of him and was

anxious to be fit and well-rested, at his best for the great event. He made coffee, boiled two eggs, went on to eat a hearty breakfast; then leaving the remains for Mrs. Bracken to clear when she came, he retired to his study, sank on his knees for a few minutes in prayer, rose and took down two books from the shelf, the life of Amos Pounder and the little vellum-covered notebook. He sat poring over them, raising his eyes from time to time to stare abstractedly across the room. At last he drew up a chair to the desk, reached for some sheets of foolscap, wrote slowly and carefully. The document bore the heading, *Evidence to be given at the inquest on Kate Evans*:

"By Oswald Brink—I expected the deceased at the rectory on Saturday evening for the dress rehearsal of the midsummer play to be given the following day. She had warned me she might be late as she was fetching a horse from Golstondale in the afternoon, so I was not surprised at first when she failed to appear. The rest of the cast assembled, and we waited for her. At ten as she was still missing I became anxious and rang up Saint Ursula's School where she worked. I was told that she had sent a message by a stranger she met on the way; it was to say that the horse was lame, and she was leading it home and would not be back till dark. The cast left, unwilling to wait any longer, but I stayed up for her an hour or so in case she arrived after all. Then as there was no sign of her I assumed she was too tired to think of it and had gone straight to bed. I went to bed myself."

"By Aidan Clegg—I was cycling on a path across the moor on Saturday afternoon when I met a girl leading a horse. I did not know at the time who she was; but I can identify her now as the deceased, whose body I have been shown in the mortuary. She told me that the horse was lame, and she was afraid that her people would be anxious about her because she would not be home till dark. I offered to carry a message, and she directed me to Saint Ursula's School. I rode off there at once."

"Further statement, if needed, by Oswald Brink—I have been shown the wounds and other marks on the body of the deceased, and it is my opinion founded on a study of religious aberration that they were inflicted in the course of the ritual of the Black Mass. For some time I have suspected the presence of a coven indulging in practices of this sort in Kemsdale Wood, but I had insufficient evidence on which to lay information. I believe that the leader of the coven is Albert Dockin, a man already wanted by the police on a criminal charge. I have had some slight acquaintance with this Dockin, and from hints that he dropped it is likely that the deceased was his chosen victim."

He put down his pen, read the document through, smiled at it in satisfaction; then the sound of footsteps caught his ear, he glanced furtively out of the window, whisked the document away into a drawer. Albert ran past outside.

Before he reached the door Brink opened it, stood ready to greet him:

"What's the matter, Albert? I thought we weren't to meet again till I sent for you."

"You mean, I'm too hot for your company. You're not being straight with me. I don't like it, Mr. Brink."

"You're talking nonsense." He drew him indoors, glanced along the passage to make sure that Mrs. Bracken was not yet in the kitchen, then led him into the study:

"Sit down now and calm yourself. You do love a grievance."

"I could do without this one. Was it you set the cops on me?"

"Of course not. Why should I?"

"How else should they know who it was drove the car on Sunday?"

"They don't. When Bracken came to see me he'd no idea."

"He'd enough idea this morning to come along with the chap from the garage at Freeborough, and he identified me."

"The man who served you with the oil? Dear me, what a piece of bad luck."

"Bad luck, my arse. I was framed. They came marching together across the camp site, hell-bent for my tent, the Freeborough guy still in his overalls. I remembered him, and he remembered me. That's him, says he, pointing his finger, and the busy grabs me by the collar. I've one in for that nosy-parker, he's the same who nabbed me in the wood."

"How did you get away from him?"

"I asked him what bloody right he'd got to touch me, told him to show me his warrant. That shook him, he let go. So I took my chance; a clean pair of heels is better than a stretch in clink."

"You bolted?"

"Straight through the hedge. There's a hole I know, they don't, and by the time they found it I was down to the harbour. The tide's coming in, but there was room to pass under the wall." He stared in disgust at his shoes and the cuffs of his trousers sodden and caked with mud: "Filthy stuff to walk through. Christ knows how I'm going to scrape it off."

"All I know," Brink retorted, "is that it stinks." He rose and opened the windows: "Get on with your story. Did your pursuers wade after you along the foreshore?"

"They thought I'd turned up on to the railway line; so I left them to it and climbed out at the bridge. There were too many people about to take notice. I mixed in the crowd, crossed the bridge and came up the steps here as sharp as I could."

"You couldn't have chosen a more unsuitable bolt hole."

"All right, you needn't fear for your precious reputation. No one saw me once I was past the church."

"I only hope that's true. Look, Albert, this misadventure may even be a blessing in disguise. If you can keep Bracken on the run, chasing round the country after you, he'll have enough to occupy him without spying on us in the wood."

"Yes, and what about me? Am I to play hide-and-seek with the busy, while you and the others celebrate the great rite?"

"Don't be afraid, you'll be there; but you've plenty of time before evening. You can spend the afternoon on your bike laying false trails for the police."

"You'll give me the part you promised? You won't let me down?"

"You can rely on my word, if you do as I tell you. Go off and play will-o'-the-wisp with Harry Bracken, but towards the end of the afternoon, not later than six, I want you in the Devil's Churchyard ready for the girl when Aidan's done his part."

"You talked to him, did you, and he's willing?"

"Less willing, perhaps, than resigned. Aidan's a man of strict principles, a bit narrow-minded, but he yielded to persuasion when I spoke of the spiritual benefits that the rite confers. I appealed to his higher nature."

"Did you tell him what's in store for the girl?"

"My account of the proceedings was abbreviated, following the example set by the admirable Doctor Bowdler and other eminent Victorians. It'll be too late to draw back when he sees how the ritual develops."

"He'll need something to pep him up. Cocoa's his booze, but if I get a chance I'll lace it with a drop of meth."*

"Why not? Dionysus is a useful ally. I'll see to it that the others are suitably refreshed at the rectory."

"Can't you spare me a few of them in the wood? She's a brawny wench, she'll fight like a wildcat. Aidan isn't enough."

"I'm sorry, Albert, I'm afraid I can't even spare you Aidan. He'll have to go straight to the school with a message to explain why she's late, not the truth of course but plausible fiction."

"Leaving the rough-and-tumble to me alone? What do you take me for? I'm a brain-worker, not a plug-ugly."

"Use your brain then to outwit her, it shouldn't be difficult."

"She's not so soft, she outwitted you over that book."

"I admit it, she was too clever for me; but she won't be too clever for you, Albert. I've every confidence in your skill."

"I'll do my best."

"That's all I ask, and when Aidan's delivered his message he'll join you in the wood, and you two can keep watch together. I'll send the others soon after sunset. They'll strip her and bind her to the altar."

"That's when the fun begins?"

"Not till I come myself. Remember that, Albert; you must wait. It'll be well worth waiting for, I promise you."

"You swear I'll get a swig of her blood?"

"What reason have you to doubt me?"

Albert was silent, and Brink fixed his eyes on him sternly:

"I need an assurance from you that, in the elation following the consummation of the sacrament, you won't forget your final duty."

"To dispose of the body?"

"Exactly."

"She'll be quite a weight. Why can't the others lend a hand?"

"The sooner they scatter and disappear the better. I've told them to lie low near the station. There's an early train

---

* Wood alcohol.

that leaves even on a Sunday morning, and they'll have more than enough out of the money I'm giving them to pay their fares home."

"So off they go out of the picture, while Aidan and I trudge up through the wood with ten or eleven stone of dead girl."

"You've only to carry her to the road, it isn't far."

"Is it too look as if a car had run over her?"

"No, there are too many difficulties, she'll have no clothes on. Dump her on the verge, and unless I'm mistaken the coroner's jury will find that she was the victim of an unknown maniac, some sexual pervert."

A door swung to in the passage, they heard the clatter of dishes.

"Mrs. Bracken?" Albert asked.

"Yes, she's clearing my breakfast things, and in another minute she'll poke her head in here to ask what I want for lunch. You'd better make yourself scarce."

Albert moved to the door.

"No." Brink spoke sharply: "Not that way. You'll meet her in the hall."

"How else am I to get out?"

"Through the window." He opened it wider: "Quick now, and be careful you aren't seen in the drive."

Albert scrambled over the sill, fell sprawling among the tulips beneath, swore loudly. Brink leant out with a frown:

"For God's sake, be quiet. Are you hurt?"

"I've hurt your bedding plants more, but their colour's given me a notion. I'll ring up the cops from a call box." He raised his voice to a shrill falsetto: "This is Snooker's Garage speaking, Miss Gloria Wigglebottom, the lady at the pumps. I've spotted the man you're after, he's here in the marketplace."

"Make it less facetious, and they might believe you." He slammed down the window, and Albert slipped away along the drive and out at the gate.

There was no one in the lane; but when he reached the abbey ruins a cluster of sightseers waited at the turnstile, queuing for tickets. The day more than fulfilled its promise at dawn; the sun shone resplendent, the sky was a vault of clear blue except for wisps of cloud far out at sea, low on the horizon. It was weather to draw holiday-makers to the sands round the corner of the cliff; but there were still numbers
180

energetic enough to climb the steps for the historic interest of the church and abbey or for a walk on the cliff path, bordered on one side by the sea and on the other by pasture golden with buttercups.

Albert making for the town moved against the flow of the crowd. As he dodged through the oncoming parties, many dressed like himself, his figure became lost among them, indistinguishable and anonymous.

There was a call box at the bottom of the steps; but it was occupied, and he was unwilling to linger. He passed on down the street and across the bridge, found another at the road junction. This was empty, and he put through a call to the police station.

He asked to speak to Serjeant Cleaver. He had a gift for mimicry when he tried in earnest, and his imitation of a woman's voice was very much more convincing than the facetious example submitted at the rectory.

"This is Snooker's Garage at Freeborough," he announced. "The manager's secretary speaking. I believe you're looking for the man who bought oil here on Sunday."

"Yes, he's given us the slip. We thought we'd got him."

"Well, he's here."

"What? In the garage?"

"No, in the town. One of our mechanics saw him in the marketplace."

"Can I speak to him—your mechanic, I mean?"

"Sorry, he's gone out; but that's all he can tell you, the chap cycled past too quick."

"I'll come over to Freeborough. Yes, and Constable Bracken too, he knows this bloke by sight. Thank you, miss."

"Don't mention it." Albert rang off.

He emerged grinning from the call box, much pleased with himself. Then his face fell, and he turned quickly to press his nose against a shop window, seemingly absorbed in contemplation of the groceries displayed there, but keeping out of the corner of his eye a close watch on the bridge, across which Harry Bracken approached him.

Harry advanced glancing keenly from side to side, but he failed to observe the hunched window-gazer in the crowded distance ahead. At the junction he hesitated, then turned towards the railway station, and Albert at once darted away along the street beside the harbour leading to the pier and the sands. He looked back from time to time, could see only parties of tourists, and he breathed again, paused to lean against the rails guarding the water's edge. As he stared about him a momentary gap in the crowd revealed who walked behind. Harry changing his mind was coming in this direction.

Albert sprang up, broke into a run. The street diverged here from the harbour to enclose a block of residential property. A bend screened the farther end; but as he hurried on a figure in dungarees appeared round the corner of the buildings. Even from the distance he was sure that it was the employee from Snooker's Garage.

He saw himself trapped, stopped so abruptly that a woman following bumped into him.

"Oh, I do beg your pardon," she exclaimed. "How clumsy of me. I'm just at my house, and I was fumbling in my bag for the key, not looking where I was going."

He recognised Molly Corrington. She opened the gate leading into the flagged parterre between the pavement and her door.

He made a rapid decision, capture approached inexorably from in front and behind: "You remember me, don't you, Mrs. Corrington? We met at the rectory. Name of Albert Dockin."

She stared at him: "Yes, of course. On Sunday afternoon. You were one of the party that's going to act in Mr. Brink's play."

"Yes, I'm a friend of Mr. Brink's; he'd speak for me, I know. I'm in trouble, Mrs. Corrington. There's a gang wants to do me in. Can I come into your house for a minute or two till they've gone?"

She had the key in her hand to insert in the lock; she hesitated.

"They're Mr. Brink's enemies too," he added desperately.

She opened the door, and he bundled in after her. She closed it behind him.

He breathed a sigh of relief: "Thank you, m'm. It's very good of you."

She glanced doubtfully at his muddy shoes and led him into the kitchen: "I'm not sure that I'm doing right. I know nothing really about you."

"I was at the rectory, you saw me. You can't think Mr. Brink would have anything to do with a wrong 'un."

182

"I can't. That's why I'm helping you. There's no one else in the town for whose sake I'd have taken the risk."

"There's no risk, m'm, I assure you."

"I hope not." She stared helplessly round the room: "I'm alone in the house."

"Miss Corrington away?"

"She'll be back to lunch, and I've still to cook it. How long do you want to stay here? You said, a few minutes."

"Couldn't you make it a bit longer? I could do with half-an-hour."

"I don't know where to put you, and I'm sure my daughter won't approve when she comes."

"Isn't there a shed or something? I'm not fussy."

"There's the garage of course, and it's empty. My daughter had an accident yesterday, and she's taken the car to be repaired. They'll do nothing to it over the weekend, but she couldn't bear to leave it as it is."

"The garage suits me fine."

"Yes, it does seem the best solution." There was relief in her voice: "It's across the road."

She led him back to the door; but as she opened it he pushed past, thrust his head out, peered up and down the street.

"O.K.," he muttered. "All clear." The garage stood diagonally opposite; he dashed across, pulled the door open, plunged inside. Molly followed more slowly:

"You won't be disturbed."

"Not by Miss Corrington?"

"She'll have no reason to go there. She'll come straight into the house."

She went back with an uneasy mind to the kitchen. Her nerves needed soothing, she groped in her bag for a packet of cigarettes. As she extracted it a slip of paper fluttered out with it and fell to the floor. She stooped, picked it up, studied the leering smile of the green man in Brink's engraving. Suddenly she raised it to her lips, kissed it passionately, burst into tears.

Pearl returned in sour humour from the largest firm of motor engineers in Easby, having failed to convince the foreman of the need to retain men on duty at overtime rates on Saturday afternoon to fit a new wing to her car. He promised that it should receive attention on Monday, pointed out that, as engine and controls were undamaged, she could drive it home again and use it in the meantime with safety. It was advice the more unpalatable as it confirmed what her mother had said before she set out. She rejected it with scorn, trudged in martyred gloom back across the town, carrying the rugs over her arm. When she reached the house she turned off to store them in the garage.

She opened the door, sprang back with a scream, fled indoors into the kitchen:

"There's a man in the garage, a burglar."

Her mother looked up from the custard pudding that she was mixing: "Whatever did you want to go there for?"

"To put the rugs away of course. You don't suppose I'd leave them in the car for anyone working on it to steal? I don't trust those mechanics."

"I'm sure they're all quite honest, dear. I only hope that Albert Dockin is too."

"Albert Dockin?"

"That's his name, the man you took for a burglar. I met him at the rectory with Mr. Brink."

"What's he doing here?"

"He's in trouble, he told me. He's got enemies, and he asked me to let him hide here to escape them."

"You mean to say you agreed?"

"Why not? He's Mr. Brink's friend, and I do know there are mysterious people around who're planning some wickedness. Mr. Brink himself said so; he's trying to prevent them, so they're furious against him and anyone else on his side."

"He's been filling you up with a lot of twaddle. There's no mystery at all about the trouble Albert Dockin's in. He's wanted by the police."

"Oh no, Pearl. Why do you say that?"

"It's the talk of the town, they're hunting for him everywhere. Harry Bracken nearly caught him, but he got away. No wonder he's glad to hide in our garage."

"I hope they don't come looking."

"It'll be no joke if they find him here. You fool, Mother, what a mess you've made just when I've at last got Jim to come to dinner."

"What has Jim to do with it? I don't understand."

"You will, if you listen. The reason the police are after this man is they've found out it was he who put the oil on the road, so that Jim's car would skid into the quarry."

"Oh dear. Oh dear." Her mother sank into a chair, trembling.

Pearl watched her sternly: "So you see. We're sheltering Jim's murderer, or as good as, if his scheme had come off."

"I never guessed. How could I?" She rose with an effort to her feet: "I'll go at once and ring up the police station."

"No, Mother, stop. It won't be easy to explain. They'll ask awkward questions."

"I'll tell them the truth, it's quite simple."

"Yes, and Jim will hear every word of it. Harry Bracken's sure to pass it on to him, they're always hobnobbing."

"I can't help it. What else can I do?"

"Anything instead of spoiling our dinner party. How can I look my best and make an impression on Jim if he thinks I'm in league with this ruffian, hiding him and helping him to escape?"

"He won't. I'll explain how it happened."

"Your precious Mr. Brink won't come too well out of it, if you say you were doing a good turn to his friend."

"Mr. Brink, I'm sure, was as much deceived in the man as I was."

"I'm not so sure of that myself, but it's no business of mine. Live and let live. It's enough for me that he wants Jim to get over his infatuation for Kate. I agree entirely, so we're allies."

"How nice to hear you say so. He cares so much for your happiness."

"What would make me happiest at the moment is to be decently rid of this nuisance without a lot of fuss."

"I wish we could be, but I don't see how."

"Why not tell the man just to clear off?"

"Without informing the police? Oh no, dear, you mustn't do that."

"I shan't, but you must. You got us into this hole, you can get us out of it."

"But you said yourself this is the man who tried to kill Jim. If I let him go he'll try again."

"They'll catch him before he does, they're sure to; but he won't be caught in our garage." She pointed to the door: "Hurry up, Mother. It's the least you can do to make up. Go and get it over. Don't be a coward."

Her mother obeyed reluctantly, peeped out into the street: "Pearl," she called, "did you leave the garage open?"

"Of course I didn't. Not with him inside."

"Well, it's wide open now." She hesitated no longer, crossed over boldly, looked in: "Why, he's gone."

Pearl followed: "That solves our problem for us."

"I still think we should tell the police. He can't have gone far yet."

"If you do, Mother, I'll never forgive you, and remember when Jim comes this evening you're not to breathe a word of this."

"I'll try not to, but I'm not very clever. They're sure to talk of the man's escape, and it's so easy to say the wrong thing."

"The less you say the better. Leave the conversation to me. I'm looking forward to this party, it's going to be a great success." Her thin lips were tightly compressed: "Mrs. Buttle will have to find new premises for Saint Ursula's. When I'm married to Jim we'll live at Easby Hall."

Lunch was over at Saint Ursula's when Jim arrived with the Land-Rover. Children were pouring out of the house, there were no classes on a Saturday afternoon. Kate left them as they flocked towards the playing field. She ran to him where he waited at the door:

"I shan't be a minute changing. Would you like to come in?"

"If the transformation takes no longer than on Sunday I'll wait here and smoke a cigarette."

"You won't have time to finish it."

She was gone. When she reappeared in blouse, jeans and riding boots he had an inch still left at the butt. He threw it away:

"Finished."

"It wasn't. There were three more puffs at least, and I hurried so I didn't even brush my hair properly."

"It shines like spun copper."

"You're being sarcastic." She sat beside him, and they drove off out of the grounds.

He was silent till they turned into the lane, then he spoke gravely: "I've just come from the police station. Quite a lot's happened this morning. I saw Harry before breakfast, and he told me he found a label from those drums in Brink's car. He suggested confronting Albert with one of the men who

186

sold them, to see if he recognised him. Well, he did, so we know for certain it was Albert who bought the oil."

"Can the police do anything about it?"

"They tried. Harry grabbed Albert by the arm as soon as the man gave the word; but at that stage he hadn't a warrant, and there was a bit of an argument and Albert got away."

"He wriggled, I expect. Harry's strong, but it would be like trying to hold an eel or a worm."

"I don't blame Harry. It was awkward for him, he knew he'd no right to arrest. Anyhow, Albert gave them the slip, and they've been hunting him ever since. When I was at the police station just now Serjeant Cleaver told me he'd had a call from Snooker's Garage, someone there had seen Albert in Freeborough on his bicycle. So the serjeant drove the hounds over, Harry and his pals, to draw that covert; he's left them there, and they'll ring him at the station if they pick up the scent."

"What's the use, if they can't arrest him when they catch him?"

"They can now. They've got a warrant, I've signed it."

"I forgot you're a magistrate."

"I don't look like one, do I?"

"You haven't the stuffed-shirt manner. Perhaps you'll grow into it."

"Do you want me to?"

"I'd hate it."

"Even if you become a socialite too?"

She shook her head, and her hair swayed against his shoulder. He took his hand off the wheel to stroke it:

"Don't worry, darling, you couldn't. The raggle-taggle would always show through."

"You were telling me about Albert. Hadn't you better go on with the story?"

"There's nothing more to tell till he's caught." He frowned: "Yes, there is. I overheard an interesting conversation in the goods yard when I left you yesterday. I'd parked this old bus there and was sitting in it when Brink and Albert came by, they didn't see me. They were talking of their plans for tomorrow when they celebrate what they call the great rite."

"It's called that in the book about Parson Amos."

"Listen, Kate, this is deadly serious. I don't care what the words are you're learning, they aren't what Brink means you to act. When it comes to the point he's Amos Pounder, and you're Bess Atkins on the altar waiting for the knife."

"Yes of course, and I'll take good care to be out of his reach. I've told you I won't go on with this after the dress rehearsal."

"I'm not sure about the dress rehearsal even. I'd rather you'd nothing to do with him at all. Will Doris be there with you?"

"No, I didn't ask her. She'd be in the way if a chance comes for any sleuthing. I want a free hand when I meet the gang."

"That's what they want themselves, a free hand with you."

"Don't be silly. This is only a rehearsal. How can anything happen to me when they need me alive tomorrow to act in the play?"

He shook his head: "I don't know, but the man's raving mad. I heard him as good as admit while they talked that it was he who put Albert up to that business in the quarry."

"There you are. Wasn't I right that you're in more danger than I am? We've got to find out what his plans are, you must see that."

"We'll know soon enough once we lay hands on Albert. We'll get it out of him, if need be by third degree."

"You haven't caught him yet, but I might. Perhaps he'll be there with the rest of them this evening at the rectory."

"He's got more sense. You're on a fool's errand, Kate. Brink suspects you already, I heard him say so to Albert. You'll get nothing out of either of them."

"All the same, Mr. Brink will have to give us instructions, explain the programme for tomorrow. At present I know nothing more than what's on the notices in the town, that the play will be performed in church after the games in the rectory garden."

"Neither place sounds ideal for the great rite as practised by Amos Pounder."

"I'm sure in my own mind that the place chosen for the climax is the Devil's Churchyard."

"If the play begins in church the cast will have quite a journey from the first act to the second. What does Brink propose? A fleet of taxis?"

"I'll know, I suppose, this evening, and if all goes well a lot more too."

"In any event this is the end, as far as you're concerned. Whatever the plans are, you'll play no part in them. That's agreed?"

She nodded.

"You'll tell Brink?" he persisted.

"When the time comes. But I've been thinking; it's better to lead him on, encourage him to expect me till he's gone too far to draw back, and you and Harry can pounce."

"I suppose so." His tone was dubious: "But I don't like it. The sooner you're out of the business the better I'll be pleased. I wish to hell I wasn't going to this dinner party at the Corringtons. Perhaps I could slip away early and come on to Saint Ursula's to see you after you get back from the rectory."

"No, you'd spoil the party, and Mrs. Corrington's a dear."

"She may be, but she's too thick with Brink for my liking. An odd thing happened last Sunday. I found a note left in my car in his writing, and when I opened it, thinking it was for me, it was meant for her to ask her not to give away some secret of his to Doctor Buttle."

"Why did he put it in your car?"

"He didn't, Pearl did. She'd two notes to deliver, it seems, one for me and this for her mother, and she mixed them up."

"I can well imagine doing it myself, more than Pearl." She laughed: "Anyhow I'm sure the secret was something quite innocent. Poor Mrs. Corrington, it's pathetic to see how she adores him. She'd make him such a good wife."

"I'm less interested in choosing him a wife than in thwarting his plan to murder you. If you won't let me break up the party I'll pay a late call at Saint Ursula's, perhaps between eleven and twelve, just to know you're safe."

"No, I'm sure Mrs. Buttle wouldn't like that. Come in the morning, and I'll tell you everything then. I'm in no possible danger till tomorrow, you're making a fuss about nothing."

"I hope so, but something Brink said to Albert preys on my mind. They were talking about you; Albert asked if you were double-crossing them, and Brink told him there was still an important piece of information hidden from you, zero hour."

"Zero hour? What's that?"

"The time, I suppose, when the real show starts. There's some trap, but till I know more of his programme I can't guess what."

189

"When the time comes I'll be nowhere near."

"I'm taking no chances. You'll have Harry to keep an eye on you all day."

"He can't if he's hunting for Albert."

"Before tomorrow morning, let's hope, Albert Dockin will be cooling his heels in a cell."

"You don't think, if Albert's arrested, Mr. Brink will change his mind?"

"Why should he? Albert isn't the only pebble on the beach. You saw them yourself that night when you were in the wood with Flossie. She counted at least a dozen dancing, she said."

"Thirteen, including the goat-headed man, the Devil, who was almost certainly Mr. Brink himself."

"So if Albert falls out he can be replaced. In fact there was a bit of an argument between the two of them while I was listening, because a certain Aidan was to be given a job Albert thought should be his."

"Aidan?"

"Do you know him?"

She shook her head.

"I want you to look out for him. It's his job to set the trap."

"I can't look out for someone I've never seen."

"Flossie has, and I've told her if she sees him again to let me know at once."

"I'm sure she will. She was splendid that night in the wood."

"She was scared to death, according to old Jane, refused point-blank to go into it alone."

"I don't blame her. It was brave of her to go even with me to keep her company, and she was such a comfort when those horrors were dancing. I shut her up for fear they'd hear her, but her jokes and giggles made them so much less uncanny."

"Flossie's sense of humour tends to be earthy."

"They were ridiculous and disgusting at the same time. Part of me wanted to laugh, part of me felt sick. There was such a smell of evil." She shuddered.

He drew up at the side of the road, put his arm around her: "Don't let's smell it any more, let's get away from it, darling. The man's diseased in mind, he defiles whatever he touches."

190

She shuddered again. He clasped her waist more tightly:

"He's raving mad. Remember what he looked like that time when we saw him in the thunderstorm, when we sheltered in the Devil's Parlour and he stood in the old circle of stones. Remember what he did to the lamb, and to poor Fan when she tried to stop him."

"I do remember. Don't rub it in."

"I must rub it in. Madmen are notoriously cunning. We know that he's setting a trap, and however watchful I am it may catch you. Don't have anything more to do with him, don't even go to this dress rehearsal. He's a homicidal maniac, a case for an expert psychiatrist, a cell in a madhouse."

"He can't be shut up without evidence. We've got to obtain it, or he'll keep on till he's found a victim, some wretched girl who doesn't know what I do and hasn't you to help her, and he'll kill her and drink her blood." Her voice broke in a sob, and she disengaged herself, opened the door and stepped out into the road: "Let's talk of something else. It's such a lovely afternoon. Why need we spoil it?"

He left the car and joined her.

They stood at the foot of a steep hill where the road descending from the high moor into Golstondale dropped sharply to a stone bridge across a stream. The upper slopes of the gill were bare and craggy, with pockets of heather interspersed; but clustered bushes filled the bottom, birch, holly and rowan, mats of flowering gorse and aromatic juniper.

He pointed: "There's a waterfall a little way upstream. Shall we go and look?"

"Yes, let's."

"Does it matter what time you get to the farm?"

"Not in the least. Dinah won't mind." She ran across the strip of short turf into the bracken, and he followed.

The only path was a track made by sheep, and when it turned aside to slant uphill they left it, making their own way beside the watercourse. The bracken rose waist-high, breast-high; they parted it with their arms as if they were swimming. It petered out under the bushes, only to yield to a stiffer obstacle as these closed in ahead, a tangle of interlaced branches.

"Why is it," Kate asked, "that our walks always end up on hands and knees?"

"It's what comes of falling in love with a wood nymph."

"Blast. I'm sorry, I didn't mean you."

"Sat on a whin bush?"

"No, the other end, burrs in my hair."

They crawled on, the lilt of water gathered insistence in their ears. The ripple of the stream beside them was reinforced by an echo louder and more sonorous not far away. At last, scratched and dishevelled but jubilant they emerged into the open, a bowl of grass, daisies, ladies' slipper and cuckoo flowers sunk in the deep embrace of crags and heather-clad banks. At the upper end the stream swollen in force and volume by confinement in a narrow gorge poured over a wide shelf into the pool beneath. The waterfall had an unexpectedness that made it seem larger than it was, such was the contrast with the size of the stream from which it issued.

They climbed to the ledge, a slab of rock ample enough to afford room for them to sit dry, out of reach of the torrent, whose song echoing from cliff to cliff encompassed them in sound. From their high seat they looked down over the gill up which they had come, over the moors beyond to a nick between the shoulders of the farthest hill, through which the sea sparkled blue in the sunlight. A ship steamed slowly across the view as they watched.

Jim turned from it, fixed his eyes on Kate instead. He put his arm round her, drew her face to his:

"Ever since I first saw you, Kate, I've loved you. Do you love me too?"

She could not reply, his lips pressed hers too closely.

They drew apart, but he still gripped her: "When shall we be married, Kate? Soon?"

She nodded.

"Very soon? Here at once?"

"How can we?"

"I'll show you."

The waterfall was their witness, the god of the river their priest.

Chapter 10

Kate urged Dinah into a brisk trot as she set off home from Rowantree Farm. She looked at her watch; nearly seven o'clock, and she had a long ride ahead of her, a horse under her heavy with grass, disinclined to exertion. While she assured herself that she had neither reason nor wish to consider Brink's convenience, it pricked her conscience to think how late she would be at the rectory. She was not accustomed to keep people waiting.

Dinah's pace soon fulfilled her forebodings. The trot became slower and slower, sinking into a walk at the least excuse afforded by a rise in the ground. The flaming sun of the early afternoon was beginning to mellow into a glow of evening, but the day was still very hot. Kate herself was tired, it was not worth the effort to arouse Dinah to greater speed. She gave up the attempt, content to sit passive and let the mare have her will.

She took a bridle path across the moor. The distance was less this way than by the road on which she drove with Jim. The surface was grassy turf soft under Dinah's feet; heather enclosed her on either side to the skyline. Lulled by the solitude she lost consciousness of place and time, rode in a dream of her own, a shining world of delight.

She awoke with a start when a man approached on a bicycle. The track was not made for wheeled traffic; he swerved precariously to avoid the bumps, and she pulled aside into the heather to let him pass.

Instead, as he drew level, he dismounted: "Miss Evans?" he asked.

"Yes." She stared at him in surprise, she had no idea who he was.

"Mr. Tranmire sent me to look for you, miss, to give you a message."

She stared, more surprised than ever: "Hasn't he gone to Mrs. Corrington's? Do you work for her?"

He shook his head: "It wasn't there I met him, it was on the road just above the wood. I happened to be passing, and he stopped me and asked me to find you and send you to help him. He looked upset, he was as white as a sheet."

"Did he say what he wanted help for?"

"He seemed to think you'd know."

"I'll go at once to Kemsdale Farm and find out."

"No, not to the farm."

"Why ever not?"

"I don't know, miss. I'm only repeating what he told me. You're not to go near the farm, he said, you're to meet him in the wood."

"Where did he go himself when he left you?"

"Straight back into the wood, darted in as if someone was after him. If you ask my opinion he's hiding there to be out of the way."

She hesitated, frowning, too bewildered to take in fully what he said.

"You're thinking perhaps," he asked, "that this will make you late at the rectory?"

"I wasn't, but of course it will. How do you know of the rehearsal? Are you a friend of Mr. Brink's?"

"Not a close friend, but I've spoken to him once or twice. Shall I tell him you'll be late, or aren't you going to bother with Mr. Tranmire?"

"I most certainly am. Yes, if you're near the rectory, it would be kind of you to warn Mr. Brink not to wait for me. You needn't explain too much."

"Would you care to write him a message? You can put it in your own words."

"There's no need, and I've nothing to write with."

"I have." He brought out a sheet of paper and unclipped a pen from the pocket of his coat.

She took them, still dazed, and did as he wished. Dinah fidgeted, the writing was barely legible.

"Sorry I'll be late," she wrote. "Please don't wait for me. Kate Evans."

She handed him the note, and he reached for it eagerly, folded it and stowed it carefully away:

"Thank you, miss. I'll make sure the rector gets it." His voice and smile held an unctuous satisfaction. He reminded her of a curate whom she knew at home, earnest, bashful, glorying in a deed of merit.

"Thank you," she replied, "for telling me about Mr. Tranmire. I'm afraid you've had a lot of trouble."

"It's no trouble, it's all in a good cause."

He picked up his bicycle, mounted and rode back the way he had come. In spite of the uneven going he travelled faster than Kate on horseback and was soon far ahead of her. When he was hidden by the crest of a hill he drew up, dismounted, took the note from his pocket and read it through; then he sat down on a tussock of heather, unclipped his pen and added a preliminary sentence. Her handwriting was such a scrawl that he had little difficulty in achieving a passable imitation. The amended message began: "Dear Mrs. Buttle. Dinah lame," then Kate's own words followed: "Sorry I'll be late. Please don't wait for me. Kate Evans." He remounted, rode as fast as he could to Easby and delivered the note at Saint Ursula's.

Kate too made haste. She no longer allowed Dinah to dawdle, urged her on with knees and heels. Her bewilderment persisted, she was still unable to make sense of Jim's summons. Looking back on their parting at Rowantree Farm she recalled only a glow of happiness, on which nothing discordant had power to intrude. She had refused his offer to catch and saddle Dinah; Mr. Alsyke seeing them approach was waiting for her in the yard to help. Screened by the Land-Rover Jim had kissed her; then he got in, drove away. He had plenty of time to drive back to Kemsdale, change his clothes and go to dinner with Mrs. Corrington.

What had happened to divert him from his purpose? Why was she forbidden to go to the farm? Why was he hiding in the wood? Her mind groped vainly for answers, lost in a maze of improbability. While it pleased her that he should appeal to her for help she felt that it was most unlike him, quite out of keeping with his character. She even wondered whether there was some misunderstanding, whether the message was garbled. There was uneasiness in the thought that the messenger knew Mr. Brink. She thrust aside the fear that was rising in her; a greater fear swallowed it up as she remembered the attempt on Jim's life in the quarry, the anxiety nagging her on his account ever since. This was no time to ask questions, to explain the inexplicable. The facts were too urgent; he was in danger, he needed her.

She reached the crest of the ridge, from which she looked down into Kemsdale. She was in familiar country now; she left the track, struck across the moor straight for the road. As she approached it she chose a low place in the wall, pulled Dinah together for the effort, put her at it and leapt it. She had to hold her up sharply on the other side to allow a lorry to pass, travelling towards Easby. Then she crossed the road, plunged into the wood along the same path as a week ago.

Although she had not been told where to meet Jim an irresistible conviction assured her, as urgent as if it spoke aloud, that she would find him in the Devil's Churchyard. The easiest approach was round the edge of the wood and across the fields; but it was a way that would lead her within sight of the farm, and his instructions forbade it. The only other choice known to her was the path that she followed, the old track that formerly gave access to the field at the bottom, and this time, knowing what obstacles to expect, the patches of bog, encroaching saplings, she was more successful in avoiding them. The summer evening mellowed the green of trees and grass, added potency to the fragrance of elder-blossoms and wafts of honeysuckle. Even in her distress of mind her senses responded with pleasure.

As she rode she glanced keenly from side to side. Nothing, not even a sheep, intruded on her solitude; but at moments her heart beat more quickly when a rustle of leaves, a crackle of twigs defied explanation, too far from her to be attributed to her own movement. She assured herself that the cause was only a bird alighting or a small animal, a stoat or a weasel, on the prowl; but she was not entirely convinced, and Dinah even less so. The mare's ears were pressed back, she was ready to shy at the least provocation, and her pace became slower and slower the deeper they penetrated into the wood, till Kate had to urge her persistently to advance at all. It was no longer the sluggishness of the journey from Golstondale; it was active protest, manifest disapproval.

When they reached the overgrown hedge, the boundary of the derelict field, Kate forced her to leap and scramble through; but the open ground failed to reassure her, she remained as uneasy as ever.

The spot was near that at which Kate and Jim first met, and Kate stared round, almost expecting to see him standing there still. In vain, the field was empty. Disappointed and desolate, she rode across to the fringe of alder by the river and dismounted. The tree that she chose for Dinah was well away from the litter containing the debris of the trampled devil mask. Even so, Dinah showed reluctance, strained at the halter by which she was tethered. Kate patted, soothed her, then set out anxiously in trepidation on foot through the bushes.

An irresistible impulse urged her on, a voice that spoke in her mind telling her clearly and for certain that she would find Jim in the Devil's Churchyard. As she crawled through the thicket she strained her ears to listen. No sound either natural or supernatural came to disturb her. She clambered up the bank where she and Flossie sat to spy, and taking care to avoid the nettles she peered over. The sacred stones stood silent, deserted. The altar lay tinted with gold by the westering sun, unattended by priest or victim.

The solitude reassured and at the same time puzzled and disappointed her. She stood up, walked forward boldly across the turf. She had a sense of frustration, almost of bathos, not knowing what to do next.

Then as she hesitated the sound began, low at first, barely distinct, but gathering strength as she listened, the moan of a human voice. She moved into the circle, seeking the direction from which it came. Its source lay beyond her, the cromlech known as the Devil's Parlour. There could be no doubt any longer that someone lurked there, moaning in pain, not only moaning but calling. The voice was muffled, unrecognisable, but the word was plain to hear, "Kate, Kate, Kate."

"Jim," she called back, ran forward to the dark entrance of the cave, flung herself on hands and knees, plunged in.

She gasped. An evil-smelling rag was crammed into her mouth, choking her. The loop of a rope passed over her head, the slip knot tightened, pinning her arms to her side. She kicked fiercely, and a muttered curse gratified her, told her that her boots found a target. Then her legs were grabbed, roped together. She could neither speak nor move.

As her eyes grew accustomed to the darkness she saw that her companion was Albert Dockin.

He picked her up, dragged her deeper into the cave; but after a few heaves he tired of the effort and dropped her. She

197

fell on her face, and as she struggled to rise he smacked her hard across her upturned seat:

"Kick me in the jaw, would you? If it weren't that he told me to leave it I'd make you smart. Just wait, my girl, till you feel what's coming to you tonight."

Gagged by the cloth, she was unable to reply.

He stooped to test and tighten the knots, then crept to a recess, a cranny between adjoining megaliths, from which he extracted a small portable stove, a saucepan, a tin of cocoa, a bottle of milk and another of methylated spirits, and two cups without saucers, one of them plain, the other adorned with a coloured picture of Windsor Castle. He filled the saucepan with milk and lit the stove, turning the flame down to keep the milk at a gentle simmer. Then he poured a splash of spirits into one of the cups, that with the pictorial design, and set it on the ground, scooping a hollow for it to stand upright. The plain cup he kept beside him.

When his arrangements were complete he sat down, leaning his back against the wall and glancing at intervals at Kate, who lay on her face no longer trying to move. Neither spoke; she was unable, he unwilling. He relieved the silence by humming the Pilgrims' Chorus from *Tannhäuser*.

They remained like this for a long time; it seemed at least twice as long to Kate choked by the unsavoury gag. Then a voice was heard outside:

"Coo-ee, Albert."

"Coo-ee, Aidan," he called back.

The name echoed in Kate's memory, recalled Jim's warning: "It's his job to set the trap." As the man came in head first under the low lintel of the cromlech she recognised the cyclist who brought her the message on the moor.

Albert turned up the flame of the stove: "Like some cocoa?"

"Nothing better."

There was little room; he squatted on the floor beside Albert, who spooned cocoa into the saucepan and stirred it.

"You needn't ask how things went. There's the answer." He pointed at Kate with his spoon: "My compliments, Aidan."

Aidan kept his own eyes averted from her: "Can she hear us?"

"Who cares? She'll have no chance to blab."

"Why? What are you going to do to her?"

The saucepan boiled over. Albert took it from the stove, filled the prepared cup for Aidan, then the plain cup for himself.

"What are you going to do to her?" Aidan persisted. "You haven't told me yet."

"Never you mind, Aidan, my lad. Whatever we do, you can be sure it's sanctified by tradition. Drink up your cocoa like a good boy."

Aidan sipped: "There's an odd taste to it."

"You're fussy." He sipped his: "Mine's all right."

Aidan tried again, stared at his cup doubtfully: "Are you sure it's cocoa in that tin?"

"Look for yourself." He passed it to him: "Cadbury's cocoa in plain letters for anyone to read. I don't say the saucepan's all that clean. What do you expect in a place like this? A five-star restaurant, A.A. and R.A.C. recommended?"

Aidan gulped down the beverage without further protest.

"Did you meet anyone as you came?" Albert asked.

"Only the land-girl. I passed her in the field."

"Did she recognise you?"

"She was too far off. She paid no attention, she isn't very bright."

"You shouldn't have gone near the farm at all. Why didn't you come by the wood?"

"It's quicker across the fields, and you might have needed help."

"Well, I didn't. Look at her." He pointed again at Kate: "Let me tell you this, Aidan. When I'm given a job I do it; I need help from no one, least of all from you."

"I'm sorry, Albert." He fidgeted uncomfortably.

"What's the matter? Have you any fault to find?"

"None, except that I wish she weren't so near."

"Can I help it if the place is poky?"

"No, of course not. Did you have a fearful struggle?"

"What do you take me for? It was a victory of brain over brawn, will over matter." He patted himself on the chest: "I summoned the power, sent it to fetch her, and it gripped her mind, filled her with delusion, forced her to come to me like iron drawn to a magnet."

"I do envy you. I'd give anything to be as proficient myself in the secret arts."

"You will, if you keep on at it. Above all, you must do

199

what you're told tonight. Remember the rules I gave you, say nothing, hear nothing, see nothing."

"Can't you find less nothing, more something for me to do?" His eyes shone, there was defiance in the jut of his chin: "You aren't fair to me, Albert. I'm capable of anything if I'm given the chance. I've never felt like this before, so full of spunk."

Albert watched him shrewdly: "Don't worry, you'll get your chance when the time comes."

"A real chance, something big to make people admire and obey me?"

"Yes, Aidan, of course. This is your night; you'll be the star, you've only to wait an hour or so. What about a stroll in the fresh air to see that all's quiet?"

"Suits me. It's stuffy in here." He staggered as he rose.

"Steady," Albert warned him.

"What do you mean, steady? There's nothing wrong with me. It's this hole, it gets on my nerves." He glared at Kate: "That girl, like something out of a slave market."

"Gets you, does she? A tasty piece for your harem."

"I'm not interested in girls."

"You don't know what you're missing."

"There you go, jeering at me because I'm a queer; but I'll show you, Albert, I'll show you. There's more in me than you think."

"I'm sure there is, Aidan." He grasped him by the sleeve to support him, steered him skilfully out of the cromlech.

Both vanished, Kate was alone. She lay tense, motionless, listening. She could hear their voices outside; but the sound grew fainter as they walked away, and at last it faded altogether from her ears. She held her breath, waited to make sure, then applied herself to free her mouth of the gag. It was a thick pad wedged behind her teeth; she screwed her jaws, pushed with her tongue, coughed and kept on coughing, unable to control the impulse. The effect was all to the good, the impediment was loosened, slipped forward. She filled her lungs with air, puffed with all her force, spat out a ball of rag, Albert's handkerchief. She continued to spit to rid herself of the disgusting taste that it left, but no amount of saliva washed it away.

Fearing that the noise would attract attention, she lay still again and listened; but all remained quiet outside, and she turned to her next task, to loosen the ropes binding her arms and legs. She rolled this way and that, bent herself double, jerked her wrists and feet. Nothing yielded, Albert's knots held fast, ineluctable. She tried to fray the rope by rubbing her legs against the edge of a stone. She tore her jeans, the rope suffered no damage.

Nevertheless she persisted till the sound of someone approaching stopped her. She froze motionless, silent. A face peered in, hidden by the shadow, but the long hair was a girl's:

"Is anyone there?"

"Flossie," she sobbed. "Oh, Flossie, I'm so glad."

"What's he been doing to you, the bastard?" Flossie crept in, came to her side.

"Quick," Kate gasped. "They'll be back soon. Undo these knots."

Flossie bent to examine them: "I guessed he was up to no good there in the pasture field. Mr. Tranmire told me to watch out and let him know if I saw him again; but I couldn't, he's out for the evening. So I thought I'd better peep for myself."

"It was brave of you."

"I was scared stiff, but I was more scared for you when I came on the mare."

"Dinah? Is anything wrong with her?"

"She'd tewed herself into a mucksweat riving at the halter till she parted it, and when she saw me she cantered up as human as you like to tell me I'm wanted."

"Poor Dinah."

"She knew all right what was happening to you."

"Where is she now?"

"I took her gear off and turned her into the pasture field. You've no cause to worry."

"Except for myself. How are you getting on with those knots?"

"Not too fast, the blighters. I've had a go at each, but my, they've got me beat. Pliers they need, not finger nails, and it's that dark you can't see what you've hold of."

"Haven't you anything in your pocket? A knife perhaps?"

"It would be today of all days. Mrs. Torgill borrowed mine off me to chop plug for her man to smoke."

"Try again with your fingers then."

Flossie tried again, fumbling ineffectively. She turned away, stooped to the floor:

"I'll see if there's a chip of stone with a sharp edge."

"Do hurry. They'll be back any minute."

"Here's a bit that might do." She straightened herself, came back with it.

"Hush," Kate exclaimed. "Listen. What's that?"

Voices could be heard in the distance, growing louder.

"Run, Flossie, quick before they come."

"Leave you here?"

"What else can you do? If they catch you they'll tie you up too. Run to the farm and fetch help."

"There's no one at the farm but me. Mrs. Torgill and her man have gone across to her sister's, and Mr. Tranmire's out with friends. Where the lad is I don't know, slipped off home as like as not."

"Listen, Flossie, get Mr. Tranmire on the phone. He's dining with Mrs. Corrington at Easby, the number's in the book."

"I'm no great hand at the telephone, it flusters me."

"Well, it damn well won't have to this evening. Go quick and do what I say before it's too late."

The voices were already dangerously close. Flossie peered out, took her chance and fled. In spite of her bulk she moved with the elusiveness of a wild creature. The capricious light of sunset, the lengthening shadows disguised her; she slipped across into the shelter of the trees unseen by the men approaching, Albert and Aidan reinforced by supporters.

Albert pointed to the cromlech: "In there. Strip the victim, bring her out."

They rushed in, seized Kate; their knives cut the ropes without difficulty. As soon as she was free she struggled, kicking out with her boots; but ready hands pulled them off, others gripped her arms, tore off her clothes. She dug her teeth into the nearest, and as he released her she screamed at the top of her voice.

"Damn the bitch," Albert shouted angrily, he was waiting outside. "They'll hear her a mile off. What's she done to her gag?"

"A muzzle, that's what she needs before we catch rabies." The speaker sucked an ugly wound on his wrist.

Another produced his own handkerchief, stuffed it into her mouth, and her scream died away in a gurgle.

"All right," he called. "I've switched her off."

When they carried her out she was naked. Her arms were roped again to her sides, her legs together. A red scarf tied at the back of her head covered her mouth and held the gag in place. They laid her prostrate across the altar, reinforcing the posture with ropes made fast over her body to stakes driven into the ground. Her legs dangled on one side of the stone, her long hair on the other, gleaming copper in the sunset.

"Fetch the paint," Albert commanded, "and I'll inscribe her."

When he had finished he stood back to survey his work: "Tetragrammaton." He rolled the word on his tongue and turned to address his companions, a new Albert transformed by his sense of the occasion: "Look there, the Tetragrammaton, and if you don't know what that means I'll tell you. Power it stands for, power as great as any in hell. Take off your clothes, every stitch; but no larking, mind, with the victim, or you'll be sorry. Wait in holy obedience till the moon rises, and the high priest comes to initiate you, to celebrate the rite."

Not even the excellence of the dinner cooked by Molly Corrington reconciled Jim to his surroundings as he sat in the drawing room afterwards in an arm-chair with a glass of port at his side, Leslie Potts in a chair facing him and Pearl and her mother together on the sofa. Leslie bored him, Pearl's amiability alarmed him, and he detested the clothes that he wore, boiled shirt and dinner jacket; he cursed himself for accepting an invitation to a house where they were obligatory. Above all he longed to be with Kate, or at least to be left alone to think of her.

"You're very glum, Jim. A penny for your thoughts." Pearl smiled archly, triumphant in black velvet and a towering hair-do, a masterpiece created by the lady stylist who reigned in the fashionable salon adjoining her own botique in the grounds of the Angel.

He shook his head, spoke with strained politeness: "Nothing doing. They're not for sale."

"Not at that price." Leslie guffawed: "He's mulling a tip straight from the horse's mouth for the 4:30 on Monday."

"You read my mind like a book, Leslie."

"Are you going to the races?" Pearl asked eagerly. "Can I give you a lift, if those lazy mechanics have my car ready in time? They've promised to work on it all Monday morning, and if it isn't ready by lunch they'll get no pourboire."

"They'll do well if it is. Flossie left her mark on it."

"She's a public danger, Jim. You really oughtn't to allow her on the road."

"I'm sure she was very sorry," her mother put in appeasingly: "We've all got to learn."

"Thank you, Mrs. Corrington." He smiled at her: "She's a good girl, she can't help it if she's built like a baby elephant. She's just as clumsy on the farm."

"No wonder, if she's never corrected." Pearl's tone was acid: "You're much too easy with her, and as for Harry Bracken he deserves to be sacked from the police force. Why hasn't he served her with a summons?"

"Harry Bracken?" Leslie picked up the name with interest: "He's been busy from all I hear. Have they caught that scoundrel yet, Jim? Talk of public dangers, I'd rather meet Flossie head-on, bumper to bumper, than a filthy skunk who rigs up a skid for me, to send my new Jag crashing to kingdom come."

"Not only the car," Molly reminded him. "Jim himself might have gone with it, but for the mercy of God. We ought to be very thankful."

"Leslie wouldn't, if the mercy left him without his precious jag." Pearl glanced at him sourly: "That car's more than a wife to him."

"You aren't fair, Pearl," he protested. "You'd soon know who comes first with me if you'd give me a chance."

Molly smiled at them both: "It's a very smart car, and I'm sure it cost a lot of money. You're quite right to take care of it, Leslie."

"I do, and of my neck too." He turned to Jim: "It could have been me as easily as you in that quarry. We're none of us safe with this maniac at large."

"He won't get far. I saw Harry just now. He's back from a wild goose chase in Freeborough; but the warning's gone out over the whole county, and as soon as we get something definite he'll be off again to pick up the scent."

"Let's hope it's the right scent this time." He raised his glass, drained the few remaining drops of wine. Molly reached for the decanter to pass it, but Pearl caught her eye and shook her head.

There was an embarrassing pause, and Molly made haste to speak:

"One can't help feeling sorry for a hunted creature."

"For a would-be murderer, Mother?" Pearl's voice held grim reproof.

"He didn't look like that at all. He was too frightened."

Leslie stared in surprise: "You've seen him, have you?" Jim too watched her with interest.

"Nonsense," Pearl interrupted. "Mother's got too vivid an imagination. She persuades herself she saw what wasn't there."

"An apparition?" Jim spoke with irony: "It fits well into the stories going round the town."

"I've heard them." Leslie tittered: "Something to do with black magic. It's amazing what twaddle people believe."

Pearl tossed her head: "Ignorant locals with minds as thick as their boots. It's a warning, Jim. That's what you'll become if you don't mend your ways."

He paid no attention to her, addressed her mother: "What did you see, Mrs. Corrington? What did the man look like?"

Her mouth opened in dismay, she was unable to speak. It seemed that at any moment she would burst into tears.

The telephone saved her, ringing vociferously in the hall. Pearl leapt up, hurried out to answer it.

The three left in the drawing room sat in constrained silence. Molly was incapable of speech, and Jim watching her forbore to press his question. They could hear Pearl's voice beyond the door; the words were indistinguishable, except for the exclamation repeated with growing irritation —"What do you say?"

Leslie found the silence oppressive:

"What's come over us? A goose walking over our graves?" His tone was facetious, but neither Jim nor Molly laughed.

No one spoke again till Pearl returned.

She seated herself without comment, lit a cigarette. Jim watched her, waited for her to speak, waited in vain. At last he asked:

"Who was that?"

Her eyes meeting his were resentful: "It was Flossie."

"Did she want to speak to me?"

"I knew you wouldn't want to be bothered. I told her you were busy."

He frowned: "What did she ring about?"

"I couldn't make head or tail of it, nothing but splutter and blather. I never can understand her frightful patois."

"I can. You should have fetched me."

"I've told you, Jim, I tried to save you from being disturbed. You're dining with us, you can forget the farm for once."

"Not if it's something urgent. Flossie hates the telephone, she wouldn't call up unless she had to."

"It's nothing to do with the farm, so you can set your mind at rest. It's some business with Kate Evans, her name was the only thing I caught clearly."

"Kate?"

"There's no need to go up in flames. As soon as I got rid of Flossie I rang up Saint Ursula's to make sure there's nothing wrong; that's why I took such a time. Mrs. Buttle says they've had a message from Kate that Dinah's lame and she's leading her, so she'll be very late getting home. They're not in the least worried."

"I am. She's probably stuck in Kemsdale, can't get Dinah any farther. All the same, it's odd she didn't ring herself."

"She'll be all right; she's got Flossie to help, and your married couple, the Torgills."

He shook his head: "They've gone out to Jane's sister's, it's right over the hill in Hoggrah. No, I'll slip back at once in the Land-Rover, tell Kate to leave Dinah at the farm, and I'll drive her to Saint Ursula's myself."

Molly and Leslie sat silently, excluded from the conversation; but Jim's last words aroused Molly to intervene:

"Oh no, Jim, you can't go yet, it's so early. I'm sure Kate won't mind waiting if Flossie takes her into the house."

Pearl frowned at her: "Leave it to me, Mother." She turned to Jim: "If Kate needs a lift they can send to fetch her from Saint Ursula's. I'll ring them again, Doctor Buttle can go in his car."

"Why should he, after a hard day's work?"

"Why should you go and break up our dinner party?"

He hesitated: "I'm sure you mean all this very kindly, Pearl; but I really know my own business best. The first call to make is to Kemsdale to find out if Kate's there, and I'll make it myself and speak to her if she is. May I use your telephone, Mrs. Corrington?"

"Of course, Jim. You know where it is."

206

He left the room. Pearl drummed irritably on her lap with her fingers:

"What a fuss about nothing. If the girl's lamed her horse she can walk, it won't hurt her."

"Who's the girl?" Leslie asked.

"Kate Evans. She teaches at Saint Ursula's."

"Red hair, wide mouth, large grey eyes?"

"You seem to have made a careful inventory of her features."

"Don't take me wrong, Pearl. She was with Jim, wasn't she, last Sunday at the Angel? I can't help it if a girl's easy to look at."

"She's a sweet girl," Molly put in.

"Have it your own way." Pearl sighed: "In my opinion she's no better than she should be."

Jim came back with a worried frown: "There's no reply."

"It's what I expected," Pearl told him. "You might have saved yourself the trouble. If they're out in the yard or with the horse in the stables they wouldn't hear you."

Molly nodded comfortingly: "That's it, and if the Torgills are away there's no one else to answer the phone."

He remained standing, unhappy and irresolute.

"Come and sit down," Pearl commanded. "If you insist on it we'll try again in a few minutes when they're back indoors, but you're making a mountain out of a molehill. Let me fill your glass, you need something to steady your nerves. They're groggy still after your accident."

He sank into his chair, but as she brought him the decanter he shook his head: "No, thank you, I've had enough."

"I don't mind if I do, Pearl." Leslie not waiting for an invitation held his glass out, so that she was unable to ignore it; but before she could pour the wine the front door-bell jangled in the passage, and she put the decanter back on the table with an impatient shrug:

"Who can that be? Are we never to have any peace tonight?"

Jim leapt to his feet: "I'll go and see." He darted out of the room, and they heard him open the outer door, exchange a few words with the visitor. He was back almost at once:

"It's a lorry waiting to get past, and he's afraid of scraping your jag, Leslie."

"What an hour of the night to bother us," Pearl complained. "Can't those lorries ever be quiet?"

"He's bringing a load of crates for the fish market. They'll be needed when the boats come in in the early morning."

Leslie rose unwillingly: "What about your Land-Rover?"

"I think it's all right, but we'll ask him." They went together out of the house.

There was no need to move the Land-Rover which was parked in an offset, leaving room for the lorry to pass. Jim stood talking to the driver while Leslie drove the Jaguar on a short distance to where the street widened.

"It's a fine night," the man observed affably.

Jim nodded: "You'll be glad of it if you've come over the moor."

"Yes, some of those roads can be awkward. They're steep, and they don't get enough binding. It doesn't take much of a storm to wash it away."

"That's what I keep telling the highway people myself, but they pay no attention."

"You're from the hills, are you sir?"

"Kemsdale. My name's Tranmire."

"Mr. Tranmire of Kemsdale Farm? If that isn't a bit of luck. I was at your place above an hour ago with some bags of seed to deliver, and I couldn't see anyone about. So I dumped the bags in the barn to keep them dry; but I wanted my papers signed, and there wasn't anyone to ask."

"You'd like me to sign them now?"

"If you'd be good enough, sir." He sorted out the invoice from a sheaf in the cab of his lorry and produced a pencil from his pocket.

Jim took it and signed: "I'm sorry you drew the farm blank. There ought to have been a land-girl hanging around somewhere. Perhaps she was down the fields with the sheep."

"I saw no one, man or girl, not on the farm, that is. The only girl I saw was up on the hill as I was coming away, and she didn't look like a land-girl, she was on horseback."

"She wasn't on foot, was she, and the horse lame?" Jim spoke with sharp interest.

"She was riding, I tell you, and the horse was no more lame than I am. She came down from the moor and took the wall on to the road with as clean a pair of heels as you'd see in a show ring. It was a pretty picture."

"Could you see where she went after that?"

"Yes, I was watching in the mirror. There's a turning into the wood, and she took it."

"Into the wood? You're sure?"

"I'd take my oath on it."

Leslie having parked the Jaguar was about to go back into the house.

"Just a minute, Leslie," Jim called to him. He turned to the driver: "You're all clear ahead now, no obstacles. Good night."

"Thanks." The man climbed into his cab: "Cheerio."

He drove away.

"What's the matter?" Leslie asked. "We can go in again, can't we?"

"You can, but I want you to lend me your car."

"My Jag?"

"Yes, she's faster than the Land-Rover."

"I should bloody well hope so. She cruises at ninety, only needs a touch on the throttle for a ton."

"That's why I want to borrow her. It's urgent."

"I'm sorry, Jim; it's a rule I've made, never to let anyone drive her but myself."

"There are exceptions to every rule. Do me this favour, and I swear I'll never forget it."

"Of course if you put it that way." His voice was hesitative.

"Thanks, Leslie. You're a hero." He raced along the street to the Jaguar, shouting over his shoulder: "Make my apologies to Mrs. Corrington and Pearl."

Leslie stared after him, glum and bewildered, unaware that he had yet given his consent.

Pearl opened the door: "Whatever are you two doing out there? Haven't you finished yet?"

"Coming, Pearl," he replied.

"It's you, Leslie, is it? Where's Jim?"

"Gone."

"He can't have, not without saying good-bye."

"He asked me to make his apologies to you."

She peered out into the street: "Is this a silly joke of yours, Leslie. There's his Land-Rover."

"He's left that and taken my Jag."

"Your Jag, your precious Jag? You mean to say you let him?"

"I suppose so. I must have been barmy."

He would have blamed himself still more bitterly if he could have seen Jim driving the car, the dizzy swerve over the bridge across the Rune, the needle flickering past the hundred up the long hill on to the moor.

Chapter 11

Flossie glared at the telephone and sobbed:

"Slammed it down. Cut me off in the middle. I'd boil her in pig mash, I would, with her lah-de-dah, her hoity-toity. The bitch, the bleeding bitch."

Fan curled on the hearth-rug, having slept through the telephone conversation without the twitch of an ear, got up suddenly, walked across and licked Flossie's hand.

She bent to caress the dog's jowl: "No, I don't mean you, Fan. Bitch is too good for her, much too good. She's a bleeding murderess, she is, Fan, there's no getting over it." Tears choked her voice; she squatted on the floor, buried her face in Fan's shaggy fur and wept:

"Oh, Fan, what shall I do? What shall I do, Fan? Miss Evans, she told me to ring him, and I've tried, I've tried, haven't I? What can I do if hoity-toity slams me down?"

Fan's only reply was to lick her tear-stained cheek.

"Shall I ring the police, Fan, shall I? But I've no head for figures, they get me that flustered. I know it'll be the wrong number, they'll slam me down. If only Harry were at home I'd slip across, but they say he's gone to Freeborough. What's he need to go there for? It's here we want him, here before they murder her, the bleeders. Oh, if only Harry were here, if only Ron were. Why don't you come, Ron? I told you I'd be alone. Ron, Ron, why don't you come?" Her voice rose to a wail: "Oh, if only my fingers weren't that clumsy with knots."

Suddenly she scrambled to her feet: "Come on, Fan, we're going. I don't care if Harry isn't there. I'll talk to Maggie, she'll tell me what to do."

The decision inspired fresh confidence, energy. She fled from the room, along the passage and across the kitchen to the outer door:

"Come on, Fan. We'll talk to Maggie. She'll be putting the bairns to bed."

Fan bounded after as she ran into the yard.

Harry Bracken's cottage stood at the foot of the hill where the road dropped into Kemsdale from the moor. Zig-zags increased the distance by road from the farmstead, but it was a bare quarter of a mile as the crow flies across the fields. No crow flew more directly than Flossie ran, trampling through standing oats, flinging herself at the fence with such force that she fell rolling on the other side. She picked herself up, ran on. She carried too much flesh for a sprinter; but she had perseverance, endurance, there was more brawn than fat in her ample curves. The resemblance that Jim found to a baby elephant was unmistakable as she burst through the wicket gate into Harry's garden, with Fan at her heels.

Harry himself stood at the open door: "Why, Flossie," he exclaimed. "What's the hurry?"

"Harry," she panted. "You're here, you're not in Free-borough?"

"I'm here, but as soon as I've had a bite to eat I'm off again. Never mind, there's someone who'll please you better." He turned and spoke into the room: "It's Flossie. She's saved you a journey, Ron."

He stood aside, and Ron came out, smarter and cleaner than in the goods yard; he had the swarthy good looks of a gypsy.

"Ron," Flossie cried. She ran to him, threw her arms round his neck, hid her face sobbing against his yellow pull-over.

"What's the matter, lass?" He patted her tenderly on the back: "What have they been doing to you? I was just on my way to the farm, time for a cosy talk together, seeing as you're alone there."

Harry's wife, Maggie, came to the door, small and dark, with black hair falling straight to her shoulders. She held

211

a baby in her arms, and a little girl in a nightdress clung to her skirt.

"Bring her in, Ron," she called. "I'll make her a nice cup of tea."

Flossie extricated herself abruptly from his embrace, she had recovered her breath: "Thanks, Maggie; there's no time. There'll be murder done in the wood unless we look sharp."

"The wood?" Harry glanced at her keenly: "What's going on there?"

"Murder, I tell you. It's Miss Evans, the lass on the white mare. They've got her tied fast in that cave, and I found her; but I couldn't loosen the knots nohow. So she told me to ring Mr. Tranmire; but it's no use, they wouldn't let me speak to him. Be quick now, Ron, Harry, both of you, or she won't be alive when we get there."

Ron stared at her in bewilderment, and from her to Harry: "What's come over her? Is it a touch of sun, do you think?"

Harry shook his head: "She's all right. Leave her to me." He turned to Flossie: "Was this in the old circle, the Devil's Churchyard?"

"That's right."

"Did you see the men, recognize them?"

"There's one called Aidan; that's all I know, and he's a friend of the parson's."

"Of the parson's, is he?"

"Yes, Mr. Tranmire told me to watch out for him."

Harry strode forward: "Come on, Ron. We'll see what they're up to. Where's your bike?"

"Hi," Flossie exclaimed. "I'm coming too."

"No, you'd better stay here with Maggie."

"I'm staying bloody nowhere till I know that poor lass isn't dead."

They did not stop to argue. All three ran to the gate leading out on to the road.

Ron's was a motorbike, Harry wheeled out his own pedal cycle from the shed: "Take Flossie behind you, I'll keep pace. Through the farm and down to the bottom. That's as far as we can ride."

Flossie nodded: "A bike's no use in the wood."

On the rough road with frequent bends Ron's engine gained little over Harry's pedals. They were close together, slowed down by a zigzag, when a car came roaring behind them, swerved to a halt with a screech of brakes.

"Sorry," Jim shouted. "No time for excuses. Jump in, all of you." He flung the door of the car open.

"You've heard, sir, have you?" Harry asked.

"She's in the wood, and that's where we're going."

Harry pushed his bicycle into the ditch, and Ron followed his example. All scrambled into the car, Harry and Ron at the back, Flossie beside Jim. At the last moment Fan who had followed bounded in on to her lap.

The Jaguar sprang forward again, and there were no more obstacles till they reached the yard gate. Flossie got out to open it, Fan accompanied her.

"Prop it," Jim called, "and run on to open the next."

"What about the sheep?"

"Damn the sheep."

She did what she was told, and as he drove into the field she scrambled back into the car before it lurched forward again. Fan returning too late raced frantically after them, barking.

Rocking and bouncing, dodging among gorse and outcrop, they plunged down the steep grassy slope.

"Sorry for the Jag," Ron gasped. "Bit of a change from the motorway."

Harry grinned, he recognised the car: "Lucky job Mr. Potts can't see us."

At the bottom Jim slackened speed, swung in towards the wall and drew up where the hurdle blocked the gap into the wood. Almost in simultaneous movement he switched off the engine, leapt out of the car. He was scrambling over the hurdle before the others had time to collect themselves. They ran to catch him up.

The waning moon shone from a clear sky on the Devil's Churchyard, where Kate lay bound across the altar and Brink towered over her, a figure of nightmare in the late Ernest Corrington's crimson and green dressing gown, crowned with a headpiece representing goat or devil that hid his face. His followers stood in a semicircle behind him. They wore no clothes at all except black masks.

He raised the switch of hazel that he carried:

"Father, Son and Holy Spirit, avaunt, avaunt, avaunt."

At each imprecation he struck the victim with his switch across the characters inscribed in red on her body. Then he

213

lowered it, turned to address the congregation in a formula in which English and Latin were indiscriminately mixed:

"*Adeste, fideles, adeste.* The threefold Adversary flies, chastised by my sacred wand. *Gloria in infernis,* glory to the dark Archangel, the Holy One in whose name I celebrate the greatest of the rites."

"Holy, holy, holy," the worshippers chanted in unison.

On the farther side of the altar under Kate's dangling hair lay a silver pyx from the church and the bronze-handled knife from the chimney piece in the rectory. He leant across, reached for the pyx, took out two wafers and pressed them to the twin cushions of flesh of the victim's seat:

"*Caro verbum facta est.* Glory to the Two in One."

"Hosanna, hosanna," the worshippers replied.

He laid a palm over each of the wafers, and they clung to his hands as he lifted them. Then he stood with arms outstretched:

"Draw near with faith and receive the bread of life to nourish you in remembrance of him who was cast out of heaven."

Two of the congregation approached, and to each he offered a hand to be kissed. As they kissed they licked up the wafers. He repeated the performance till all had partaken.

"Rejoice, my sons," he cried. "Rejoice and give thanks. Bow your heads, servants of the mysteries. Keep silence for the secret of secrets, miracle of miracles, the transubstantiation of blood into wine."

He turned from them, bowed to the altar, then pacing with solemn steps round it to the other side he stooped to pick up the knife, which lay partly covered by Kate's drooping hair. As he groped his arm inadvertently brushed her face, and the bandage over her mouth, already loosened by her posture, was dislodged and fell off. She chewed with desperate resolution at the gag stuffed behind it.

Unaware of this, he returned to his place in front of the altar, and standing behind her he held the knife poised over her back:

"Angels and archangels, hear me, illuminate, transfigure me. *Vinum praebeo aeternae vitae.*"

With convulsive effort Kate spat. The saliva-soaked rag shifted, flopped out suddenly on the ground. Her mouth was clear and she screamed. She screamed and screamed, and all the echoes of the wood screamed in sympathy, screamed in

Jim's ears as he struggled in frantic haste through the thicket.

Brink stood with knife still poised: "Silence," he thundered. "Silence I command you in the name of all that's holy."

She paid no heed, screamed louder and louder.

"Silence," he repeated, but with less authority than irritation. He turned to the worshippers: "Can't one of you stop her? This noise is sheer blasphemy, an outrage at the celebration of the holy sacrament."

"Leave her to me." The voice was Albert's: "If you can't jab the girl yourself and stop her squealing, give me the knife and I will." He tried to seize the knife, but Brink wrested it out of his grasp.

"No, no, Albert. Don't touch that. Do you want to bring the rite to disaster?"

"I'll make it a bigger success than ever you could."

"Get back." He clung to the knife: "You betray my trust."

"Trust, you say? Your trust isn't worth a fart. I'm your pal when it suits you; when it doesn't you'll pull a fast one and hand me over to the busies."

"Hush, Albert, I implore you, this is holy ground. Beware of the vengeance of the great ones whose spirit you defile."

"I respect them as much as you do, Mr. Brink. Haven't I studied and sweated to become an adept? You're not going to rob me of my chances now. Give me the knife, let me stick it into the girl myself and drink her blood. You're not fit for it, I am. It's Albert Dockin tonight who'll join the great masters." He gripped the knife again by the handle.

Kate, bound fast with head drooping over the altar, could see nothing of what was happening; but she checked her screams to listen to the altercation, then to the struggle as the two men fought for possession of the weapon to kill her. A third voice, Aidan's, broke in; he spoke in an aggressive tone very different from his habit, with slurred syllables:

"Get away, both of you. What's this, a religious service or a brawl? Give the knife to me. I thought as much, your sacrifice is unworthy. The great powers reject your screaming girl; they want a man, a willing victim, to offer his manhood on their altar."

"You're canned, Aidan," Albert exclaimed in disgust. "Tight as an owl. Who'd have thought a drop of meth would last so long?"

215

"Stop him," Brink yelled. "He intends abomination, the rite of Attis."

Already Aidan had snatched the knife from both of them. He ran with it to the altar, slashed at the ropes:

"Get off, bitch, get out of my way, make room for your betters."

Very willing to obey, Kate lifted herself; her arms were free, but she was still roped round the thighs and ankles. As Aidan turned to release them Albert caught his arm, dragged him back. The two wrestled, fell to the ground together, fighting. Aidan still clasped the knife, Brink stooped to retrieve it.

Anchored by the legs but free to move the upper part of her body, Kate wriggled herself to lie less across than on top of the stone, and as Brink bent down for the knife his head came within her reach. She rose on her knees, stretched her arm and grabbed the devil's mask by one of its plastic horns. He shrank back with a cry of horror, not knowing what touched him. She held tight, and for a moment they tugged against each other; then the whole goatlike integument came off in her hand.

His face was revealed, his complexion no longer rubicund but blanched to a ghastly pallor, his eyes bulbous and panic-stricken.

"Sammael, Azazel," he muttered. "Lords of darkness, spare me. Mercy, mercy; it wasn't your servant's fault."

His terror was such that she pitied him: "Of course it wasn't, Mr. Brink. You did your best."

"Peccavi, peccavi." His distress overflowed into Latin: *"Rex tremendae maiestatis.* The bread was made flesh. Am I unworthy of the blood?"

"No, you can't have that," she told him, "so it's no good thinking of it."

He stared at her without recognition, striving to make sense of her words. His face screwed up like a frightened child's, he burst into tears, and the knife slipped from his hand.

Hitherto, except for Albert and Aidan, the masked worshippers had kept their places, watching events with interest but without attempt to intervene. It was as if they were unaware of anything unusual in the struggle for the knife, the recriminations, Kate's partial release, took it for granted that all this was part of the canon of the Black Mass. Now however they pointed, shouted:

216

"The cops, police. Scoot."

Jim, Harry, Ron and Flossie emerged over the crest of the bank, raced forward towards the circle of stones. Jim's dinner jacket and starched shirt-front crumpled and bespattered with mud gave him an air of raffish authority. Harry in uniform added official confirmation. The devotees of black magic scattered and fled, with Harry and Ron in pursuit.

Jim ran to the altar: "Kate," he called. "Kate darling." She waved to him.

"You're alive? Thank God."

"I can't get up," she explained. "My legs are tied."

"I'll see if Harry has a knife."

"No, not Harry, till I'm dressed." She pointed to the sacrificial knife lying on the grass: "Use that. Be careful, it's terribly sharp." She shuddered.

He grabbed it, severed her remaining bonds; but she still lay prostrate.

"Are you hurt?" he asked anxiously.

"No, but I'm quite naked, less indecent back view than front."

"It's all right, my sweet. Both Harry and Ron have gone chasing those devils into the wood."

"What about Mr. Brink?"

"I'd like to lay my hands on him. Where is he?"

"He was here beside me till you came, then he vanished." She raised herself on hands and knees to peer over the end of the altar stone: "Gosh, he's there. Is he dead?"

Jim moved round to look. Brink lay stretched in the grass, motionless, flat on his back. His crimson dressing gown, garish even in the moonlight, wrapped his body in imperial splendour.

"Is he dead?" Kate repeated.

"I couldn't care less. He can damn well stay dead till I've seen about you. Where are your clothes?"

"In the cromlech, I expect. That's where they took them off me."

"Shall I fetch them? No, better still; here's Flossie."

"Flossie? She's with you, is she? Thank goodness for that."

Flossie came up, panting. She showed more surprise at Brink's appearance than Kate's:

"My, if it isn't the parson. Did you do him in?"

"Serves him right," Jim declared, "if she did."

217

"But I didn't," Kate protested. "I never touched him, except to pull that disguise off." She pointed to the empty goat's-head lying on the ground.

Flossie recognised it with a peal of laughter: "Well, that fair caps it. So the Devil was the Reverend Brink? He's better to know by his face than by what he showed t'other night."

"Flossie," Jim interrupted. "Take Miss Evans to the cave where her clothes are, and help her to dress."

"Right-o." She turned to Kate: "Wait, and I'll lift you on my back."

"You'll do nothing of the sort. I'm not a corpse yet."

"Thanks be. I'd sooner carry you quick than dead."

"You don't know how much I weigh. Jim, shut your eyes; I'm going on foot."

Flossie grinned: "If I'd your figure I'd want him to keep them open."

Kate seized her by the hand, and they ran together to the cromlech.

Jim, left alone with Brink, knelt at his side, lifted his head. The eyes opened.

"Ah," Jim muttered grimly. "So you aren't as dead as we thought."

"Retro me, retro me," Brink sat up, glaring wildly: *"Retro me, Satana."*

"If you're seeing devils," Jim told him, "I hope they get you."

Brink paid no attention, he chanted with eyes fixed on the sky: *"Tuba mirum spargens sonum per sepulcra regionum."* He broke off; his jaws worked, but no sound issued.

"I haven't an idea what you're talking about." Jim frowned: "I need Kate to interpret."

The name pierced the trance, Brink stirred: "Kate, the chosen of the gods, fountain of the red wine of life." He turned suddenly, stared Jim in the face, but without recognition. His eyes glistened with terror, his brow with sweat:

"Forgive me, Lord, spare me. She was yours, a peach chosen from the garden of delight for your enjoyment, for yours alone. I sinned and am justly punished, a false priest. While I prayed to you, Lord, to accept her I lusted for her in my heart."

Jim stood up, stepped back, watching. There was still hostility in his face, but a troubled curiosity was added. Brink persisted engrossed in his own prayer:

"Mercy Lord. I sinned in the flesh, but my purpose was free from pride. I invoked the hidden power to spread happiness among those around me, content for my own part to live unregarded, a humble parish priest. The great ones turned from me, my invocation they rejected. Punish me, but with mercy, for my presumption. Others have presumed from motives worthier of vengeance."

He rose to his feet, tall, crimson-robed, a priestly phantom revisiting the moonlit shrine of a forgotten cult, and as if indeed he lived in a world of his own he remained unaware of Jim beside him. He moved to the altar:

"Grant me this last favour, Lord. Save me from public shame. Let me punish myself."

He reached for the sacrificial knife left there by Jim after cutting Kate free; but Jim, unseen and vigilant, forestalled him, grabbing it and snatching it away. Brink groped staring in dismay, understanding neither how nor where the knife had vanished. He groaned, staggered, sank huddled in the grass.

Jim carried the knife to the cromlech, laid it on the coping stone over the entrance. He could hear the girls talking inside, Flossie giggling:

"What's this? A pair of breeks? They stink like a midden."

Then Kate's voice: "They certainly aren't mine. They're probably Albert's."

"Either his or that Aidan's. Right-o, I'll rummage again, but it gives me the creeps what I'll come on."

"What's the matter?" Jim called.

"A great dump of clothes," Kate explained. "This must have been the cloakroom when the congregation got ready for the Black Mass."

"Are yours mixed up with them?"

"I'm praying hard they aren't, but it's too dark to see properly."

"Wait a sec. I've a box of matches."

He fumbled in his pocket, and her head protruded from the aperture, followed by a bare arm. She clutched the box, withdrew, and he heard a match struck, then Flossie's voice:

"Here you are, miss. Green blouse, white jeans and riding boots."

"Bra and tights too?"

"You're lucky. They've chucked them all here together in the corner."

"Of course. It comes back to me. I heard Albert tell them to burn them. He said I'd never need them again."

"What's that?" Jim asked. "What were they to burn?"

"My clothes. Incriminating evidence; but it's all right, they haven't, I'm putting them on."

A moment later she crawled out fully dressed.

He surveyed her with a grin: "I'm glad you've chosen the right ones."

"I'd rather stay naked all night than wear what they'd worn."

Flossie emerged behind her: "You should just take a sniff. If ever clothes needed burning those do."

"A bonfire?" He nodded: "Why not? It's quite an idea, Flossie."

"You'll roast enough fleas to fill a pie," she told him.

Kate's eyes rested on the knife on top of the cromlech: "Why did you put it there?"

"The knife? So that Brink can't get hold of it."

"Isn't he dead?"

"No, he came round after you left; but he's quite off his head, raving. He wanted to kill himself."

"Poor man, it must have been a shock to him when I screamed."

"A shock I wouldn't have spared him for the world."

She glanced at the altar and shuddered: "I can't believe I was lying there. It's as if it was just a nightmare, and I've woken up."

She ran ahead, bent over Brink's huddled form. His eyes were shut, but as she stared at him he opened them:

"Frenato delphine sedens, Theti nuda."

"No, Mr. Brink, I'm not any longer, and the dolphin's turned out in the field, fast asleep—at least I hope so."

He shut his eyes again, then opened them to meet hers still fixed on him: "The green man dies, the Midsummer Goddess lives on." His eyes shut, and this time they remained shut.

She turned in alarm to Jim standing behind her: "He's really dead now, I'm certain."

"No, darling. He'd like to be, but he isn't. Look, he's breathing. It's only a coma, and the kindest thing you can do is to leave him to it."

Harry and Ron appeared out of the trees and crossed the clearing.

"I'm afraid they've given us the slip, sir." Harry's voice held disappointment and vexation.

"Not entirely they didn't." Ron pointed to Fan following at their heels: "The old bitch got her teeth into one of the bastards, a fair treat."

"I hope it was Albert," Jim replied.

"Tallish bloke, wobbled as if he'd had a drop too much."

"Sounds like Aidan," Kate declared. "That'll teach him to treat bitches with more respect."

"Whatever are you talking about?" Jim asked.

"Never mind." She stooped to caress Fan, who came bounding up to her: "We're all the same, aren't we, Fan? We get in the way and we bite."

"I'll not get in his way, never fear." Flossie caught Ron's eye and giggled: "I've seen as much as I want.'

Harry frowned at her: "You be quiet, Flossie. We want no sauce from you when we're on police work." He caught sight of Brink lying in the grass and turned in surprise to inspect: "Has something happened to him, sir?"

"Yes, I'm afraid he's lost his reason. Our suspicions were true, Harry."

"The rector, a gentleman like him." He clicked his tongue: "Who'd have believed it? Sunday after Sunday preaching in church, and all the time he's bent on murder."

"It's no use upsetting ourselves. He's off his head. Thank God, we stopped him, and he can be certified."

Harry stared at the figure supine on the ground: "Does he need attention? Should I go for a doctor?"

"It won't hurt him to wait."

"He won't get away, from the look of him." Harry spoke grimly: "I wish I could say the same of the rest of the gang."

"You'll catch them. They can't travel far without being recognised in their birthday suits."

"I doubt they'll have found their clothes and put them on."

"They can't as long as we're here. That's where they left them." He pointed to the cromlech.

"In the hole there, the Devil's Parlour?"

"Yes. Miss Evans and Flossie came across them, and we were just planning when you turned up to make a bonfire."

"Burn their kit?" His tone was doubtful.

"Why not? If you can't get them for attempted murder you can always bring a charge of indecent exposure."

Harry still hesitated: "Destruction of property by the police? Is it in order?"

"It's damn well going to be."

Ron grinned: "It won't half make folks laugh to see them."

"Very good, sir. You know best what the law is." Harry's scruples were melting, easily reconciled to an entertaining departure from his duties.

"If the stuff won't burn," Kate told him, "there's a bottle of meth in the cave."

"Fine," Jim exclaimed. "Souse the filth well, and it won't stink so. Go along, Harry, and take Ron with you. Bring the whole wardrobe out, and we'll offer burnt sacrifice to Baal."

Harry and Ron obeyed, and Flossie accompanied them to help. They returned with their arms full of shirts, pullovers, trousers and soiled underwear, which they piled in the grass in front of the altar. The cloth sodden with sweat was not easy to kindle; but they nursed the flame with splashes of methylated spirit and an abundant supply of twigs and dry leaves till the pyre was well alight, a censer of fetid smoke in the ancient circle.

Kate shuddered as she stared at the belching fumes: "It's too like a scene from the past, from that book about Parson Amos."

Jim's arm was round her waist: "With the difference that I'm holding fast to Bess Atkins."

Brink left the Devil's Churchyard with three men and two girls to sustain and propel him. For much of the way he was able to walk on his own feet, firmly gripped by an arm on either side. He had enough control of his body to obey the direction of others, but neither strength nor will to resist. There were difficult moments where thickets could not be avoided. His escort pushed, pulled, sometimes lifted him through. He submitted without protest, convinced that his companions were spirits of the underworld summoning him to judgement. He addressed Fan as Cerberus, Kate as Proserpine.

At last they reached the wall, untied the hurdle and conveyed him through into the field. While the men heaved him into the car Kate and Flossie tied the hurdle back into place, and Dinah who stood in the shadow of the wall watching them came up and nuzzled Kate's hand.

Kate kissed her nose: "Thank you, Dinah, for fetching help. You were quite right. I needed it badly."

At the farm Harry put through a call to the police station. An ambulance arrived to collect Brink and remove him to hospital, and a warning was sent to all police in the district to look out for twelve naked men and arrest them. Harry insisted that this was sufficient identification, that there was no likelihood of their reclothing themselves. He did not explain the reason, that their clothes lay, a heap of smoking ashes, in the centre of the ancient circle of stones in Kemsdale Wood.

Jane Torgill was back from her sister's. As Jim and Kate passed through the kitchen they interrupted an eager clatter of conversation, Ron and Flossie telling their story, Jane and Alf Torgill asking questions.

"Is the water hot, Jane?" Jim asked. "Miss Evans is going to have a bath, and I'd like one myself afterwards."

"There's water enough, Master James, and if anyone ever needed it you do. All dressed up too for dining out. If I scrub from now till doomsday I'll never get those stains off your party suit."

"Save yourself the trouble, Jane, and save me a splendid excuse for refusing invitations to dinner."

"You'll get as good food at home without dressing up for it." She chuckled: "Be off now, and when you're both washed I'll have your supper ready."

"You're not going to start cooking at this hour? It's nearly midnight."

"I'll start when and as I like, I'd have you know. If you want to starve you can find someone else to mind your kitchen. Look sharp, Flossie, and you Ron too, you can give your tongues a rest and help me. You'll not ask to go hungered to bed, not if I know you."

Ron and Flossie grinned agreement.

Although Kate had her bath first she found Jim waiting for her when she came downstairs. He himself had only to put on clean clothes, a sweater and trousers, she to repair as best she could those which had shared her adventures, thrown aside in the cromlech when she was stripped for the Black Mass. They had taken less harm however than she feared, and there were brushes and lotions on the dressing table in

223

the room allotted her. The brushes had ivory handles with intertwined initials chased in silver, HCT. She guessed that they had belonged to Jim's mother, Henrietta Caroline Tranmire.

If she was doubtful of the success of her efforts his eyes reassured her as she joined him.

"The bath was heavenly," she told him as she seated herself.

"All black magic washed down the waste pipe?"

She shook her head: "There wasn't any turps. I'm still sitting on the Tetragrammaton."

"Tetra what?"

"The Holy of Holies, the four consonants of the secret name of God. At least that's what I think he wrote there."

"Shall I look to make sure?"

"No thank you. It's probably in Hebrew characters anyhow."

"Which you can read, and I can't. What's the use of a first in Greats, my sweet bluestocking, if you can't see behind you?"

"I don't want to see." She shuddered: "I hate it."

"I'm sorry, Kate. There's nothing funny about it at all."

"There's nothing funny in knowing you're going to be killed; but even that wasn't the worst part. It's horrible to have to die with people like that looking on."

"I curse myself for letting them get as far as they did. There was I making elaborate plans to guard you tomorrow, and all the time the event was fixed for today. That's what Brink meant by zero hour."

"His important secret?"

"Yes, I knew there was a catch in it; but I never guessed zero hour was the dress rehearsal, the play itself just a hoax."

"As things turned out, I never went to the dress rehearsal."

"You did; but it was held in the Devil's Churchyard, and it wasn't to rehearse amateur theatricals, it was to celebrate the Black Mass."

"I see now why Mr. Brink was so keen on my attending it and meeting the rest of the cast."

"You certainly got to know them."

"I wasn't looking forward to it at the rectory, it was far worse in the wood."

"Why did you go to the wood at all?"

"To look for you. That man called Aidan met me on the

moor, and he said you'd sent him with a message, you were in the wood and wanted me to help you."

"Good Lord, why should I? You knew I was dining with Mrs. Corrington."

"Yes, it was all most mysterious, but worrying too."

"So you went to the wood to help me and rode straight into the trap?"

"It wasn't very intelligent of me, I'm afraid."

"I don't know about intelligence, but it does great credit to your heart."

She shook her head: "I was stupid, but there was something in my mind that wasn't me, a voice telling me I'd be sure to find you in the Devil's Churchyard."

"What sort of voice?"

"It didn't speak aloud till the end when I heard moans from the cromlech, and then it was just Albert pretending, and I was caught."

"The swine. I only hope he's caught too. The pity is we've given up the pillory. That's where he needs putting, naked as he is, a public laughingstock."

"He's disgusting, I couldn't bear him to touch me. I try not to believe that the voice all the time was his calling me, his thoughts mixing with mine."

"It's a power that Parson Amos was said to possess."

"Yes, I read it in your book, he sent evil spirits to make people do what he wanted. Perhaps Albert can too, but they'd no success with Dinah."

"Dinah?"

"She broke loose from the tree where I tied her, and she went to fetch Flossie."

"And Flossie tried to fetch me, to ring me up. I'll never forgive Pearl for what happened. She took the call herself, choked Flossie off and came to me with a story that Dinah was lame, and you were leading her home and likely to be late."

"Where on earth did she get that from?"

"She said she couldn't understand what Flossie was talking about, so she rang up Saint Ursula's, and that was what she was told, that you sent the message yourself."

"I sent no message to Saint Ursula's, there was no need; but I did send a message by this Aidan to tell Mr. Brink I'd be late for the rehearsal, not because Dinah was lame, which she wasn't, but because Aidan said you needed me."

"There's been dirty work on Aidan's part. I don't know how he managed it; but the effect was to let the Buttles think you were taking your time across the moor, and if they sent to look for you it would be on the road towards Golstondale."

"I do hope that isn't what they're doing. I've my own key, so they don't usually bother how late I am; but if they've heard something's wrong they may. I ought to let them know."

"It's all right. I rang Saint Ursula's before you came down, and it's well I did. Doctor Buttle answered, and he was worried, he was just going to get the car out and drive to Golstondale. So I gave him the facts, or as much as I'd time for, and you can fill in the rest yourself."

"Oh dear, I'd better see him at once and explain." She rose sadly to her feet: "I wonder what Flossie did with Dinah's saddle and bridle."

"Stop talking nonsense, Kate." He put his hands on her arms and pressed her back into the chair: "Sit tight on that Tetragrammaton, or you'll get it smacked. The Buttles aren't worried any longer; they'll have gone to bed, and they won't thank you for waking them up with your story at this time of night. Nor will Dinah, who's found herself a nice snug corner in the field to snooze in."

"She'll have to be woken up some time to take me home."

"You're not going home till you've eaten the supper Jane's cooking for us, and when the time does come you're going by car. Didn't you notice that smart Jaguar we put Brink in?"

"I did. Is it yours?"

"Guess again; but it needn't stand idle till I give it back to Leslie Potts."

Her last scruples of conscience vanished when Jane Torgill brought in their supper, an immense dish of bacon and eggs, fried liver and kidneys, and homemade sausages flavoured with herbs. She put it on the table, returned to the kitchen and came again with supplementary dishes of roast potatoes and broad beans.

"Will you have enough?" she asked. "There's more in the pan."

"Good gracious, Jane. I've eaten one dinner already, and you expect me to have the appetite of a famished wolf."

"Well, I have." Kate laughed: "My last meal was lunch,

226

and I hurried over it. Thank you ever so much, Mrs. Tor-gill, this is just what I longed for."

"That's right, miss," she replied. "Eat your fill. There's nothing like good food to give a lass what a man wants to look at."

Kate obeyed the advice with much willingness, and Jim quickly forgetting that he had dined fell little short of her example. A bottle of Burgundy which he brought from the cellar encouraged a mood to drown even the terrors of the Devil's Churchyard.

When the dishes were empty he lit a cigarette. Kate glanced at the mirror opposite on the wall and tugged a gilt compact from her hip picket. He watched her with a smile:

"By the pricking of my thumbs."

The pocket gripped, she tugged impatiently, and the com-pact slipped from her fingers, fell and burst open, scattering powder.

"Damn." She bent to pick it up.

"Does this happen every time," he asked, "or only once a week?"

"Why?" Then her brow cleared: "Yes, of course, the first time we met."

"You've even kept the green man." He reached for a disc of paper on the floor and handed it to her.

"Only because I'd forgotten it was there." She stared at the engraving with distaste: "He's much younger and he hasn't a paunch, but he's not unlike Mr. Brink himself, or Parson Amos either."

"He's a nasty bit of work, that's certain."

"Not nasty but terribly vain, the sort of man to be daz-zled by ideas because they're his own, and let them grow on him till they become an obsession."

"Leading to a grand climax in the Black Mass. Isn't nasti-ness the right word for it?"

She shook her head: "In his eyes it was sublime. He saw himself as a priest performing a sacred duty."

"You're too open-minded, Kate. Be careful, it's a vice of the academic."

"I felt anything but academic lying across that altar."

"I'm sorry, darling, I shouldn't have said that; but you'll never make me believe it's Brink's duty to stick a knife in your heart."

"Of course it isn't, or in anyone else's." She still held the engraving of the green man. She scrunched it up and threw it into the wastepaper basket: "He thought it was; but thank goodness he'll be put where he can't try, he'll have no more victims."

"Thanks to you. If you'd shirked it, as I wanted, he'd still be on the prowl, no one would know of his madness."

"He'd have got worse and worse as his vanity became more and more wrapped up in itself."

"In my opinion there was as much sex in it as vanity. Doctor Buttle suspected prostate trouble."

"Poor Mr. Brink, he can't help that."

"He can't help it that you're much too desirable, but it doesn't excuse him."

"He'd have been the same with any girl. I wasn't a person to him, I was an erotic gadget."

"A gadget of charming design, far too good for his blasphemies."

"I'm not a gadget at all. Anyhow, I was too frightened to be shocked by them."

"Same here." He nodded: "Murder was what I worried about, the rest didn't matter."

"It would have to any devout churchpeople, if they'd been present."

"Was he very blasphemous?"

"Yes, very, and so childish too, quite amazing in a man of his learning."

"I suppose he gets the same kick from it as one of your brats at school cocking a snook at you behind your back."

"And I'm sure God pays no more attention than I should."

"Brink wouldn't like that at all."

She laughed: "It spoils the fun for the Titan defying Zeus. He's left to look foolish."

"I wonder how much he believes of his hocus-pocus."

"He must have persuaded himself he does. The whole point of black magic is to pride yourself on believing the opposite to anyone else. It's like any other cosy sect of superior people."

"Not so cosy for the victim, was it?"

"I'd rather have been the victim than one of the flock, stuffed with silly nonsense till my mind hadn't room to think. Murder and blasphemy are bad enough; but the ideas were even worse, they were so bogus."

"Nothing's worse than murder. You're talking nonsense yourself, Kate."

"My academic vice? Yes, perhaps I am. It was dreadful waiting to be murdered, and it's wicked to upset people by insulting the symbols they've built their faith on. I only hope nothing gets known of what went on at the Black Mass. It certainly won't from me."

"Or from Brink himself, not in his present condition."

"Poor man. Will they keep him long in a mental hospital?"

"I hope so. It's the right place for him."

"I'm sorriest for Mrs. Corrington. It'll break her heart."

"Yes, poor old thing, she's a faithful soul. At one time I thought she'd a finger in this pie of his; but I doubt it now, it doesn't go with her character."

"It doesn't, the least bit. She'd be appalled at the very idea. She'd never believe him capable of it, not if the evidence stared her in the face."

"Well, it will when she hears about tonight."

"She'll hear too he's out of his mind, that he's been certified. Perhaps that'll make things easier for her. I hope it does."

He nodded: "You know that gaudy dressing gown he wore as high priest of the Devil? I lifted him when he fainted, and I couldn't help noticing. It had Ernest Corrington in the collar. She must have given him it."

"How pathetic."

"Yes, she little knew what he'd use it for. Chasubles may be her line, but not for the Black Mass."

"It's so sad to think what she was hoping, what she'd every right to hope. She wasn't at all happy, I've heard, with her first husband."

"A prize bounder, from what the Buttles tell me. She seems bent on acquiring another for her second choice."

"I shouldn't call Mr. Brink a bounder, it's just that he's too eccentric to be easy to live with."

"You excel at understatement, Kate."

"Anyhow, he might have been different with Mrs. Corrington to look after him. She's longing for someone to mother."

"Well, this is her chance."

"Yes, I see what you mean. She'll visit him in hospital, and that'll help him to get well, and they'll let him out so that he can go back with her to Easby and marry her."

229

"The perfect idyll, and they all live happily ever after, except Pearl."

"Wouldn't she like it?"

"Do you honestly think she would?"

"There's only one solution then. You'll have to marry Pearl yourself."

"Commit bigamy? Have you forgotten a wedding, Kate, held at a waterfall with Pan and the naiads for witnesses, and the bride the prettiest of them all?"

As their eyes met the blood rose to her face.

"Have you forgotten it, Kate?"

She shook her head.

"Nor have I, and never shall." He picked her up from her chair, carried her to his own and set her on his knees.

"I'm heavy," she protested. "You'd find Pearl much lighter."

"Thank you, I know what else I'd find."

"Something I haven't got?"

"You'll never persuade me yours is a bony seat."

The waning moon was long past the zenith when the Jaguar glided out of the farmyard, crept cautiously round the zigzags in the lane, gathering speed past Harry Bracken's sleeping cottage for the steep hill up on to the moor.

"How lovely the night smells." Kate let down the window as far as it would go; the handle was stiff, and she had to use force.

Jim watched her with a smile: "I doubt if that window's been opened since Leslie bought the car."

"What a pity we can't take the roof off."

"That would need a saw and a file, and I don't want to quarrel with the Potts clan, I've lambs for their Michaelmas sales."

"No, of course we mustn't damage the car, it was very kind of him to lend it."

"He didn't mean to, but I gave him no time to argue."

"I'm glad you didn't. You'd have been too late."

His answer made the car swerve. He restored his hand in haste to the wheel.

At the top of the hill they turned on to the main road. There was no traffic at this hour; the Jaguar leapt forward, not at the reckless speed demanded earlier in the night, but